"Damn, that's a big cat," Ben said, staring at the feline hulk at his feet.

"That's no cat, that's my bodyguard," Mercy answered.

"I can see that." Ben squatted down to scratch the top of his head. "What's his name?"

"Depends on the day and my mood. Today I'm leaning toward Dumbbutt."

"Because?" Ben asked.

"Because he's too stupid to know when he's got it good. If he sticks around, he's got heat and my bed to sleep in. But no, that would apparently cramp his style. So he takes off, for days at a time. Then he has the nerve to drag his carcass back here, all matted and hungry, and beg for my forgiveness."

Silence.

"You wouldn't be trying to make a point here, would you?" At Mercy's smile, he added, "Because I'm not hungry. Or matted."

"Yeah, well, you're not getting back in my bed, either."

Dear Reader,

After thirty years of marriage and five kids, Valentine's Day has become pretty much just another excuse to eat chocolate. Oh, and those cheesy little candy hearts that say "U R Fine" and "Be Mine." If I get flowers, fine; if not, no biggie. At this point, I don't need no stinkin' Valentine's Day to remind me that I'm loved.

But, oh, how I remember those Valentine's Days when I didn't have a significant (or even insignificant!) other, when the only way I'd get a box of chocolates was to buy them myself. And how pathetic was that? Once I stumbled onto the real thing, however, the symbols weren't nearly as important—something Mercy Zamora finally figures out, even before Ben Vargas makes it clear that this Valentine's Day is going to be like no other.

Still, if someone wants to give me a box of Godiva, I wouldn't turn it down....

Karen Templeton

THE PRODIGAL
VALENTINE

KAREN TEMPLETON

SPECIAL EDITION®

Published by Silhouette Books

America's Publisher of Contemporary Romance

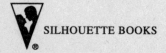 SILHOUETTE BOOKS

ISBN-13: 978-0-373-24808-7
ISBN-10:   0-373-24808-3

THE PRODIGAL VALENTINE

Copyright © 2007 by Karen Templeton-Berger

Visit Silhouette Books at www.eHarlequin.com

Printed in U.S.A.

Books by Karen Templeton

KAREN TEMPLETON

is a Waldenbooks bestselling author and RITA® Award nominee, a mother of five sons and living proof that romance and dirty diapers are not mutually exclusive terms. An Easterner transplanted to Albuquerque, New Mexico, she spends far too much time trying to coax her garden to yield roses and produce something resembling a lawn, all the while fantasizing about a weekend alone with her husband. Or at least an uninterrupted conversation.

Acknowledgments

With many thanks to Mary Jaramillo,
whose contributions to this book
have hopefully kept this gringa
from sounding like a complete *pendeja* (dumbass)

As always, to Jack, my Valentine
for twenty-eight years and counting

Chapter One

"How hard can it be," Mercedes Zamora muttered through chattering teeth as she elbowed her way into the mammoth juniper bush bordering her sidewalk to retrieve her Sunday paper, "to hit the frickin' *driveway? Crap!*" A flattened branch slapped her in the face; on a growl, she dove back in, thinking she had maybe three seconds before her bare feet fused to the frosty driveway, only to let out a shriek when something furry streaked past her calves and up to the house.

The cat plastered himself to her front door, meowing piteously.

"Hey. Nobody told you to stay out last night," she said as she yanked the paper out of the greenery, swearing again when she discovered her long, morning-ravaged curls and the bush had bonded. She grabbed her hair and tugged. "I feel for you but I can't…quite…*reach you!*"

The bush let go, sending her stumbling backwards onto the cement, at which point a low, male, far-too-full-of-himself chuckle from across the street brought the blood chugging through her veins to a grinding halt. Frozen tootsies forgotten, Mercy spun around, wincing from the retina-searing glare of thousands of icicle lights sparkling in the legendary New Mexican sunshine.

Oh, no. No, no, no…this was not happening.

Ten years it had been since she'd laid eyes on Benicio Vargas. And seared retinas notwithstanding, it was way too easy to see that those ten years had taken the shoulders, the grin, the cockiness that had been the twenty-five-year-old Ben to a whole 'nother level.

Well, hell.

What effect those years might have had Mercy, however— stunning, she was sure, in her rattiest robe, her hair all juniper-mangled—she wasn't sure she wanted to contemplate too hard. Not that she was ready to be put down just yet—her skin was still wrinkle-free, her hair the same dark, gleaming brown it had always been, and she could still get into her size five jeans, thanks for asking. But the last time Ben had seen these breasts, they hadn't had their thirtieth birthday yet. Quite.

Not that he'd be seeing them now. She was just sayin'.

Ben flashed a smile at her, immediately putting her father's glittering Christmas display to shame. Not to mention his own parents', right next door.

Mercy wasn't sure which was worse—that once upon a time she'd had a brief, ill-advised, but otherwise highly satisfactory fling with the boy next door, or that here she was, rapidly closing in on forty and still living across the street from the lot of them in one of her folks' rental houses. But hey—as long as she was leading her own life, on her own terms, what was the harm in keeping the old nest firmly in her sights?

As opposed to Mr. Hunky across the street, who'd booked it out of the nest and never looked back. Until, apparently, now.

"Lookin' good over there, Mercy," Ben called out, hauling a duffle out of his truck bed, making all sorts of muscles ripple and such. Aiyiyi, could the man fill out a pair of blue jeans or what?

"Thanks," she said, hugging the plastic-wrapped paper to the afore-mentioned breasts. "So. Where the hell have you been all this time?"

Okay, so nuance wasn't her strong suit.

"Yeah, about that," Ben said, doing more of the smile-flashing thing. If she'd rattled him, he wasn't letting on. Behind her, the cat launched into an aria about how he was starving to death. "I don't suppose this is a good time to apologize for just up and leaving the way I did, huh?"

Huh. Somebody had been spending time in cowboy country. Texas, maybe. Or Oklahoma. "Actually," she called back, "considering you've just confirmed what half the neighborhood probably suspected anyway…" She shrugged. "Go ahead, knock yourself out."

His expression suddenly turned serious. Not what she'd expected. Especially since the seriousness completely vanquished the happy-go-lucky Ben she remembered, leaving in its place this…this I-can-take-anything-you-dish-out specimen of masculinity that made her think, *Yeah, I need this like I need Lyme disease.*

"Then I'm sorry, Mercy," he said, the words rumbling over to her on the winter breeze. "I truly am."

She shivered, and he waved, and he turned and went inside his parents' house, and she drifted back up to her own front door, her head ringing as though she'd been clobbered with a cast-iron skillet. And, she realized, in her zeal to get her digs in first, she had no idea why he was back.

Not that she cared.

The cat, who couldn't have cared less, shoved his way inside before she got the door all the way open. Her phone was ringing. Of course. She squinted outside to see her mother standing at the two-story house's kitchen window, her own phone clamped to her ear, gesticulating for Mercy to pick up. There was something seriously wrong with this picture, but she'd have to amass a few more brain cells before she could figure it out.

"Yes, Ma," she said as soon as she picked up her phone. "I know. He's back. Opening a can of cat food right now, in fact. Sliced grill, yum, yum."

After an appropriate pause, Mary Zamora sighed loudly into the phone. "Not your stupid cat, Mercy. *Ben*."

"Oh, *Ben*. Yeah, I saw him just now, in fact. Talk about a shock. Got any idea why he's here?"

"To help his father, why else? Because his brother broke his foot the day after Christmas on that skiing trip?" she added, rather than waiting for Mercy to connect the dots. "Yes, I know Tony's not exactly your favorite person—"

"Did I say anything?"

"—but since the man is married to your sister, I really wish you'd try a little harder to like him. For 'Nita's sake, at least. Did she tell you, they're adding to the back of the house? And that new wide-screen TV they bought themselves for Christmas…not bad, huh?"

Mercy rolled her eyes. Tony did okay, she supposed, but her mother knew damn well that if it weren't for Anita's second income as a labor and delivery nurse, most of that extra "stuff" wouldn't happen.

"But anyway," Mary Zamora said, "now that Tony can't drive for at least a month, and God knows Luis couldn't possibly handle all those contracts on his own, Ben's come home to fill in."

Something about this wasn't adding up. Three or four years back, Tony had been down with mono for nearly six weeks, and Ben hadn't come home then. So why now? However, having developed a highly tuned survival skill where her mother was concerned, Mercy knew better than to mention her suspicions.

Just as she knew better than to mention her hunch that all was not well in Tony-and-Anita land. Seriously not well. But her parents would be crushed if Anita's marriage went pffft, especially since they hadn't completely recovered from Mercy's oldest sister Carmen's divorce two years ago. The two families had been tighter'n'ticks for more than thirty-five years, from practically the moment the Zamoras had moved next door. Two of their children marrying had only further cemented an already insoluble bond.

Since Anita hadn't confided in Mercy, all she had was that hunch. Still, the Zamora women, of which there were many, all shared a finely-honed instinct for zeroing in on problems of the heart. And right now, Mercy's instinct was saying yet another fairy-tale ending bites the dust.

"He looks pretty good, don't you think?"

Mercy jerked. Okay, so one check mark in the why-living-across-from-the-parentals-is-a-bad-idea box. Clearly, four weddings (and one messy, nasty divorce) hadn't been enough to put her mother off the scent. Until Mercy was married as well, the world—and all the unattached, straight males who roamed its surface in blissful ignorance that they were marked men—was not a safe place.

"Don't suppose there's much point in denying it."

"No, there isn't. And you're not seeing anyone at the moment, are you?"

"Ma, I've been working nearly nonstop at the store, you know that. I've barely seen myself in the past two years. But to head you off at the pass—fuggedaboutit. Me and Ben…not gonna happen."

No need to mention that she and Ben had already happened. Not that she had any complaints on that score. In fact, if she remembered correctly…

And she would open the rusty gate to that path, why?

"Mercedes," her mother said. "You may have been able to stave off the ravages of time up until now—"

"Gee, thanks."

"—but it's all going to catch up with you, believe me. A woman your age…how can I put this? You can't afford to be too particular."

Because obviously a woman of Mercy's advanced years should be rapidly approaching desperate. Brother.

"Actually," Mercy said, "I can't afford not to be. And believe me, some thirty-five-year-old guy who's still blowing where the breeze takes him, who hasn't even been home

since the last millennium, doesn't even make the running."
The odd stirring of the old blood notwithstanding.

"So what are you saying? You're just going to give up, be
an old maid?"

Mercy laughed. "Honestly, Ma—that term went out with
poodle skirts. Besides, you know I'm happy with things the
way they are. Business is great, a dozen nieces and nephews
more than feed my kid fix, and I actually like living alone.
Well, as alone as I can be with you guys across the street and
Anita and them two blocks away. There's no big empty hole
in my life I need to fill up."

"But think how much more financially stable you'd be,
married."

Mercy pinched the bridge of her nose. "Which I suppose
is your way of saying you could be getting twice as much for
this house as I'm paying you."

"Now you know your father and I are only too happy to
help out where we can. But, honey, it has been six years…."

Yeah, Mercy's teeter on the edge of poverty while she and
her two partners got their business up and running hadn't
exactly left her parents feeling too secure about her ability to
take care of herself.

"I know it's been a struggle," she said quietly. "But we're
doing okay now. In fact, I can start paying you more for the
house, if you want. So I'm over the worst. And it was *my*
struggle. You should be proud, you know?"

"I am, *mija.* I am. 'Nita with her nursing degree, and
Carmen getting that good job with the state. And now you,
with your own business… No mother could be prouder of her
girls, believe me. It's just that it kills me seeing you alone. And

I worry that…well, you know. That if you wait too long, you'll lose out."

"Geez, Ma…did Papito sneak something into your coffee this morning? Look, for the last time—" Although she seriously doubted it would be "—I like being alone. And I'm not lonely. Okay?" At her mother's obviously uncomprehending silence, she added, more gently, "So, yes, maybe back in the day, when everybody else was falling in love and getting married and having babies, I felt a little left out that it wasn't happening for me. But I'm not that person anymore. And at this point, if I were to consider marriage, it would have to be to somebody who's going to bring something pretty major to the table, you know? Somebody…well, perfect."

"Nobody's perfect, Mercy," her mother said shortly. "God knows your father's not. But I love him anyway. And I thank God every day for sending him to me."

"But don't you see, Ma? Pa *is* perfect. For *you*. Okay, so maybe you had to whip him into shape a bit," she said with a laugh, and her mother snorted, "but the basics were already all in place. And besides, you were both so young, you had the time and energy and patience on your side. I don't. I'd rather stay single than expend all that energy on either ignoring a man's faults or trying to fix them. So the older I get, the less I'm willing to settle for anything less than the best. And I can tell you right now, Ben Vargas doesn't even make the short list."

And at that moment, the man himself came back outside to get something out of his truck, and Mercy let out a heartfelt sigh at the unfairness of it all.

"Well," her mother said, clearly watching Ben as well, "when you put it that way…no, I don't suppose he does."

"*Thank* you. So does that mean you're off my case?"

"For now. But damn, the man's got a great backside."

Mercy hooted with laughter. "No arguments there," she said as the clear winter sun highlighted a jawline much more defined than she remembered. And since when did she have a thing for wind-scrambled hair? And—she leaned over to get a better look—beard haze? "But butt or no butt," she said, still staring, "as soon as Tony's back in the saddle, so's Ben. Riding off into the sunset."

Her mother chuckled.

"What?"

"You're watching him, too, aren't you?"

Mercy jerked back upright. "Of course not, don't be silly."

"Uh-huh. So maybe you're the one who needs to remember he's not going to be around long."

With her luck, Mercy thought after she hung up, her mother would live to a hundred. Which meant she had another forty years of this to go.

And wasn't that a comforting thought?

Seated at the tiny table wedged into one corner of his parents' kitchen, Ben tried to drum up the requisite enthusiasm for the heavy ceramic plate heaped with spicy chorizo, golden hash browns and steaming scrambled eggs laced with green chile his mother clunked in front of him.

"If you've been driving most of the night," Juanita Vargas said over the whimpering of a trio of overfed, quivering Chihuahuas at her feet, "you should take a nap after you eat. I'll make sure your father keeps the volume down on the TV when he gets back from his golf game."

Still trying to wrap his head around the odd sensation of having never left—he could swear even the orange, red and yellow rooster-patterned potholders were the same ones he remembered—Ben smiled, picked up his fork. "That's okay, I'm fine."

"You don't look fine. You look like somebody who hasn't had a decent meal in far too long. Did I give you enough eggs? Because I've got plenty more in the pan…here," his mother said, reaching for his plate, "I might as well give them to you now, save me the trouble later—"

"No, Mama, really, this is plenty," he said, shoving a huge bite of eggs into his mouth. "Thanks."

The phone mercifully rang. The minute the wisp of a woman and her canine entourage shuffled and clickety-clicked to the other side of the kitchen, Ben quickly wrapped half of his breakfast in his paper napkin to sneak into the garbage later. He'd die before he hurt her feelings, but he'd also die if he ate all this food.

Why, again, had he expected this trip home to provide him with the peace he so sorely needed? Not only was his mother fussing over him like he was a kindergartner, but the minute he got out of his truck he could feel all the old issues between him and his father rush out to greet him, as bug-eyed and overeager as the damn dogs. And then, to top it all off, there was Mercy.

Oh, boy, was there Mercy.

Ben took a swallow of his coffee, wondering how a ten-second interaction could instantly erase an entire decade. For one brief, shining moment, as he'd watched her battling that bush—he chuckled, remembering—he was twenty-whatever and about to combust with need for the hottest tamale of a woman he'd ever known. Who, physically at least, seemed to be in the same time warp as his mother's house. Except he was glad, and surprised, to see she'd finally given up on trying to tame her insanely curly hair. Not much bigger than one of the Chihuahuas—although a helluva lot cuter, thank God, he thought as the biggest one of the lot returned to cautiously sniff his ankles—Mercedes packed a whole lot of punch in that thimble-sized body of hers.

Except, her appearance aside, he doubted she was the same woman she'd been then. God knows, he wasn't the same man. Why he'd thought—

Stupid.

Yeah, his mother had wasted no time in telling him Mercy was still single, but Ben somehow doubted his abrupt departure all those years ago had anything to do with that. Mercy as a torch-carrier? No damn way. A grudge-nurser, however…now that, he could see.

Not that he'd broken any promises. After all, she'd been the one who'd made it clear right from the start that it had only been about itch-scratching. Because he knew she wanted what her sisters had—marriage, babies, stability. And she knew the very thought made him ill. So there'd never been any illusions about permanent. Still, that didn't excuse Ben's taking off without giving her at least a heads-up. She'd deserved better than that.

She'd also deserved better than a pointless affair with some *pendejo* who'd been convinced that running away was the only way to solve a problem he didn't fully understand.

Too long it had taken him to realize what a dumb move that had been.

"You're finished already?" his mother said at his side, going for his plate again. "You want some more—?"

"No! Really," Ben said with a smile, carefully tucking the full napkin by his plate. "I'm fine. It was delicious, thank you."

She beamed. "You want more coffee?"

"I can get it—"

"No, sit, I'm already up."

After handing Ben his coffee, Juanita sat at a right angle to him, briefly touching his hand. Although her stiff, still-black hair did nothing to soften the hard angles of her face, her wide smile shaved years off her appearance. "It means a lot to your father," she said softly in Spanish, "that you came back. He's missed you so much."

Ben lifted the mug to his lips, not daring to meet his mother's gaze. He'd known how much his leaving would hurt Luis, but staying simply hadn't been an option. Now, however…

"Just doing my duty," he said, only to nearly choke when his mother spit out a Spanish curse word. Now he looked up, not sure what to make of the combined amusement and concern in her ripe-olive eyes.

"For ten years, you stay away," she said, still in Spanish. "As if to return would contaminate you, suck you back into something bad—"

"That's not true," he said, except it was. In a way, at least.

"Then why didn't you even come home for holidays, Benicio? To go off and live your life somewhere else is one thing, but to never come home…" Her face crumpled, she shook her head. "What did we do, *mijo?*" she said softly. "Your father adored you, would have done anything for you—"

"I know that, Mama," Ben said, ignoring his now churning stomach. He reached across the table and took his mother's tiny hand in his, taking care not to squeeze the delicate bones. "I was just...restless."

Not the entire truth, but not a lie, either. In fact, at the time he might even have believed that *was* the reason he'd left. Because he'd never been able to figure out why, after he'd been discharged from the army, he couldn't seem to settle back into his old life here. But time blurs memory, and motivations, and reasons, and now, sitting in his mother's kitchen, he really couldn't have said when he'd finally realized the real reason for his leaving.

But for damn sure he'd always known exactly what he'd left behind.

His mother smiled and said in English, "Considering how much you moved around inside me before you were born, this is not a surprise." Then her smile dimmed. "But now I think that restlessness has taken a new form, yes? Something tells me you are not here because of Tony, or your father, but for *you.*"

A second or two of warring gazes followed, during which Ben braced himself for the inevitable, "*So what have you really been doing all this time?*"

Except the question didn't come. Not then, at least. Instead, his mother stood once more, startling the dogs. She took his empty mug, looking down at it for a moment before saying, "Whatever your reason for coming back, it's good to have you home—"

"Ben!"

At the sound of his father's voice, Ben swiveled toward the

door leading to the garage, where Luis Vargas, his thick, dark hair now heavily webbed with silver, was attempting to haul in a state-of-the-art set of golf clubs without taking out assorted wriggling, excited dogs. Ben quickly stood, tossing his "napkin" into the garbage can under the sink as his father dropped the clubs and extended his arms. A heartbeat later, the slightly shorter man had hauled Ben against his chest in an unabashedly emotional hug.

"I didn't expect you for another couple of hours, otherwise I would've stayed home!" The strong, builder's hands clamped around Ben's arms, Luis held him back, moisture glistening in dark brown eyes. Slightly crooked teeth flashed underneath a bristly mustache. "You look good. Doesn't he look good, Juanita? *Dios,*" he said, shaking Ben and grinning, "I've waited so *long* for this moment! Did you eat? Juanita, did you feed the kid?"

"Yes, Pop," Ben said, chuckling. "She fed me."

His father let go, tucking his hands into his pockets, shaking his head and grinning. A potbelly peeked through the opening of his down vest, stretching the plaid shirt farther than it probably should. "I see you, and now I'm thinking, finally, everything's back the way it should be, eh?" He slapped Ben's arm, then pulled him into another hug while his mother fussed a few feet away about how he shouldn't do that, the boy had just eaten, for heaven's sake.

Now the house shuddered slightly as the front door opened, followed by "For God's sake, woman! I'm okay, I don't need your help!"

Ben stiffened. Damn. Would another hour or two to prepare have been too much to ask?

Apparently not, he thought as, in a cloud of cold that briefly soothed Ben's heated face, his brother and sister-in-law, along with their two kids, straggled into the kitchen.

"Look, Tony!" Luis swung one arm around Ben's shoulders, crushing him to his side. "Your brother's finally come home! Isn't that great?"

His brother's answering glare immediately confirmed that nothing had changed on that front, either.

Chapter Two

"So…" Tony banged his crutches up against one wall and collapsed into the nearest kitchen chair, stretching out his casted foot in front of him and glowering. Shorter and stockier than Ben, Tony resembled their father more than ever these days. A neat beard outlined his full jaw, obliterating the baby face Tony had detested all through high school. "You made it."

His mother was too busy fussing over the kids to notice the vinegar in her oldest son's voice, but Ben definitely caught his sister-in-law's irritated frown.

"Don't start, Tony," she said softly, and his brother turned his glower on her.

"Yeah, I made it," Ben said, taking the coward's way out by turning his attention to his niece and nephew. A sliver of regret pierced his gut: Although his mother had e-mailed photos of the kids to him, he'd never seen them in person before this. His chest tightened at the energy pulsing from lanky, ten-year-old Jacob, at little Matilda's shy, holey half-smile from behind her mother's broad hips.

"Come here, you," Anita said, shucking her Broncos jacket and holding out her arms, her fitted, scoop-necked sweater brazenly accentuating her curves. Ben couldn't remember Mercy's next youngest sister as ever having a hard angle anywhere on her body, even when they'd been kids. A biological hand Anita had not only accepted with grace, but played to full advantage. Her embrace was brief and hard and obviously sincere. "Welcome home," she whispered before letting him go.

"You haven't changed a bit," Ben said, grinning. "Still as much of a knockout as ever."

Her laugh did little to mask either her flush of pleasure or the slight narrowing of her thick-lashed, coffee brown eyes as she gave him the once-over. Masses of warm brown curls trembled on either side of her full cheeks. "And you're still full of it! Anyway…little Miss Peek-a-Boo behind me is Matilda, we call her Mattie. And this is Jacob. Jake. Kids, meet your Uncle Ben."

Since Mattie was still hanging back, Ben extended his hand to Jake, gratified to see the wariness begin to retreat in his nephew's dark eyes. "I hear you play baseball."

A look of surprise preceded a huge grin. "Since third grade, yeah. Short stop. Do you?"

"After a fashion. Enough to play catch, if you want."

"Sweet! Dad's like, always too tired and stuff."

"That's crap, Jake," Tony said, and Anita shot him a look that would have felled a lesser man.

"And when's the last time you played with him, huh?"

"For God's sake, 'Nita, my leg's broken!"

"I meant, before that—"

"Are you the same Uncle Ben that makes the rice?"

In response to his niece's perfectly timed distraction, Ben turned to smile into a pair of wide, chocolate M&M eyes. Twin ponytails framed a heart-shaped face, the ends feathered over a fancy purple sweater with a big collar, as the little girl's delicate arms squashed a much-loved, stuffed something to her chest. Ben was instantly smitten. "No, honey, I'm afraid not."

"Oh." Mattie hugged the whatever-it-was more tightly. The ponytails swished when she tilted her head, her soft little brows drawn together. Curiosity—and a deep, unquestioning trust that makes a man take stock of his soul—flared in her eyes. "Papi talks about you all the time," she said with a quick grin for her grandfather. "He says you usta play with Aunt Rosie and Livvy a lot when you were little."

"I sure did." Ben nodded toward the thing in her arms. "Who's your friend?"

"Sammy. He's a cat. I want a real kitty, but Mama says I can't have one until I'm six. Which is only a few weeks away, you know," she said to Anita, who rolled her eyes.

"You must take after your mom," he said, with a wink at Anita, "'cause you're very pretty."

"Yeah, that's what everybody says," Mattie said with a very serious nod as her mother snorted in the background. "I'm in kindergarten, but I can already read, so that's how come I know about the rice." She leaned sideways against the table, one sneakered foot resting atop its mate, then closed the space between them until their foreheads were only inches apart. "My daddy broke his leg," she whispered, like Tony wasn't sitting right there.

"I know," Ben whispered back. "That's why I'm here, to help your grandpa until your dad can go back to work."

"Never mind that it's totally unnecessary," Tony said to his father, not even trying to mask his irritation. "For a few weeks, one of the guys could drive me around. Or you could," he directed at Anita, who crossed her arms underneath her impressive bust, glaring.

"And I already told you, I don't have any vacation time coming up—"

"And maybe," Ben's mother said, clearly trying to keep her kitchen from becoming a war zone, "you should be grateful your brother is back home, yes?"

"Yeah, about that," Mattie said, startling Ben and eliciting a muttered, "God help us when she hits puberty," from Anita. "If you're my uncle, how come I've never seen you before? And are you gonna stay or what?"

Ignoring the first question—because how on earth was he supposed to explain something to a five-year-old he didn't fully comprehend himself?—Ben gently tugged one of those irresistible ponytails and said, "I don't know, bumblebee," which was the best he could do, at the moment.

An answer which elicited a soft, hopeful "Oh!" from his mother, even as his brother grabbed his crutches, standing so quickly he knocked over his chair.

"We need to get goin'," he said. "'Nita, kids, come on."

"But you just got here!" Ben's mother said as his father laid a hand on his arm.

"Antonio. Don't be like this."

"Like what, Pop?" Tony said, halting his awkward progress toward the door. "Like *myself?* But then, I guess it doesn't matter anyway now. Because it's all good, isn't it, now that *Ben's* back. Kids...*now.*"

Both Jake and Mattie gave Ben a quick, confused backwards glance—Mattie adding a small wave—before Anita, apology brimming in her eyes, ushered them all out. In the dulled silence that followed, Ben's mother scooped up one of the whimpering little mutts, stroking it between its big batlike ears. "It's Tony's leg, he's not himself, you know how he hates feeling helpless."

Ben stood as well, swinging his leather jacket off the back of his chair. At the moment, it took everything he had not to walk out the door, get in his truck and head right back to Dallas. Why on earth had he thought that time in and of itself would have been sufficient to heal this mess, that everyone would have readjusted if he took himself out of the equation...?

"Where are you going?" his father demanded.

"Just out for a walk. Get reacquainted with the neighborhood."

"Oh." His father's heavy brows pushed together. "I thought maybe we could watch a game or something together later."

"I know. But..." Ben avoided his father's troubled gaze, tamping down the familiar annoyance before his mouth got away from his brain. Knowing something needed to be fixed didn't mean he had a clue how to fix it. Not then, and not, unfortunately, now. He smiled for his mother, dropped a kiss on the top of her head. "I'm not going far. And I'll be back for that game, I promise," he said to his father.

"Benicio—"

"Let him go, Luis," his mother said softly. "He has to do this his own way."

Ben sent silent thanks across the kitchen, then left before his father's confusion tore at him more than it already had.

For maybe an hour, he walked around the neighborhood, his hands stuffed in his pockets, until the crisp, dry air began to clear his head, until the sun—serene and sure in a vast blue sky broken only by the stark, bare branches of winter trees—burned off enough of the fumes from the morning's disastrous reunion for him to remember why'd he come home. That he'd made the decision to do so long before he'd gotten the call from his father, asking for his help.

So even if everything he'd seen and faced and overcome during his absence paled next to the challenge of trying to piece together the real Ben out of the mess he'd left behind, he still felt marginally better by the time he turned back on to his parents' block…just as Mercy's garage door groaned open.

From across the street, he watched her drag a small step stool outside, wrench it open. Now dressed in jeans and a bright red sweater small enough to fit one of his mother's dogs, she plunked the stool down in the grass in front of her house. She jiggled it for a few seconds to make sure it was steady, then climbed and started to take down the single strand of large colored Christmas lights at the edge of the roof. In a nearby bald spot in the lawn, that Hummer-sized cat of hers plopped down, writhing in the dirt until Mercy yelled at it to cut it out already, she'd just vacuumed. Chastened, the beast flipped to its stomach, its huge, fluffy tail twitching laconically as it glared at Ben.

Speaking of a mess he'd left behind. If he knew what was good for him, he'd keep walking.

Clearly, he didn't.

* * *

"Need any help?"

Mercy grabbed the gutter to keep from toppling off the step stool, then twisted around, trying her best to keep the *And who are you again?* look in place. But one glance at that goofy grin and her irritation vaporized. Right along with her determination to pretend he didn't exist. That he'd never existed. That there hadn't been a time—

"No, I'm good," she said, returning to her task, hoping he'd go away. As if. All too aware of his continued scrutiny, she got down, moved the step stool over, got back up, removed the next few feet of lights, got down, moved the step stool over, got back up—

"Here."

Ben stood at her elbow, the rest of the lights loosely coiled in his hand. A breeze shivered through his thick hair, a shade darker than hers; the reflected beam of light from his own truck window delineated ridges and shadows in a face barely reminiscent of the outrageous flirt she remembered. Instead, his smile—not even that, really, barely a tilt of lips at once full and unapologetically masculine—barely masked an unfamiliar weightiness in those burnt wood eyes. An unsettling discovery, to say the least, stirring frighteningly familiar, and most definitely unwanted, feelings of tenderness inside her.

She climbed down from the stool. "You started at the other end."

"Seemed like a good plan to me."

"Creep."

That damned smile still toying with his mouth, he handed the lights to her.

On a huffed sigh, she folded up the stool and tromped back to the garage. The cat, wearing a fine coating of dirt and dead grass, followed. As did Ben.

She turned. "If I told you to go away, would you?"

He shrugged, then said, "How come you're taking down your lights already? It's not even New Year's yet."

Mercy and the cat exchanged a glance, then she shrugged as well. "I have to help Ma take her stuff down on New Year's day, I figured I'd get a jumpstart on my own, since the weather's nice and all. And they're saying we might have snow tomorrow. Although I'll believe that when I see it. Not that there's much. Which you can see. I still have my tree up, though—"

Shut up, she heard inside her head. *Shut up, shut up, shut up.* Her mouth stretched tight, she crossed her arms over her ribs.

"And why are you over here again?"

"I'm not really over here, I'm out for a walk. But you looked like you could use some help, so I took a little detour. Damn, that's a big cat," he said as she finally gave up—since Ben was obviously sticking to her like dryer lint—and dragged a plastic bin down off a shelf, dumping the lights into it.

"That's no cat, that's my bodyguard."

"I can see that."

Mercy glanced over to see the thing rubbing against Ben's shins, getting dirt all over his jeans, doing that little quivering thing with his big, bushy tail. Ben squatted to scratch the top of his head; she could hear the purring from ten feet away. "What's his name?"

"Depends on the day and my mood. On good days, it's

Homer. Sometimes Big Red. Today I'm leaning toward Dumbbutt."

The cat shot her a death glare and gave her one of his broken meows. Chuckling, Ben stood and wiped his hands, sending enough peachy fur floating into the garage to cover another whole cat.

"Because?"

"Because he's too stupid to know when he's got it good. If he sticks around, he's got heat, my bed to sleep in and all the food he can scarf down. But no, that would apparently cramp his style. Even though the vet swore once I had him fixed, he wouldn't do that. She was wrong. Or didn't take enough off, I haven't decided. In any case, he periodically vanishes, sometimes overnight, sometimes for days at a time. Then he has the nerve to drag his carcass back here, all matted and hungry, and beg for my forgiveness."

Silence.

"You wouldn't be trying to make a point there, would you?"

Mercy smiled sweetly. "Not at all."

"At least I'm not matted," he said, his intense gaze making her oddly grateful the garage was unheated. "Or hungry. My mother made sure of that."

"How about fixed?"

He winced.

"Yeah, that's what I figured." She turned to heft the lights bin back up onto the shelf. "But you're not getting back in my bed, either."

Funny, she would have expected to hear a lot more conviction behind those words. Especially the *not* part of that sentence.

"I lost out to the cat?"

There being nothing for it, Mercy faced him again, palms on butt, chest out, chin raised. As defiant as a Pomeranian facing a Rotty. "You lost out, period."

They stared at each other for several seconds. Until Ben said, "You know, I could really use a cup of coffee."

"I thought you were out for a walk?"

"Turned out to be a short walk."

More gaze-tangling, while she weighed the plusses (none that she could see) with the minuses (legion) about letting him in, finally deciding, *Oh, what the hell?* He'd come in, she'd give him coffee, he'd go away (finally), and that would be that. She led man and cat into her kitchen, hitting the garage door opener switch on the way. Over the grinding of the door closing, she said, "I'm guessing you needed a break?"

The corner of his mouth twitched. "You could say."

"I don't envy you. God knows I couldn't live with *my* parents again. What are you doing?"

He'd picked up her remote, turned on the TV. "Just wanted to check the news, I haven't seen any in days. You get CNN?"

"Yeah, I get it. And you're gonna get it if you turn it on."

On a sigh, he clicked off the TV, moseyed back over to the breakfast bar. "You still don't watch the news?"

"Not if I can help it. Feeling overwhelmed and helpless ain't my thang." She pointed to one of the bar stools. "Sit. And don't let the cat up—" Homer jumped onto the counter in front of Ben "—on the bar."

Long, immensely capable fingers plunged into the cat's ruff, as a pair of whatchagonnadoaboutit? grins slid her way. On a sigh, Mercy said, "Regular or decaf?"

"What do you think?"

No, the question was, what was she *thinking,* letting the man into her house? Again. When no good would come of it, she was sure. And yet, despite those legion reasons why this was a seriously bad idea, the lack of gosh-it's-been-a-long-time awkwardness between them was worth noting. Oh, sure, the atmosphere was charged enough to crackle—surprising in itself, considering her normal reaction (or lack thereof) to running into old lovers and such. *That was fun...next?* had been her motto for, gee, years. So who'd'athunk, that in spite of the unexpectedness of Ben's reappearance, the sexual hum nearly making her deaf, in the end it would be a completely different bond holding sway over the moment, lending an *Oh, yeah, okay* feeling to the whole thing that made her feel almost...comfortable. If it hadn't been for that sexual hum business.

Which led to a second question: If yesterday—shoot, this morning—she'd been totally over him, what had happened since then to change that?

Digging the coffee out of the fridge, she glanced over, noticed him looking around. Then those eyes swung back to hers, calling a whole bunch of memories out of retirement, and she thought, *Oh. Right.*

"Cool tree," he said.

Grateful for the distraction, Mercy allowed a fond smile for the vintage silver aluminum number she'd found at a garage sale. Some of the "needles" had cracked off, but with all the hot pink marabou garland, it was barely noticeable. Well, that, and the several dozen bejeweled angels, miniature shoe ornaments and crosses vying for space amongst the feathers. This

was one seriously tarted up Christmas tree, and Mercy adored
it. "That's Annabelle. You should see her at night when I've
got the color wheel going. She's something else."

Ben shook his head, laughing softly, and yet more
memories reported for duty. Including several that fearlessly
headed straight for the hot zones.

"I just met Mattie and Jake," he said.

Whew. "Yeah? Aren't they great? That Mattie's a pistol,
isn't she?"

"She is that." He sounded a little awestruck. "Took to me
right away."

"Don't take it personally, the child doesn't know the
meaning of 'stranger.' A second's glance in her direction and
you're doomed. Drives my sister nuts."

"She wouldn't…Mattie knows better than to go off with
someone she doesn't know, I hope."

"With Anita for her mother? What do you think?"

Ben's shoulders seemed to relax a little after that, before he
said, "I can't believe you're still here. In this house, I mean."

A shrug preceded, "Why not? It's home." She spooned
coffee into the basket; took her three tries to ram it home. "It's
just me, I don't need a huge house. And the landlord gives me
a good deal on the rent."

"You've made some changes, though."

"Not really," she said, wondering why she was flushing.
"Oh, yeah, those lamps by the sofa are new—Hobby Lobby
specials, half off. And I did paint, about three years ago.
During my faux-finishing phase. That lacquered finish was a
bitch, let me tell you."

"Huh." He paused. "The walls are certainly…red."

"Yeah, I almost went with orange, but thought it would be a bit much with the sofa."

"Good point." Another pause. "Never saw a sofa the color of antifreeze before."

"Do I detect a hint of derision in that comment?"

Ben's mouth twitched again. "Not at all. But the walls… your father must've nearly had a coronary."

"To put it mildly. Until I pointed out that since I'll have to be blasted out of here, painting over the walls is moot."

He chuckled, then asked, "How are your folks?"

"Fine," she said, even though what she really wanted to do was scream *Stop looking at me like that!* "Dad's finally retired, driving Ma nuts. Her arthritis has been acting up more these past couple of years, which is why I have to help her take down her decorations."

"She still turn the place into the North Pole?"

"You have no idea. And every year she buys *more* stuff. For the grandbabies, she says."

"How many are there?"

"Twelve. Although Rosie's pregnant with her fourth. A fact my mother never tires of shoving down my throat. That I'm the only one without kids. Oh, and a husband."

His expression softened. "Guess there's no accounting for some men's stupidity."

Uh…

Mercy spun back to the gurgling coffeemaker. "No matter. What can I say, that ship has sailed."

After a silence thick enough to slice and serve with butter and jam, Ben said, "So what are you up to these days?"

The coffeemaker finally spit out its last drop; Mercy pulled a pair of mugs down from a cabinet, filled them both with the steaming brew. She handed him his coffee, then retreated to lean against the far counter, huddling her own mug to her chest. "Actually, I finally got my business degree, opened a children's gently used clothing store with two of my classmates, about six or seven years ago. Except it grew, so now we carry some furniture and educational toys, too."

He held aloft his mug in a silent toast. "And you're doing well?"

"Fingers crossed, so far, so good. We were even able to hire an assistant last summer. A damn good thing since both of my partners have babies now. Had to find a larger place, too. One of those old Victorians near Old Town? Your father's company did the remodel, actually."

"No kidding? I'll have to drop by, check it out."

"You, in a kid's store?"

"Why not? Hey, I've got a niece and nephew to spoil. Especially…" His eyes lowered, he thumbed the rim of his cup, then looked back up at her. "Especially since I've got a lot of lost time to make up for."

"And whose fault is that?"

"You know, you could at least pretend to be diplomatic."

"I could. But why? And since we're on the subject…so what exactly *have* you been doing for the past ten years?"

His eyes narrowed, a move that instantly provoked a tiny *Hmm* in the dimly lit recesses of her mind. "This and that," he finally said. "Going where the work was."

"Whatever that's supposed to mean."

He looked at her steadily for a long moment, then said quietly, "I didn't vanish without a trace, Merce. My family's always known where I was, that I was okay. And I'm here now, aren't I?"

"But *why,* is the question? And don't give me some song-and-dance about your father needing you. Because I'm not buying it."

Ben leaned back on the bar stool, gently drumming his fingers on the counter, as he seemed to be contemplating how much to tell her. "Let's just say events provided a much needed kick in the butt and let it go at that."

"A kick in the butt to do what?"

One side of his mouth kicked up. "Thought I said to let it go?"

"Not gonna happen. So?"

He slid off the stool, moseying out into the living room and picking up a family photo of her youngest sister Olivia and her family, including four little boys under the age of nine. "I needed some time to…reassess a few things, that's all." He set the photo back down and turned to her, his hand in his back pocket, and something in his eyes made her stomach drop.

"Ben…? What's wrong? Did something happen?"

"You always could see through me, Merce," he said softly, a rueful grin tugging at that wonderful, wonderful mouth. "Even when we were kids. But this isn't about something happening nearly as much as…well, I find myself wondering a lot these days how I got to be thirty-five with still no idea how I fit in the grand scheme of things."

Yep, she knew that feeling. All too well. Only, up until a few minutes ago, she could have sworn she'd left that "Who the hell am I?" phase of her life far behind her. Apparently, she'd been wrong.

Not only because the grinning, cocky, nobody-can-tell-me-nuthin' dude of yore had morphed into this man with the haunted eyes who'd clearly been knocked around a time or two and, she was guessing, had come out all the stronger, and perhaps wiser, for it. But because, in the time it took to drink a single cup of coffee, whoever this was had turned everything she'd thought she'd known about herself on its head.

On a soft but heartfelt, "Dammit," Mercy sidestepped the breakfast bar and crossed the small room, where she grabbed Ben's shoulders and yanked him into a liplock neither of them would ever forget.

Chapter Three

He'd been as powerless to stop their mouths' colliding as he would have been a meteor falling on his head.

But nothing said he'd had to wrap his arms tight around her and kiss her back, with a good deal of enthusiasm and no small amount of tongue. Or lower her onto that hideous green sofa—except his back, which wouldn't have taken kindly to bending over like that for longer than a second or so. Damn, she was short. Even so, he could still stop, no sweat, any time he wanted to, still pull away from that warm, wicked mouth and the warm, wicked woman that came with it.

Which eventually he did, if for no other reason than they both needed air, bracing his hands on either side of her shoulders and searching her eyes before once again lowering his mouth to hers, this time going slow, so slow, so mind-druggingly slow, pulling back whenever she tried to cozy up to his tongue, gently nipping her lower lip, her chin, her neck…remembering how it had been between them.

How good.

She made a sound that was both growl and whimper as her long, pale fingernails dug into his arms, as one leg snaked around his waist, trapping him, claiming him, even as his body completely ignored his brain's strident protests, that this was stupid and wrong and what the hell was he thinking?

Breathing hard, she pushed him slightly away, even as she clutched his shirt. "So, how long are you here again?"

Right.

His heart pounding, Ben waited, silently swearing, for the testosterone haze to clear. Then he pushed himself up, and away, walking back into the kitchen to get his coat.

"Four weeks," he said, flatly. Because damned if he was going to hold out the same bone to Mercy he never should have to his family. Because he had no idea what his plans were. What came next. "Maybe six."

She sat up, her hair as knotted as her forehead, and need and regret and a whole mess of pointless, inappropriate feelings got all tangled up in his head. He'd missed that bizarre mixture of vulnerability and toughness that was Mercedes Zamora. Missed it way too much to risk screwing things up now.

"What are you doing?" she asked.

"I think it's called coming to my senses."

"Uh-huh." Laughing, she shoved her hair out her face with both hands. Her swollen lips canted in a crooked smile, she slumped against the cushions, propping one foot on the brightly painted wooden trunk she used for a coffee table. The shiny red walls made the air seem molten, flooding his consciousness with possibilities he had no business considering. "And just what do you think," she said, "the odds are of our keeping our hands off each other while you're here?"

"That's not the point." His hands shot up by his shoulders. "I can't do this, Mercy."

"Yeah? Could've fooled me."

"No. I mean, I can't do this again. Mess around. With you."

"Because…?"

"Because it wouldn't be right."

"Yeah, well, it wasn't right the first time. Don't recall that stopping us."

He squeezed shut his eyes against the onslaught of memories. "God, Merce," he said, opening them again, "what is it about you that makes me so hot my brain shorts out?"

She shrugged, then grabbed a bright blue throw pillow, hugging it to her, looking uncannily like a very grown-up version of their niece. "I'm easy?"

This time, he laughed out loud. "Oh, babe, one thing you're not is easy."

"Fun, then. And by the way, that thing where you said I made you hot?" She gave him a thumbs up.

"Like men don't say that to you all the time."

"Ooh, somebody's just racking up the brownie points right and left today." Two heartbeats later she stood in front of him again, her thumbs hooked in his belt loop, tugging him close. "No, really, that's a very sweet thing to say, considering I'm not exactly the nubile young thing I used to be. But what other men might or might not say to me isn't the point. The point is…" Her gaze never leaving his, she let go to skim a fingernail down his chest, smiling when he involuntarily flinched. "The point is, it's been a long, long time since anyone made me hot enough to short out my brain, too."

"Oh, yeah? How long?"

The fingernail slid underneath the front of his shirt, gently scraping across his skin. "Guess."

He pulled away.

"Would it put your mind at ease," she said behind him, "to know I'm not looking for the same things I was ten years ago?" When he turned, she added, "Not with you, not with anybody else. I'm not looking for forever, Ben." Her mouth stretched into an almost-smile. "Not anymore."

He frowned. "You don't *want* marriage? Kids?"

She walked over to the same photos he'd been looking at earlier, straightening out the one he'd apparently not put back correctly. "It's like when you're a teenager, and you just *know* if you don't get that album, or dress, or pair of shoes, you'll expire. Then one day you realize you never did get whatever it was you thought you couldn't live without, and not only did you survive, you don't miss it, either."

And clearly she'd forgotten just how well he'd always been able to see through her, too. Her reluctance to make eye contact was a dead giveaway that she was skirting the truth. But this wasn't the time to call her on it, especially since he was hardly in a place where he could be entirely truthful with her, either.

So all he said was, "You're one weird chick, Mercy," and she laughed.

"Not exactly breaking news," she said, facing him again. "Look, whether we should have let things get out of hand or not back then, I can't say. But I've never regretted it. Have you? No, wait," she said, holding up one hand. "Maybe I don't want to know the answer to that."

Ben realized he was grinding his teeth to keep from going to her. "Not hardly," he said, and she smiled.

"Well, then. Ben, I knew from the moment you came home after the army that you'd never stick around. Yeah, I was supremely annoyed that you took off without saying anything, but I always knew you'd leave." She did that thing where she planted her palms on her butt, and Ben's mouth went dry. "Just like I know you'll leave this time. But while you're here, we could either drive ourselves nuts pretending we're not interested, or we could enjoy each other." Her shoulders bumped. "Your call." When he shook his head, she said, "Why not?"

"*Porque nadie tropieza dos veces con la misma piedra,*" he said softly, repeating an old Mexican proverb he'd heard a thousand times as a kid. *Because nobody trips over the same stone twice.*

They eyed each other for a long moment, then she returned to the kitchen, collecting their mugs.

"You're angry."

"Don't be ridiculous." The dishwasher shuddered when she banged it open. "It was just a thought."

"Merce. A half hour ago you gave the very distinct impression you'd rather eat live snakes than start something up again with me. So why the sudden change of heart?"

She slammed the dishwasher shut, turned around. "That was my wounded pride talking. So good news—guess I'm a faster healer than I realized."

"And I'm just getting started," he said, and her brows

plunged. "Honey, I'm not rejecting you. I'm rejecting the past. Because I *don't* want to pick up where we left off. Because, yeah, I want you so much I can't think straight, but it's more than that with you." His throat ached when he swallowed. "It was always more than that with you."

In the space of a heartbeat, her expression changed from confusion to stunned comprehension to bemusement. The cat jumped up on the counter beside her, bumping her elbow to be petted. Being obviously well-trained, she obeyed, then said, "You remember the scene early in *It's a Wonderful Life* where Jimmy Stewart finds himself in Donna Reed's living room, and her mother hollers down the stairs, asking her what he wants, and Donna Reed says, 'I don't know,' then turns to Jimmy Stewart and says, 'What *do* you want?' and he gets all mad because he doesn't really know?" She cocked her head. "Well?"

"I don't know," Ben ground out, stuffing his arms into his jacket. "But I can tell you I'm not looking for the same things I was before, either."

Then he strode to her door and let himself out, not even trying to keep from slamming the door.

The forecast had called for a slight chance of snow on New Year's Eve—pretty much an empty threat in Albuquerque, which, Ben mused as he listened to his mother fuss at his father at their bedroom door, rarely had weather in the usual sense of the word. Muttering in Spanish, his mother trooped down the hall, all dressed up for her night on the town.

"You sure you're going to be okay?" Juanita said, wrapping a soft, fuzzy shawl around her shoulders, half concealing the glittery long-sleeved dress underneath. Her eyes sparkled as brightly as the diamond studs in her ears—his parents and Mercy's were spending the night at one of the fancy casino resorts on a nearby Indian reservation, and she'd spent most of the day primping in preparation. When he'd been a kid and money had been tight for both families, "doing something for New Year's" meant getting together to play cards, or, later, watch videos. Apparently, though, their parents had been celebrating in grand style for some years now, and seeing how excited they were tickled Ben to death.

"I imagine I'll muddle through somehow," he said with a smile.

The doorbell rang; his mother opened it to let Mary and Manny Zamora inside. "Luis!" she tossed over her shoulder as Ben and the Zamoras shook hands, exchanged hugs and small talk. "They're here!" She minced to the end of the hallway in high heels she wasn't used to wearing. "What *are* you doing?"

Grumbling under his breath, his father appeared, still adjusting the ostentatious silver-and-turquoise bolo on his string tie. After a burst of chatter, the Zamoras and his father headed back out, but his mother lagged behind.

"Now there's plenty of food in the refrigerator," she said, "and you know how to use the microwave—"

"Juanita! *Per Dios!*"

"I'm coming, I'm coming!"

Ben stood in the doorway, watching them drive off, the headlight beams from his father's brand new Escalade glancing off a handful of tiny, valiantly swirling snowflakes. As he was about to close the door, he noticed Mercy's Firebird in her driveway, its lightly frosted roof glistening in the light from the street lamp several houses over. Ben frowned—the quintessential party girl, alone on New Year's? Now that was just wrong.

Close the door, Ben. None of your business, Ben. Stay out of it, Ben…

A minute's raid on the family room bar produced a bottle of Baileys he hoped didn't predate Nixon. If nothing else, they could spike their coffee.

Or, he considered as he stood on her doorstep, ringing her doorbell, she could—justifiably—tell him to take his Baileys and stick it someplace the sun don't shine—

"No!" he heard Mercy say on the other side. "Never, ever answer the door without first making sure you know who's on the other side!"

The door swung open (because clearly Mercy didn't take her own advice, which provoked a flash of irritation behind Ben's eyes). From inside floated the mouthwatering scents of baked chocolate and popcorn. "Ben! What are you doing here?"

Her hair sprouting from the top of her head in a fountain of ringlets, the party girl was dressed to kill in a three-sizes-too-big purple sweatshirt that hung to midthigh, a pair of clingy, sparkly pants, and blindingly bright, striped fuzzy socks. Not surprisingly, considering the way they'd left things the day before, her eyes bugged with total astonishment, which pleased Ben in some way he couldn't begin to define.

"I, um, didn't like the idea of you being by yourself on New Year's?" he said as Mattie, swallowed up in a nearly identical outfit and crying, "Uncle Ben! Uncle Ben!" launched herself at his knees, adhering to him like plastic wrap. Then she leaned back, giving him her most adoring, gap-toothed smile.

"Aunt Mercy an' me're watching *Finding Nemo* but Jake doesn't wanna, he says it's a sissy movie." The squirt latched onto his hand and dragged him across the threshold. "Wanna come watch with us?"

Ben's gaze shifted to Mercy, who shrugged. The sweatshirt didn't budge. "Welcome to Mercy's Rockin' New Year's Eve. I'm babysitting," she said, standing aside to keep from getting trampled as Jacob yelled from the back of the house, "I'm not a baby!"

"Get a job and we'll talk," Mercy called back as they all returned to the living room.

No reply except for the muffled pings and zaps of some video game.

"Popcorn's ready," she yelled again, plopping a plastic bowl as large as a bathtub in the middle of that trunk with identity issues. Over in her corner, Annabelle shimmered red…blue…green…red as the color wheel did its thing, while a small fire crackled lazily in a kiva fireplace in the opposite corner, and Ben felt a chuckle of pure delight rumble up from his chest.

Mercy reached up to adjust her hair, her hands landing on her hips when she was done. Her nails were as red as her walls, with what looked like little rhinestones or something imbedded in each tip. Amazing. Ben's gaze shifted to her face; she looked more befuddled than ticked, he decided. "We've already had the first course—brownies—but I think there's still a few left in the kitchen."

"Thanks, but I think I'll pass. Um…" Ben slipped off his jacket, flinging it across the back of a chair. "Are you okay with this?"

One eyebrow hitched, just slightly. "That you crashed my party? Yeah, I should've had the dude at the door check the guest list more carefully. But hey, no problem, we've got chaperones and everything."

"What's a chaperone?" Mattie asked.

"Somebody who makes sure nobody does something they shouldn't," Mercy said, never taking her eyes off Ben's, the eyebrow hiking another millimeter. Okay, definitely not ticked. Not that having the kids here meant a whole lot in the tempering-the-sexual-tension department. Apparently.

"What's that?" the little girl said, latching on to the Baileys. "C'n I have some?"

"Not if you want your mother to ever, ever let you come here again," Mercy said, taking the bottle from Ben and nodding in approval. "Later," she said, holding it up, then setting it on top of the fashionably distressed armoire housing a regular old TV and DVD player. She walked the few steps to the hall, pushing up the sleeves of the sweatshirt. They fell right back down. "Jacob Manuel Vargas! If you don't get out here *right now* and get yourself some popcorn, your uncle Ben's gonna eat it all up!"

"Uncle Ben's here? All *right!*" he heard from down the hall, followed by pounding footsteps and a grinning kid in a hoodie and jeans. He high-fived Ben; Mercy stuck another plastic bowl in his hands with the warning that if he got a single piece on her bed his butt was going to be in a major sling.

"Wanna play games with me later?" he asked Ben around a mouthful of popcorn, looking less than terrorized by his aunt's threat. "I got this really cool racing game for Christmas, I'm already at the third level."

"Sure thing," Ben said, feeling a little like the new kid at school getting picked for the best team. "But in a sec, okay? So," he said to Mercy, imbuing his words with as much meaning as he dared. "Tony and Anita went out?" He settled on the sofa, swiping the bowl of popcorn off the coffee table. Mattie wriggled into place beside him, grabbing a far-too-large handful that promptly exploded all over her, the sofa and the floor.

"Sorry, Aunt Mercy!"

"Don't worry about it, cutie-pie, it happens." Mercy bent over to pick up the scattered kernels, her hair and face glimmering red...blue...green...red. "Yeah," she said. Deliberately avoiding his eyes? "They'd already made reservations at the Hilton, so it seemed a shame to give them up just because Tony broke his leg. But the real party's here—right, munchkin?" she said to Mattie, lightly tapping her niece on the nose with a piece of popcorn. The child giggled, snuggling closer to Ben and swiping a piece of popcorn out of his hand.

"We get to stay up until midnight—" she yawned "—and watch the ball drop in Tom's hair."

"*Times Square,* stupid," Jacob said, prompting an immediate "Don't call your sister stupid," from Mercy.

Apparently unfazed, the little girl twisted around to look up at Ben with big, solemn, slightly sleepy eyes. "It's funner over here. Mama 'n' Daddy've been fighting a lot. I don't like it when they do that."

Mercy's eyes flashed to Ben's as Jacob, instantly turning beet red, muttered, "Shut up, Mattie."

"Well, they have. An' you're not supposed to say 'shut up,' Mama says it's rude."

"Guys!" Mercy said. "Enough. But you know what? Your mama and I used to fight like crazy when we were kids, and it didn't mean anything."

"Really?" Mattie said.

Mercy laughed. "Oh, yeah. Yelling, screaming…ask your grandma, she used to swear it sounded like we were killing each other. And then it would blow over and we'd be best buddies again—"

"C'n I have a Coke?" the boy said, bouncing up out of the chair.

"Sure, sweetie," Mercy said. "You know where they are. And by the way," she said to his back as he walked away, "what happens here, stays here, got it?"

That got a fleeting grin and a nod. Only Ben wasn't sure if Mercy was talking about the questionable menu or the even more questionable conversation. He stuffed another handful of popcorn into his mouth, staring at the slightly trembling image of a red-and-white fish on the screen in front of him. As Jake traipsed back to Mercy's bedroom with his popcorn and soda, Mattie dug the remote out from under Ben's hip, punched the Play button and the red fish started talking to a blue fish that sounded oddly like Ellen deGeneres.

"So you really think that's all this is?" he said softly over Mattie's giggles as Mercy sank into the cushion on the other side of her niece, tucking her feet up under her.

Her silence spoke volumes as she reached across their niece to pluck several kernels from the bowl. "No," she said, her eyes on the screen. "Unfortunately."

"You think somebody should go talk to Jake?"

"I've tried, but…" She shrugged, her forehead puckered.

"Guys, shh," Mattie said, poking Ben with her elbow. "This is the best part, when Dory pretends she's a whale."

Out of deference to Mattie, they stopped talking. But Ben wasn't paying the slightest attention to the movie, and he somehow doubted Mercy—whose mouth was still pulled down at the corners—was, either. Under other circumstances, he would have been perfectly fine with staying right where he was, with this goofy little girl cuddled next to him and her goofy aunt not much farther away, munching popcorn and watching a kid flick.

But sometimes, life has other ideas.

So he gently extricated himself from the soft, trusting warmth curled into his side, shifting the child to lean against her aunt instead, then followed the sound of engines roaring and tires screeching until he reached Mercy's bedroom. Sitting cross-legged on the end of Mercy's double bed, Jake was intently focused on the game flashing across the smaller TV sitting on the dresser in front of him, his thumbs a blur on the controller as he leaned from side to side.

Ben leaned against the door frame, his thumbs hooked in his jeans pockets. "Hey," he said softly, acutely aware that, as far as Jake was concerned, Ben was a stranger. Not to mention he was venturing into potentially explosive-ridden territory. No doubt Tony would see Ben's attempt to help as blatant, and extremely unwelcome, interference.

Attention riveted to the car zooming and swerving wildly on the screen, Jake bumped one shoulder in acknowledgment. "Soon as I'm done—" he hunched forward, pounded one button a dozen times in rapid succession, then whispered "*Yes!* I can set it up…for two players…"

"No hurry."

The room was dark except for a single bedside lamp, but he could see she'd gone with the orange in here, Ben noted with a wry smile. Sort of the same color as that clownfish, actually. But for a woman as unabashedly female as Mercedes Zamora, her bedroom was almost eerily frou-frou free. Even more than he remembered. No lace, no filmy stuff at the windows, no mounds of pillows or—God bless her—stuffed animals on the unadorned platform bed, covered with a plain white comforter. Nothing but clean lines as far as the eye could see.

And all that color, drenching the room in a perpetual sunset.

Ben turned his attention to his nephew, then eased over to sit next to him. The cat, who'd been God knew where up to that point, jumped up and butted his arm, then tramped across his lap to sniff Jake's hand.

"Go away, Homer," he said, giggling. "Your whiskers tickle."

Yeah, that's how kids are supposed to sound. "Wow," Ben said, sincerely impressed. "You really rock at this."

A quick grin bloomed across the kid's face. "Thanks. Okay," he said a minute later, his fingers again flying over the buttons as the image changed to a split screen. "The other controller's in my backpack, if you want to get it?"

"Sure." Ben dug through a wad of rumpled, detergent-scented clothes, pulled it out, plugged it into the console. "You have to promise to go easy on me, though," he said. "I think the last video game I played was Mario on Nintendo."

"You mean, like Game Cube?"

"No, I mean the *original* Nintendo. Way before your time."

"Oh, yeah…my dad still drags that out every once in a while. But mostly he likes my PlayStation, 'cause it's way cooler."

Ben chose his car—a red Porsche, what else?—and they were off. Twenty seconds in, Ben realized his reaction time needed some serious retooling. The kid was beating the crap out of him. "Your dad play games with you?"

"Yeah, sometimes. Mom doesn't like it much, though."

"Oh?" Ben said carefully.

"She keeps saying…he needs to…grow up." Apparently realizing his gaffe, the kid flicked a glance in Ben's direction, only to then say, "Why's Dad mad at you?"

Ben stiffened, tempted to pretend he had no idea what the kid was talking about. But what would be the point? "I'm not sure I can explain." He glanced at the boy. "Why?" he asked, smiling. "Was he bad-mouthing me?"

Jake flushed. "Kind of. Papi though, he like couldn't stop talkin' about you when they were over at our house last night. He's really, really happy you came home."

"So am I," Ben said. Then he bumped the boy's shoulder with his own, earning him a quick, slightly embarrassed grin.

After another couple of seconds, though, Jake said quietly, "Mattie's right, Mom an' Dad really have been yelling a lot at each other lately."

"That must suck," Ben said after a short pause.

"Totally. Especially since it really scares Mattie, she's just a little kid. And I know what Aunt Mercy said, about how she and my mom used to fight when they were kids, but this is different."

"Why do you think that?"

"I dunno. It just is. Me 'n' Mattie fight all the time, too, but…" Jake shook his head.

Ben's game car crashed into a wall, bounced back onto the

road, righted itself and kept going. Which is exactly what this conversation was going to do if he wasn't careful. Except for the keep going part, maybe. "I don't know, maybe it's not as bad as it looks. After all, do you think they would have gone out tonight if they really weren't getting along?"

Beside him, the kid shrugged. "Dunno. Maybe."

After another few seconds—and another wipeout—Ben ventured, "Have you told your mom and dad how you feel?"

When several moments passed with no reply, Ben looked over to see the boy's jaw set much too tightly for such a small person, and his heart cramped. "Jake?" he said gently.

His breathing suddenly labored, his nephew tossed down the controller. "This game is dumb, I don't want to play anymore, okay?"

"Sure, no problem." Ben tried to lay a hand on the kid's shoulder, but he jerked away. So he lowered his head to look up into his face. "I know we only just met, but you can tell me how you feel, it's okay—"

Huge, scared eyes met his. "You're gonna tell, aren't you?"

"Is anybody actually getting hurt?"

Jake looked away. Shook his head.

"Then I swear, dude, this is strictly between you and me. So are we cool?"

After a moment, the boy nodded.

Ben thought for a moment, then said, "When your mom and dad get mad, do they yell at you? Or Mattie?"

"Uh-uh."

"You're sure?"

"Yeah, 'course. Well, Mom gets kinda crazy when I forget to clean my room an' stuff, but that's different."

Ben smiled. "Yes, it is." He sucked in a breath, then asked, "And you're sure it's only yelling? No hitting?"

Jake's head popped up at that, his entire face contorting with his incredulous, "No! Geez, why would you think that? They just argue, is all." He smacked at a tear that had trickled down his cheek. "Sometimes it's not even loud or anything. It's just like…I dunno. Like they forgot how to talk to each other an' stuff."

"Maybe this night out will be good for them, then," Ben said. "Give them a chance to be alone, just with each other. So maybe they can figure out how to talk to each other again."

"Yeah, maybe," the kid said, but he didn't exactly sound hopeful.

"Sometimes it's tough, being a parent," Ben said, and the kid frowned up at him.

"How would you know? You don't have any kids, right?"

Right to the gut. "No, I don't. But I've been around. And besides your Mami and Papi Vargas always swore your dad and I drove them crazy."

A tremulous smile flickered across the child's face. "For real?"

"Oh, yeah. And they used to argue, too, now and then. Nobody's going to get along all the time, no matter how much they love each other. Sometimes, they're going to disagree about stuff. Loudly. Like your aunt said, it usually blows over—"

From the doorway, Mercy softly cleared her throat. Both Ben and Jacob twisted around. "I thought I'd make root beer floats—how does that sound?"

"Cool," Jacob said, grabbing his controller again. "Call me when they're ready, 'kay?"

"Sure thing, your highness," Mercy said on a soft laugh,

her expression sobering when she shifted her gaze to Ben. "Come help me in the kitchen?"

Uh, boy.

"What happened to your sidekick?" Ben asked easily, warily, as he followed Mercy down the hall.

"She passed out long before they found Nemo," Mercy said in a low voice. "No, leave her, I'll put her to bed in a bit."

"Brownies, popcorn, root beer floats…" Shaking his head, Ben leaned against the front of the sink, lowering his voice as well so as to not wake Mattie. "You trying to poison these kids or what?"

"It's a party, I'm hardly going to serve them Brussels sprouts. And I overheard a lot of what you said to Jake."

Yeah, he figured this was coming. "You're not going to even apologize for eavesdropping, are you?"

The refrigerator's compressor jerked awake when she opened the freezer to get out the ice cream, then the fridge itself for the bottle of root beer. "Nope."

"And do I detect an edge to your words I should worry about?"

"It's not that I don't appreciate you trying to make the kid feel better, but…" She plunked both soda and ice cream onto the counter, frowning at him. "But giving him false hope when you don't really know the situation seems a little, I don't know. Presumptuous?"

"Because who the hell am I to come waltzing back into everyone's life and try to fix things I know nothing about?"

"Something like that, yeah."

"I was only following your lead."

"I know, I know," she said on an exhaled breath. "Reach

me those goblets over the sink, would you? Only three, Mattie's down for the count, I'm sure." As he retrieved a trio of heavy, short stemmed glasses, she said, "Somehow, hearing the BS coming out of your mouth made me realize how ridiculous it must have sounded coming out of mine."

Ben frowned, only half watching Mercy pour the root beer into the glasses. "What little I was around Tony and Anita the other day…things definitely seemed tense. But do you think their marriage is in that much trouble?"

"Honestly? I don't know. I've tried to bring up the subject with my sister, but she won't bite."

"Which isn't a good sign."

Obvious worry deepened the faint lines already bracketing her mouth. "No. It isn't."

Ben released a breath. "I guess I assumed the tension was due to Tony's breaking his leg and they hadn't quite adjusted to how they were going to get through the next few weeks." Not to mention how Tony was going to deal with Ben's taking over for him during that time. That, Ben understood. Whatever was going on between his brother and Mercy's sister though…not a clue. "Tony's being a jerk, isn't he?"

"*Oh*, no," Mercy said, vigorously shaking her head. "There's no way I'm taking sides in this. For Jake's and Mattie's sakes, if nothing else."

"It's okay, I do remember what Tony can be like. Especially around women. To tell you the truth…well, I was kind of surprised that 'Nita and he even got together. I always thought she was smarter than that."

"Tell me that didn't come out the way you meant it."

He laughed a little. "Apparently not. And anyway, I guess I hoped either Tony'd gotten his head screwed on straight, or that 'Nita would be able to screw it on for him. But he's always had this weird attitude where women were concerned."

"I think the word you're looking for is *throwback*."

"Not that you're putting yourself in the middle or anything." When she smirked, he added, "And our folks have no clue, do they?"

"Are you kidding? God knows, Anita wouldn't say anything, she'd feel like a failure. Especially considering how thrilled they all were that the two of them got together. You'd have thought they'd made the perfect royal match. And in any case, I'm sure she really loves your brother."

"And you have no idea why."

"Please. I'm the last person to try explaining the workings of the human heart. Although, to give credit where it's due, he's definitely not a slacker—your father wouldn't get half the jobs he does if it weren't for Tony's getting out there and beating the bushes. And he loves his kids. Even if he does seem to think it's mainly 'Nita's job to keep them alive. Still…" Her brow furrowed. "I'm not sure which is worse—having our parents watch the slow, painful death of their kids' marriage, or getting blindsided by a possible divorce announcement."

Mercy scooped out the ice cream, carefully dropping it into the first glass of root beer. "Can I ask you something?" she asked softly.

"Like my saying 'no' would stop you."

"True," she said, a smile making a brief appearance. Another scoop of ice cream tumbled into the second glass.

"Given everything you said yesterday…" Her gaze veered to his. "Why'd you come over tonight? Assuming you didn't know the kids were here, I mean."

She had him there. "I'm not sure. It just seemed like the thing to do."

Again, she dipped the scoop into the carton. A glob caught on her knuckle when she drew it out; she licked it off and said, "Should I leave it at that?"

"I'd be immensely grateful if you would."

A low laugh rumbled from her throat. "Oh, admit it—" Her eyes sparkling with laughter, she leaned close and whispered, "I'm the flame and you're nothin' but a big old horny moth."

He met her gaze steadily, fearlessly. "You're dripping."

She flinched. "What?"

"The ice cream. It's dripping."

Swearing under her breath, she finished off the last float, then asked him to call Jacob.

A few minutes later, they woke a very drowsy Mattie to welcome in the New Year, after which Ben scooped the boneless little girl off the sofa and carried her to the twin-bedded room next to Mercy's. A dead weight against his chest, she smelled of popcorn, chocolate, girly shampoo and Mercy's perfume.

Mercy peeled back the covers so Ben could lay her down; she grabbed that disreputable stuffed kitty and curled onto her side, mumbling, "Love you, Uncle Ben," and almost instantly drifted back to sleep. With a squeaked meow, Homer hopped onto the bed, forming a tight, furry knot at the small of her back.

Ben straightened, his throat constricting as he watched Mercy draw the covers up over those defenseless little shoulders, reveling in a sense of belonging he'd deliberately ignored for far too long in the name of the "bigger" picture.

Jake begged to stay up a little longer to finish his game. "Fifteen minutes," Mercy said at her bedroom door, then continued to the living room, where she collapsed on the sofa, her toes curled on the edge of the trunk, her eyes closed.

"I should go," Ben said. "Let you get to sleep."

"We never got to the Baileys," she mumbled, her eyes still shut, then yawned.

"Maybe we should save it for another time."

Slowly—reluctantly—her eyes opened. "*Another* time?"

"You know what I mean."

She laughed. "Not only do I not know what you mean, I seriously doubt you do, either. No, it's okay," she said, vaguely waving one hand. "No explanation necessary." Her forehead crimped. "Bet you hadn't banked on walking into the middle of a domestic crisis."

"Can't say that I did. But—" he shrugged "—that's just part of being a family, right?"

"Ain't that the truth." Her eyes lowered to her knee; she stretched forward to pick off a piece of popcorn stuck to the glittery fabric, then looked back up at him. "Actually, I'm glad you came over. I didn't realize how much I needed to talk to somebody about all this stuff until there was somebody to talk to. Somebody not totally crazy, anyway. Okay, a different brand of crazy, maybe," she said when he chuckled. Again, she leaned back, her expression speculative. "It's good to have you home."

"Even if we don't...you know."

"Yeah," she said drowsily. "Because it was always more than that with you, too."

Over the sudden buzzing inside his skull, Ben quickly leaned over to kiss her on the forehead. "It's good to be here," he whispered, then let himself out.

And it *was* good to be back, he thought later, as he lay in the far-too-small twin bed in his old room, scratching a snoring rat-dog's upturned belly. Even though, if it had been sanctuary he'd sought, the joke was on him. Between leftover issues from the past and a heap of fresh ones from the present, he hadn't exactly walked back into a fifties sitcom.

Nor would he have ever believed how quickly a couple of kisses, and a conversation or two could bring the past rear-ending into the present. But apparently he'd carried Mercy's scent and feel and offbeat sense of humor with him, inside him, all these years like an old photograph. And worn and faded and cracked though it might be, all it took was a single glance to turn memories back into reality.

To turn "What if?" into "What now?"

Chapter Four

The week following New Year's passed uneventfully enough, Mercy supposed. Decorations came down and got put away, and life returned to its usual post-holiday stuttering, sluggish semblance of normalcy. Mercy sometimes saw Ben coming out of his parents' house, and they'd wave and say "How's it going?" and the other one would say, "Fine, you?" but that was pretty much the extent of their interaction.

All things considered, probably a good thing, she mused as she leaned heavily against one of the shop's glass counters, her head braced in one palm, morosely leafing through a display catalog. Since Ben—despite his showing up on her doorstep on New Year's Eve in a cloud of super-saturated testosterone—still clearly wasn't interested in starting something nobody had any intention of finishing. Nor, apparently, in a friends-with-benefits scenario.

She slapped to the next page. So why, exactly, was she morose again?

Other than the fact that it had been far too long since she'd gotten naked with anybody, that is. Or that, now that she'd done the kissy-face thing with Ben, Ben was the only "anybody" she cared to get naked with.

Sometimes, life was just plain cruel.

The bell over the door jingled. Mercy glanced up as a young mother with two very small boys in tow pushed her way inside. "Timmy, stay with me," the mother said to the older boy, an adorable curly-headed blond, then smiled her thanks when their part-timer, Trish, helped the mother settle her youngest into a collapsible stroller before leading them back to the baby and toddler section.

"So what do you think?" said Cass, one of Mercy's partners, leaning her tall, Eddie Bauer-ified frame against the case. Cotton sweater, cord skirt, shades of beige. Her feathery blond hair swept over her shoulders when she pointed to one of the photos. "Those heart-shaped balloons would look great tied in bunches in the centers of the displays, wouldn't they? We could give them away to the kids when they came in."

"Valentine's Day sucks," Mercy muttered, slapping down the next page.

"Hey. You've been grumpy all week. What gives?"

"PMS?" Mercy said without looking up.

"Nope, your chocolate binge was two weeks ago. Try again."

"Yeesh, you keeping track of my cycles now or what? So I'm just in a weird, rotten mood, okay? And sure, the balloons are fine." She flipped another page, keeping half an eye out for the little blond dude, who'd wandered back out to the front and was now holding a low, intense conversation with a panda bear in the stuffed animal display.

"And how about," Cass said, "a bunch of large foil hearts on the wall behind the cash register—"

"Don't press your luck. I'm having enough trouble with the balloons. *What?*" she said when the blonde poked her arm.

"What's his name?"

"Who?"

"Whoever's brought on this sudden, rabid hatred for Valentine's Day."

Mercy slammed shut the catalog, folding her arms over her white fur-blend sweater. "Nobody. It's just…" Her mouth thinned, she met Cass's amused—or maybe that was bemused—blue-green gaze. "You know the last time somebody gave me a Valentine's card? Not counting my nieces and nephews? When I was *sixteen.* Is that pathetic or what?"

"Well, join the club, honey," came a chipper Southern accent from a few feet away.

Mercy glowered at Dana Turner, Great Expectations' third partner. Her happily married, undoubtedly-getting-it-and-she-didn't-mean-a-card-regularly partner. "Where the hell did you come from?"

"My, my, aren't we the cheery one this morning?" said the chestnut-haired beauty, her full cheeks adorably dimpled. "And the parking lot, actually." A long, soft cardigan skimmed a figure not dissimilar to Anita's, a thought which, seeing as Anita was married to Ben's brother, led right back to Ben. She was doomed.

They'd all three been single when they started up their little business. But in the past year both Cass and Dana had fallen in love—or in Cass's case, fallen back in love, with her first husband—gotten married, become mothers. Or close enough to count, Mercy thought as Dana whipped out the latest photo of Ethan, her husband's toddler son.

"Oooh," Trish—who happened to be not only Dana's cousin, but Ethan's biological mother—said, "Let me see."

An unorthodox arrangement, to say the least. But as long as it seemed to be working for all parties concerned, who was she to say? In any case, Mercy had been genuinely thrilled for both of her partners that they'd found something so precious. So this ridiculous and unexpected stab of...of *envy* made no sense. None. Because how could she be envious of something she didn't even want?

So what the hell, she was blaming Valentine's Day. And all the stupid, unrealistic romantic notions it engendered. Hearts, flowers, candy...piffle. She didn't need no stinkin' Valentine's Day—

"May I help you?" Mercy heard Trish say, and Mercy looked up to find herself caught in Ben's slightly lost gaze.

Heart, meet throat.

She practically mowed Trish down as she zipped out from behind the counter, but letting some twenty-something, big-eyed, sweet l'il ole Southern gal get her hooks in was not on her to-do list this morning. "Ben! What are you doing here?" Was it her, or did she seem to be asking that a lot these days?

And yes, those were three sets of eyes glued to the scene. He smiled. Behind her, somebody gulped. "I'm working on a site close by, and since it's Mattie's birthday next week, I figured this was as good a place as any to find a present."

"Oh! Right! And as it happens, she's got her eye on this really cool craft set, right over here…"

She glared at Dana's hand-waggle as she passed, ignored the *Ah…now I get it* look in Cass's eyes. Thankfully, the game and toy area was down the hall in another room entirely, and Mercy doubted whether even Dana and Cass would stoop so low as to follow. But then, you never knew.

She skimmed her fingertips along a long, wooden shelf. "Ah. Here it is."

Ben pulled it off the shelf, frowning at the box, and she stood there, inhaling him, not even caring if her brain exploded from pheromone overload. Any sane person would have moved out of range. Yeah, well…

"You sure this isn't too old? She's only going to be six."

"I know how old my niece is, Ben. Especially since I'm hosting the birthday bash. And no, it's fine. See?" She pointed to the age recommendation at the bottom of the box. "Ages four to ten. Trust me, she'll love it."

She saw Ben's head snap up as the little boy, the panda now clutched in his arms, wandered past the archway. "Is anybody keeping an eye on that kid?"

"We all are. And anyway, there's no place he can go. We keep the stairs and back hall gated. He's fine."

Still, Ben watched for another second or two until the boy's mother popped into view, taking him by the hand and steering him back into the clothing area. Ben breathed an audible sigh of relief, then distractedly put back the kit.

"About the other night…" His eyes slanted to hers, and her

heart wriggled loose from her throat to bounce back into her chest. Oh, goody—junior high flashback. "I had a great time."

"Playing video games and watching a kid's movie?"

"What can I say? I'm easily amused."

"Obviously." Their gazes wrestled for an interesting second or two before she looked away, straightening out a shelf that didn't need straightening. "And is there some reason it took you a week to tell me this?"

"Not really. I've just been busy." He picked the kit back up off the shelf. "So you really think this is good?"

Oh. Well. So much for that. Dredging up her most disarming smile, Mercy said, "Give her this and you'll be her best friend for life. Want it gift wrapped?"

"That'd be great."

She led him toward the counter, becoming increasingly annoyed with herself the longer the silence stretched between them without his asking her if she'd like to go to lunch. Or something. Gee, the you're-all-grown-up-now bolt could strike anytime now. Praise be, Dana and Cass were both in the office and thus not present to witness her humiliating regression to adolescence.

"Trish, would you please wrap this in the birthday paper? *Trish!*"

The young woman jumped, making the little crest of light brown hair fanning from the top of her head—not to mention assorted dangly earrings—frantically quiver. At least it was too cold to flash the belly button ring. "Oh, yeah, Mercy, right away. So…I take it you two know each other?"

"Our families have been neighbors forever," Mercy supplied shortly, ringing up Ben's purchase. Not looking at him. Ignoring the heat flooding her cheeks. She swiped his credit card, handed it back to him. "And my sister's married to his brother."

Behind her, Trish cut off a hunk of paper from one of the supersized rolls.

"Yeah? That's so cool, being friends that long. I don't have any friends left from when I was a kid, since I haven't been back home in, gosh, like ten years or something…."

Once again, the little boy tootled past, still hanging on to the bear, his thumb plugged into his mouth. Leaning casually against the counter, Ben said, "Hey, kiddo…where's your mama?"

Not about to let go of that thumb, the child spun around, then swung the panda in the direction of the back room.

"You think we should go find her?"

Out came the thumb with a soft pop. "I'm not s'posed ta go anywhere wif somebody I don't know, 'less Mommy says it's okay."

"Good boy," he said, and the baby grinned. Ben crouched to his level. "How old are you?"

Three fingers shot up.

"Wow. What a big kid!"

Another enthusiastic nod. "I know! I'm the big brover!" he said proudly, thumping his own chest.

Ben smiled and held out his hand, palm up. "Gimme five, big stuff." After they did the guy thing, Ben said, "But you know, it's probably a good idea not to go where you can't see Mommy, either. So tell you what—why don't you stand right here with these nice ladies, and I'll go tell her you're here, how's that?"

"'Kay."

Before Ben could straighten up, however, the mother appeared, annoyance flattening her mouth as she pushed her snoozing youngest one-handed in the stroller, a bunch of clothes draped over her other arm. "There you are! Honestly, Timmy— how many times do I have to tell you to stay with me?" She grabbed his hand and tugged him to her side, dispensing apologetic looks all around. "I hope he wasn't being a bother!"

"No, of course not," Mercy started, but one brief glance from Ben squelched her reassurance. And sprouted more than a few questions inside Data Processing Central.

"With all due respect, ma'am," he said levelly, "your son's only three. You're lucky this is a small place, and all these ladies are good at watching out for the customers' kids. But what if this had been Wal-Mart or someplace like that?"

Mercy could see the woman bristling. "Then he would have been in the cart," she snapped. "Are you implying I can't take care of my own child?"

"Not at all. But since he seems to wander so much, you might want to consider one of these…" He reached past Mercy to unhook a child's harness and tether from a display by the register.

The mother let out a gasp and visibly recoiled. "No way am I putting my child on a *leash!*" She threw the items in her hand at Trish and hustled both her children toward the door. On a gasp, Mercy hustled right after her.

"I'm so sorry, ma'am, I'm sure he didn't mean anything by it—"

Too late. She was gone.

Mercy wheeled around, flapping her hands at Trish to put everything back. "Gee, thanks, Ben," she said. "Anytime I need to clear customers out of the store, I'll know who to call."

He gave her a funny look. "Better you lose a sale than she lose her child," he said, picking up his wrapped package and sweeping past her. When he hit the door, though, he said, "And you might want to think about installing some security cameras, or at least mirrors. This setup you've got here is a nightmare waiting to happen."

Mercy was still gawking at the door when Trish returned. "Geez," she said, "what was up with the testosterone tsunami?"

Indeed.

Like sporadic bursts of gunfire, Tony and Anita's raised voices assaulted Ben's ears the minute he got out of his truck. He walked up to the front door anyway, one hand propped on the stucco wall while he waited for someone to answer the doorbell. His cell rang; he unclipped it from his belt, checked the number, his mouth pulling flat as he deliberately ignored it. For now.

Mercy's sister did the honors, greeting him with a smile as bright as the teddy bears adorning her wrinkled scrubs, one that warred with both the weariness and annoyance flooding her dark eyes.

"Just came to give Tony an update," he said as a squealing Mattie, still in her little plaid jumper and white blouse from school, zoomed over to him. Ben flew her up into his arms, grinning when she planted a big, sloppy kiss on his cheek.

"Yuck!" she said, the bridge of her nose wrinkled as she swiped the back of her hand across her mouth. "You're all scratchy!"

"Mattie, honestly," Anita said, swatting her daughter lightly on her bottom before chuckling, Ben returned her to terra firma. With a wave, the little girl scampered off. "Yeah, he said you might drop by. Come on in, but enter at your own risk. The place is a holy mess. Tony!" she hollered over the sounds of dueling televisions, their German Shepherd alternately whining and barking his head off at the patio door. "Ben's here!"

"'Nita…" He waited until he had her attention, then asked in a low voice, "Is everything…okay?"

He didn't miss the flinch. "Sure, everything's fine. Why do you ask?"

"No reason. You look beat, that's all."

She seemed to relax. "It's just been totally nuts at work. We had ten mothers give birth yesterday, and only three of us on duty. That was rough. Then I get home, and there's homework to see to and laundry and…well. I'm sure you don't want to hear about any of that, Mr. Bachelor."

"Doesn't Tony help with the homework?" Ben asked mildly. "Pop always did with us."

Wariness peered out from her eyes before she shrugged. "Yeah, well, half the time he comes to me, anyway, moaning that he doesn't get it, so he ends up confusing the kids more than helping. It's easier on everybody if I do it. Hey—wanna stay for dinner? I brought home enough KFC for an army."

"Thanks, but I think Mom said something about green chile stew. Which she apparently hasn't made in years, so my butt would be in a major sling if I don't show up."

"Hell, maybe we should *all* show up—"

"Mom!" boomed from down the hall. "Mattie's bugging me!"

"Oh, for the love of…Mattie!" Anita yelled, her voice trailing off as she disappeared down the hall, the hem of her top twitching with each movement of her round hips. "Leave your brother alone, baby, so he can do his homework!"

Ben shook his head, relieved in a strange sort of way. Maybe yelling was just the way people communicated with each other around here.

"I'm telling you," Tony said as he hobbled into the living room on his crutches. "These things are a bitch." He fell into a recliner, levering it back to prop his feet up on the rest as the crutches dropped with a clatter onto the carpet beside him. After his initial blowup that first day, Tony had apparently decided to bury his personal feelings about Ben's return at least enough for them to work together. Tension still bubbled just beneath the surface, even if everyone was choosing to ignore it. For the moment. "Did I hear something about Mom making green chile stew?"

"That's what she said."

"Man…" Tony shook his head, the very picture of sorrow-fulness. "I can't remember the last time 'Nita put something on the supper table that didn't come in a foam takeout box or outta the microwave."

Ben shoved aside the Sunday paper, Jake's backpack, and a pair of skinny, big-haired dolls with abnormally large chests—he frowned at that one—to perch on the edge of the tan leather sofa, his hands linked between his knees. "I imagine she's pretty worn out by the time she gets home from work."

"Which she wouldn't be if she quit." When Ben frowned, Tony pushed out a frustrated breath. "I keep telling her, we don't need her salary, I can take care of all of us just fine on what I bring home. But no. She's got this thing about 'keeping her hand in,' or something, says she'd go bananas if she had to stay home all day. So instead the house always looks like crap and I haven't had a decent meal in years. And why are you looking at me like that?"

"I'm trying to see the marks left from the rock you clearly crawled out from under. Where do you get these ideas? Certainly not from our parents. Mama worked, too, remember?"

"Part-time. And not until we were in middle school. And she still kept up the house and all that."

"'Nita's not Mama," Ben said, walking right into the line of fire with his eyes wide open. A character trait he was obviously never going to shake. "Which you knew when you married her. She always wanted to be a nurse, you know that. And she loves her work. So why should she give it up for the privilege of cleaning your house and cooking your meals?"

His brother's face collapsed into a glower. No surprise there.

"And where do you get off, *hermanito,* handing out family advice when you haven't even been around for the past ten years? At least I stuck around. *I* went into the business with Pop instead of drifting all over the place like a damn tumbleweed. You broke their hearts, Benny. Bet you didn't know that, did you? Hell, I bet you didn't even give them a second thought when you took off."

"That's not true, Tony." Ben pushed out through the hot, hard knot at the base of his throat. But his brother was on a tear and didn't hear him.

"An' hey—at least I *got* a family. And a home. What've you got to show for your thirty-five years, huh? *Nada.* Not a damn thing. So maybe you should stop and think about that before you go spouting off at the mouth about stuff you don't know jack about."

"Okay, you two, enough," Anita said tiredly from the entry, walking over to halfheartedly shuffle the stacks of magazines and newspapers on the glass-topped coffee table into some semblance of order. "God, I would've thought you'd both be past all this sibling rivalry crap by now."

"I'm jus' saying…" Tony started, but Anita shut him up with a glare.

"How Ben chooses to live his life is nobody's business but his," she said. Then she straightened up, her hands on her hips, as the glare veered in Ben's direction, giving him a pretty good idea of exactly how much of the conversation she'd overheard. "But Tony's right. Seems to me you're in no position to be doling out domestic advice. Now. You two got work stuff to talk about, I suggest you get on with it. 'Cause KFC is gross when it gets cold."

Which they did, because neither of them was about to let this thing between them jeopardize the business their father had spent thirty years building from scratch. Still, Tony's words had sliced a lot more deeply than Ben was about to let on, especially in the light of all those feelings that being with Mercy and the kids on New Year's had brought to the surface.

But then, wasn't this why he'd come home? To face everything he'd been ignoring for far too long?

The question plagued him all through dinner with his parents, as he talked new construction methods with his father, listened to his parents' good-natured Spanglish bickering while his mother's dogs pranced on their hind legs, begging.

"No, no, I'll get that," his mother said when they were done and Ben tried to help her clear the table as the Chihuahuas went bonkers, scurrying around like bug-eyed, big-eared bumper cars. "You go on into the family room, spend some time with your father."

Ben gathered up their plates and silverware anyway, carting it all over to the counter. "I will. I need to make a quick call first, though." Then, impulsively, he gave his mother a one-armed hug. "Thanks for dinner. It was great."

Her eyes sparkled. "If I didn't know better, I'd think you missed my cooking."

"Now why would you think that?"

"Could be the three bowls of stew you put away."

"Could be," he said, and she gently swatted his head.

He didn't bother putting on his jacket before slipping outside, ambling toward the street. The afternoon had felt almost springlike, but par for the course in the high desert, when the sun went down the temperature plummeted right with it. Within seconds, the cold seeped through Ben's flannel shirt; his nose tickled with the pungent, hot-dog-roast scent of fireplace smoke. He breathed it in, letting it settle him. Ground him. Across the street, Mercy's house was dark. Huh. It was after seven and she wasn't home yet?

Not that it was any of his business. Except for his visit to the store earlier, they hadn't seen or talked to each other since New Year's. Because, he realized after a good night's sleep—as good as could be expected, at least—how could he even begin to do something about that until he figured out what to do about *this.* He dug his cell out of his shirt pocket.

"Hey, Roy," he said softly when the man on the other end picked up.

"So. You are listening to your messages. Have you decided yet?"

Ben was silent for a moment, watching Mercy's car pull up into her driveway. "And I told you before I left, this was open-ended."

"Oh, come on, Ben—broken legs don't take that long to heal. Six, eight weeks, tops—"

"Roy. Don't."

On the other end, a huge sigh preceded, "You not coming back—you and I both know that's hogwash. This isn't about what you do, Ben. It's who you are."

"And somebody's been watching way too much daytime TV."

"I'm serious. You're one of the best. And you know it." When Ben didn't respond, Roy said, "What happened wasn't your fault. You know nobody's blaming you."

"Maybe not. But it definitely cut things a little too close for my comfort."

"Yeah," the other man said quietly. "It's hell findin' out you're not infallible."

Ben massaged the space between his eyes, then let his hand drop. "This isn't about me being infallible. Or not. It's about me realizing maybe I don't want to check out before I've had a chance to explore a few more options."

Across the street, Mercy killed her car lights, swung open her door. She climbed out of her Firebird, doing a double take when she noticed him standing there. She slammed shut her door and started in his direction, a breeze tugging at all those shiny curls.

"I've gotta go," Ben said.

"Fine. But stay in touch, you hear me?"

"Sure thing."

Ben clapped his phone shut and slipped it back into his

pocket, watching Mercy's deliberate, measured approach as she crossed the street, one hand stuffed in the pocket of her open, ankle-length red coat, the other tightly clutching the strap of one of those metallic, fish-scaly purses he saw all over the place these days. Loosely wrapped around her neck, a flimsy, pale green scarf fluttered around her, like limp bug wings. His eyes traveled down, past the tight jeans to those pointy-toed, sky-high-heeled boots.

Just looking at her, his pulse kicked up a notch.

She came to a stop a few feet in front of him; the air stirred, disseminating her musky, heady perfume, and he took a deep breath, both to drink in her scent and keep his head from exploding.

"Don't cut your conversation short on my account," she said.

"I didn't. In fact, you showing up gave me a good excuse to end it."

Curiosity flickered briefly across her features before she said, "So. Care to explain why you overreacted in the store this morning? About the little boy?"

"I didn't—"

"Uh, yeah. You did. I told you we were all keeping an eye on him. In fact, the parents who come into the store know they *don't* have to worry about anything happening to their kids while they're shopping. But I'd like to think they don't have to worry about some yahoo embarrassing the hell out of them, either."

Ben's jaw tightened. "Look, I'm sorry if I cost you a sale—"

"Oh, screw the sale, Ben. And it's not as if I don't understand how that mother's attitude might have seemed a little cavalier to you. Or ours. Just because I don't like thinking about the scary stuff doesn't mean I don't know it happens.

Or that I—we—shouldn't be on our toes. Why do you think we *sell* the harnesses, for cripe's sake? But she wasn't in Wal-Mart, she was the only customer in a small store with only one way in or out. The chances of somebody making off with her kid were virtually nil. Which you can't tell me you didn't know, your macho man act notwithstanding."

They stared each other down for several moments before, on a sharp exhale, Ben said, "I didn't mean to upset that mother. I swear. I just…" He dug through his brain for an explanation he figured she'd buy. Yeah, telling her the truth would be the obvious choice, but he wasn't ready for the fallout that would inevitably cause. "You remember the one time when we were kids, and our parents took us all to the fair? And I got separated from the rest of you?"

"I don't…oh, wait a minute! We were on the midway, right? And Carmen and 'Nita and I were arguing with our folks that we were too old for the dumb kiddy rides, and we turned around and you were gone." She laughed. "My sisters and I were already miffed at being stuck with the stupid *boys*. Then you ran off and all we could think was how much time we were losing while our fathers had to go look for you."

"And here all these years I'd envisioned tears streaming down your little faces, because you were all worried about me." She snorted. "Oh, there were tears, all right. Tears of profound annoyance. I believe Carmen called you a doo-doo head." Another laugh bubbled out of her throat. "And Livvy started singing *Doo-doo head, doo-doo head* from her stroller, which shattered our poor mothers' last nerves. Carmen was so busted." Still chuckling, Mercy shook her head. "God,

Ben, I can't believe you remember that. You couldn't've been more than what? Four?"

"Five. And for years I had nightmares about wandering around by myself…" He shuddered. "All those legs, and the bright lights, and those weird, scary dudes in the booths with all the stuffed animals…"

"Yeah, I've had a nightmare or two about those weird, scary dudes myself. But for heaven's sake, Ben, you weren't gone for more than five minutes."

"Believe me, it seemed like a lifetime. Anyway, whenever I see a little kid wandering off on his own like that, I guess I flash back a little."

After several seconds, Mercy shook her head.

"What?"

"Not a half-bad attempt at covering your butt. Except you forget—" she smiled "—I know exactly what that butt looks like. But if it makes you feel better—and yes, that would be me giving you an out—I talked it over with Cass and Dana, and they agree it wouldn't hurt to at least put in security mirrors until we can afford something more sophisticated. We probably should have done it months ago, anyway, just to mitigate the shoplifting factor if nothing else."

"Sounds like a plan to me."

"We thought so." The purse slipped, sparkling and flashing like mad in the security light; Mercy hiked it back up on her shoulder. "Well. 'Night." Then she stepped off the curb, and Ben found himself wrestling with the idiotic sensation that she was taking his breath with her.

"Hey, uh…wanna go get a cup of coffee or something?"

Already to the middle of the street, she turned. "Why?"

Ben pushed out a weary laugh. "You know, it amazes me how women can split a simple question into a thousand layers. All I'm asking is, would you like to go have coffee with me? Because it's cold out here and in there—" his head jerked back toward his parents' house "—is a minefield. And over there—" he nodded toward hers "—is even worse."

A sly smile snaked across her mouth. "Without our little chaperones, you mean?"

Damn. "They do come in handy," he said.

"I see. Don't trust yourself? Or don't trust me?"

"I don't trust…us."

Her brows shot up. "Wow. I wasn't expecting *honest.* But you see…" She walked back to stand right in front of him, her eyes deep and dark and far too discerning. "There *were* layers, weren't there? Not a thousand, maybe. But enough. Because I figured out some time ago that that whole 'simple' schtick you guys have going? It's just a ruse to get us to quit trying to dig below the surface. Because, according to male lore, this isn't anything below the surface. The surface is all there is. Well, guess what, bud?" She shoved her hair out of her face, leaned close enough for him to feel her breath, a warm, weightless caress across his jaw, and whispered, "*I don't buy it.*"

Her keys jangled loudly in the stillness when she fished them out of her pocket. "But in any case, thanks but no. I've been on my feet all day, and frankly all I want to do is take a long bath and hit the hay. Besides, I need to see if Homer's around."

Ben frowned. "He run away again?"

"Yeah," she said with a sigh. "Couple nights ago. I know he's okay, but…I miss the big lug, y'know? So, I assume I'll see you at Mattie's party on Sunday?"

"Wouldn't miss it. Hey," he called to her back as she again started across the street. "Is it just me, or was that the world's most convoluted blow-off?"

Her laughter drifted back to him on the breeze.

Doofus-brain was indeed whining piteously at the back patio door when Mercy walked into the house. Ignoring the stupid surge of relief she felt every time the thing returned, she clunked her purse and keys onto the breakfast bar and wrenched open the door. Rumbling like a power saw, the cat launched himself at her shins, peering up at her from time to time with those big, soulful, amber eyes as he pushed out yet another strained little cry. Because, you know, he was about to keel over from hunger and all.

And because Mercy was a total pushover, the instant she dumped her coat she clicked across the tiled floor to the cupboard for a can of Fancy Feast. Homer's dish filled, she hunkered down beside him, her chin resting on her knees as she stroked his smoked turkey-scented fur. Unlike some cats who didn't like to be messed with while they ate, Homer's philosophy ran along the lines of as long as the food was going in, she could do anything she wanted to him.

Come to think of it, she'd known a few guys like that in her time, too.

She sighed, twice, then slid down onto her butt on the not-as-clean-as-it-should-be kitchen floor to lean her back against the cabinet. If she were smart, she'd just grit her teeth until Ben left. Put him right out of her pretty little head. Unfortunately, he didn't seem terribly interested in vacating the premises.

"The thing is, cat," she said, plucking pieces of God-knows-what out of his fur, "I can't figure out what Ben and I are to each other. Is he an old friend or an ex-lover?" The cat looked up at her and meowed. "Oh, don't give me that scandalized look. Like you couldn't figure that out? Then again, what do you know, you're a eunuch." Homer *brrped* indignantly, then promptly hauled himself onto her lap to regale her with cat-food breath. Mercy sank both hands into his ruff and started to scratch. "But then, there's not much point in thinking about any of it, is there? Well, there was that whole 'wanna go have coffee' thing. Oh, right, you weren't around for that. Yeah, he asked me out for coffee."

Homer reared back, his eyes narrowed.

"I know, I know, usually that's manspeak for 'let's have sex.' But not this time. At least, I don't think so." On yet another sigh, she clunked her head back against the whitewashed wood. "Dammit, Home—why don't men come with user manuals—"

The doorbell sent the cat flying off her lap, leaving many little perforations on her thighs. Swearing, Mercy hauled herself to her feet and hobbled to the door, massaging her butt to get the blood flowing again. Her mind tore through the short—or in her case, fairly long—list of possibilities: Ben, her mother, any of her sisters, your friendly neighborhood psychopath...

Clutching her down jacket at her neck but still shivering in the cold, Anita gave her a weak smile. "Got anything stronger than Kool-Aid?"

Chapter Five

Uh-oh. In fact, Mercy guessed this was the Mother of All Uh-Ohs.

"A cheap California red from two Christmases ago?" she said.

"Hell, at this point I'd take nail polish remover," her next youngest sister said, coming inside and following Mercy to the kitchen. As Mercy climbed onto her kitchen stool to retrieve the hitherto-forsaken bottle of wine from a top cupboard, her sister regaled her with bits and pieces of a conversation she'd overheard between Tony and Ben earlier that evening.

"Wow," Mercy said, dusting the bottle off with a dish towel. "Ben really stuck up for you like that?"

"Yeah, but that's not the point. The point is, Tony's still

being a butt about me working. And I've pretty much given up on his ever *not* being a butt about me working."

"I take it you've talked it over with him."

"Only until I'm blue in the face. Thanks," she said when Mercy handed her a glass of wine, downing half of it before coming up for air. "Only it wasn't until tonight that it hit me—I think he's deliberately refusing to help around the house, waiting for me to crack."

"If you haven't cracked in ten years, what makes him think you will now?"

"Yeah, well, you keep dripping water on the rock long enough, eventually it wears down. And how come you don't look surprised?"

"Sweetie, I hate to break it to you, but you and Tony..." Mercy took a sip of her own wine, made a face. Maybe nail polish remover would be better. "It's pretty obvious the two of you aren't exactly lovey-dovey these days."

"But that's the weird thing. The sex is almost as good as it ever was." At Mercy's raised brows—half of her didn't want to know, but it was that train-wreck thing—Anita sighed. "After ten years, sure, things slow down. The kids, our work...they take a toll. At least on the frequency. But when they do happen, they really happen."

"So...your night out on New Year's...?"

"What can I say?" she said acerbically. "Get us away from the house and our issues, pour a few drinks in us, and it's twelve years and fifty pounds ago." She took another slug of her wine, grimacing this time. "God, this stuff really *is* awful. Whoever brought it to you should be shot. But the point is—" she swished the wine around in her glass, as if maybe that would improve it "—great sex every couple of weeks isn't enough. Not for me, anyway. And I'm tired of fighting, of trying to change things that aren't going to change. Of trying to change a *man* who's never going to change. So, as soon as Mattie's birthday's over…" Tears swam in her eyes. "I'm seriously thinking of separating."

"Oh, honey…" Mercy's glass clinked onto the counter; Anita held hers out. Mercy refilled it, waiting until Anita'd knocked it back before tucking her hand in her sister's on top of the bar. "Isn't that a little drastic? I mean, maybe you should try, I don't know, counseling or something first?"

"Already did. Tony refused to go after the second session."

"Oh. Wow. I didn't know."

"Nobody did. I'd hoped…" Anita drew in a deep breath, letting it out on a shuddering, "I'd hoped we could fix things without anybody finding out. Because you don't have to say it, I know this is going to kill Ma."

Mercy squeezed her sister's hand. "No, it won't. If she survived raising five girls, I think she'll survive this."

"But Carmen—"

"Was the first. It probably gets easier with practice?"

That got a tiny, soft laugh.

"What about the kids, though?" Mercy asked.

Anita shrugged sadly. "Part of me thinks it's better to stick it out for their sakes. At least until they're older. But I know they're picking up on the tension."

They're doing a helluva lot more than that, Mercy wanted to say. But her sister had enough to deal with without adding that to the pile. At least, not now.

"Do you still love him?" Mercy asked softly.

Her sister's eyes cut to hers, her mouth pulled tight. "Are you asking that because you hope I do, or hope I don't?"

"What *I* think has nothing to do with it—"

"C'mon, Merce—you've never liked Tony."

"Well, I wouldn't have wanted to marry him. Which, considering, I would have thought was a good thing."

Another little laugh. "I know Tony was—is—a little rough around the edges. But underneath all that…there's a good man in there, somewhere. Pig-headed, yes. But good." Then she sighed. "But this business with Ben…" She shook her head, then lifted her glass to her lips again.

"What business with Ben?"

"What do you think?" she said, gesturing with her nearly empty glass. "The way Luis always favored Ben over Tony. You never noticed?" Mercy shook her head. "Yeah. Ben could do no wrong in his father's eyes. Even after he left, even though every time Juanita or Luis talked about Ben, it was with all this disappointment in their voices, like they couldn't figure out where they'd gone wrong. Tony, on the other hand…"

Her brows knit, she ran one short-nailed finger around the rim of her wineglass. "Once Ben was out of the picture, Tony thought maybe *finally* Luis would start giving him some credit, you know? Because Tony was the good one, see, the one who stayed, the one who did follow his dad into the business. But it's been ten *years,* Merce," she said, tears crested on her lower lashes, "and Luis still won't acknowledge everything Tony's done."

Mercy reached for a tissue box by the kitchen phone, handed it to her sister. "Do you hear yourself?" she said gently. "Hate to tell you this, honey, but this does not sound like a woman ready to leave her husband."

Anita honked into a tissue. "Just because I wish Luis would see Tony for who he is doesn't mean I don't wish Tony would see me for who *I* am, too. But on that score…" One hand came up, pointing unsteadily in Mercy's direction. "You mark my words, when this hits the fan, it's not my side they're going to take."

"Why would you think that? Juanita and Luis love you."

"They love that I gave them grandkids. But Luis actually took me aside one day and said—get this—that me working keeps Tony from feeling like *the man.*"

"That's insane."

"Not to mention prehistoric. Although they do love to throw Ma's never working outside the house in my face."

"Yeah, because she had five kids in like as many minutes. And she never *wanted* an outside job. But you know damn well Ma was thrilled when you got your nursing degree."

Anita pinned her with a now slightly bleary gaze. "And from seeds such as these are family feuds grown…crap," she muttered, nearly falling from the stool to grab her coat off the end of the counter, digging into the pocket for her cell phone. "Yeah, baby," she said after she answered. "I'll be home soon, I'm just over at Aunt Mercy's… Sure, you pick out two books you want me to read, we'll do it as soon as you've had your bath, okay?… A few more minutes. See you soon, baby."

She clapped shut the phone, holding it to her chest, staring out into space as if she'd forgotten Mercy's presence. Mercy reached up and smoothed a curl off her sister's face, smiling a little when the conflicted eyes veered in her direction. "You look exhausted," she said. *And slightly drunk,* which she didn't. How the woman thought she was going to read to the kids, she had no idea.

"There's an understatement," Anita said on a sigh, then frowned. "Did I ever thank you properly for taking the kids on New Year's?"

"*De nada.* They tell you that Ben came over, too?"

"Did they ever. I think Mattie's in love. Aiyiyi, every five minutes, it's 'Uncle Ben' this or 'Uncle Ben' that. You can imagine how well *that's* going over with Tony." Anita shifted on the stool, propping her chin in her palm. "And…is that interest I see in *your* eyes?"

Okay, maybe not so drunk. Unfortunately. "What that is," Mercy said, "is cheap wine shorting out my neurons."

Her sister laughed, then slid off the bar stool to stand on wobbly legs. "You do realize we all know you and Ben had a thing before he went away."

Mercy stilled. "Excuse me?"

"Mercedes. Please. We weren't blind."

After several seconds of sparring gazes, Mercy sighed. "You *all* knew?"

"Are you kidding? Miss Nobody's-Good-Enough-For-Me gets it on with the bad-boy-next-door? That's seriously hot stuff, *chica*. We were *so* scandalized." She grinned. "And envious as hell. So…are things heating up again?"

Mercy stared her down. "Do I *look* like someone with a death wish?"

"Yeah, but what a way to go," Anita said, slipping her coat back on. At Mercy's front door, she turned and said, "By the way, I cannot tell you how grateful I am you're doing this birthday party for Mattie. At this point I think it would take me under."

"I'm sure. And hey, anytime I'm around, you want to send the kids over, feel free. I'm serious," she said when Anita made protesting noises. "I'm crazy about the little rug rats, and you need the break." Mercy hesitated, then said, "Look, God knows I'm no expert here, but maybe you and Tony just need more time alone to hash out a few things. And don't shake your head at me, I heard what you said. I also heard what you didn't say. It's not Tony you want to divorce, it's his attitude."

Again, her sister's eyes filled with tears. "Am I crazy for still loving him?"

"*Love* is crazy," Mercy said, then smiled. "Or so I've heard. So you need to fight for him, sweetie. You've got one helluva arsenal there," she said, nodding toward her sister's ample bosom. "Might as well use it."

Anita choked on a laugh, then opened Mercy's door, wiping her eyes on her sleeve. "I don't suppose I have to tell you not to say anything. To the folks."

"Last time I checked, I didn't have the word *idiot* stamped on my forehead, so I think we're good." She drew her sister into her arms, rubbing her back. "It'll work out, you'll see." Then she let go, saying, "Let me get my keys, I'll drive you home—"

"No, it's okay, I walked." Anita dug in her pocket for a stick of gum, shoving the unwrapped piece into her mouth. "The air will sober me up."

"Fine. But you call me when you get there!" Mercy called out to her sister's retreating form.

Afterwards, though, Mercy wondered where she got off reassuring her sister about something she'd become more cynical about with every passing year. At the moment, the success-in-romance ratio for the Vargas sisters wasn't looking so good—one divorce, one marriage on the rocks, and one sister with a remarkable propensity for picking losers—

Okay, run that by her again?

But it was true. Because despite her oft-sung I'm-good-with-being-single refrain, choice hadn't been the sole deciding factor in Mercy's lone wolfette lifestyle. In fact, her contentment probably spoke more to an adapt-or-die philosophy that had guided her since birth. A good philosophy to have, she thought wryly as she threw together a chef's salad, when life seems determined to toss you its dregs.

Or, when something good finally washes up on your shores, and the tide carries it right back out again.

Mercy lit a pair of candles, then sat at her dinette table, Homer stretching to hook his claws on the table's edge beside her, begging. She tossed him a pinch of ham, which he inhaled. Yeah, old Benny-boy was just like this dumb cat. A chronic wanderer, the type who skirted the edges of anything resembling a real relationship. Sure, the sparks were still there between them, which was why she definitely wouldn't have minded a reprise of their affair. And the friendship, which, she now realized, probably did complicate things too much to once again trip over that particular stone. Still, she doubted his refusal to mess around a second time stemmed as much from nobility as it did sheer self-preservation.

Mercy's land line rang; a moment later she heard, "*Just me, I'm home, don't bother answering.*" She got up anyway, forking in dressing-soaked greens as she walked across the room to close her blinds. One hand on the wand, she peered outside to catch a glimpse of Ben inside his parents' open, lit garage. He was on his phone again. Evidence, she supposed, of his life away from here. His real life, she reminded herself.

A life that had nothing to do with her.

The dozen balloons tethered to Mercy's mailbox, eye-popping bright against the grays and beiges of the winter day, brought it all back in an instant. Oh, yeah, Ben thought as he crossed the street, his present for Mattie buried in the towering stack he carried from the pair of indulgent grandparents walking beside him, these people knew how to *celebrate*.

Teeth-rattling salsa pulsed from inside when Rosie, Mercy's very pregnant next-to-youngest sister, opened the door. "Benicio!" she cried, dragging him across the threshold to strangle him in a brief hug. Shiny red lips erupted into a smile; with her short, spiked hair and funky makeup and earrings, she could have easily passed for a teenager instead of a thirty-something mother of three. And eight-ninths. "Abby!" she then called to her daughter, a skinny girl of about nine or ten who emerged from the crowd and noise, giving him a smile. "Show Uncle Luis where to put the presents, then take Aunt Juanita's food to the kitchen," Rosie said with a quick smile for Ben's mother, who'd helped raise the Zamora girls as much as Mercy's mother had helped keep Ben and Tony from running amok, more than earning her the honorary title.

"You look great," Ben said after the crowd swallowed up the girl and his parents. "When's this one due?"

"Not soon enough, unfortunately. And no, I don't know whether it's a boy or a girl, so don't ask. It's not like it matters, right? Anyway, food's on the dining table, help yourself. Mingle. Get reacquainted. The men are all huddled together

somewhere, probably in Mercy's bedroom watching a game."
And with a little wave, she was gone.

The tiny house was jammed to the gills with bodies,
laughter, music, food. As expected, the living area had been
birthdayfied within an inch of its life, balloons and twisted
streamers in every color imaginable hugging the walls, the
ceiling. Ben chuckled though, when he caught sight of Annabelle, still standing proudly in the corner, now adorned with
tootie horns and leis, a purple foil birthday hat in the place of
honor on top.

"Hey there," he heard beside him.

He looked down into Mercy's laughing eyes and it was like
seeing the warm, beckoning light in the window after hours
of trudging through a blizzard. Odd, considering the way
they'd left things. Then again, this was Mercy. Not your gal
if you liked things tidy and logical. As apparently Ben didn't,
since, as the emotional dust stirred up by his return had begun
to settle, it was becoming increasingly clear that his memories
of her, of their time together, had been far more than the
musings of a lonely man obsessing about his first really hot
relationship.

The hot pink cousin of Annabelle's tree-topper nestled
crookedly in her curls; a trio of leis practically hid—and
clashed with—a lacy top nearly the same green as her sofa.
A dozen kids of various ages streaked through the room
behind them, their shrieks of laughter knifing through the
din. In retaliation, somebody turned the music up louder.
Forget peace and quiet—it was more like being dropped into
the middle of Mardi Gras.

On impulse, he reached for Mercy's hand. One eyebrow

arched, but she didn't try to pull away. Instead, she leaned closer so he could hear her over the roar of music, children's laughter and conversation.

"You need introductions?"

"What I need is a beer."

"Follow me. But hang on tight, the undertow around here is vicious."

"These aren't *all* your nieces and nephews, are they?" he asked as she tugged him through the throng.

"No, at least ten of 'em are Mattie's friends from school. But you know us, any excuse for a party."

It seemed to take forever to navigate the twenty or so feet to her kitchen, where Vargas females of assorted ages vied for counter space and bragging rights. All conversation ceased, however, when Ben arrived, the expressions before him ranging from mild interest to rampant speculation to border-line hostility.

"Well, well, well," Carmen, Mercy's older sister, said with a slanted smile and a smoky voice. A dozen silver bangles clattered as she lifted her drink to Ben. "The prodigal has returned, in all his glory." Her dark, streaked waves tumbled across the sharp angles of her face as she set her drink on the counter, then looked up, crossing her arms over a black sweater. "And I do mean glory. My God, honey…where *did* you get those shoulders?"

"Didn't I tell you he filled out real nice?" Anita said, tossing him a grin as she uncovered his mother's dish.

"You guys have been talking about me?"

"Well, duh," Olivia, the baby sister, said from a chair by the kitchen table, spooning baby food into a little dark-haired boy's mouth, while another curly-haired imp leaned on her lap, regarding Ben with a soulful gaze. Still skinny even after four kids, Livvie flicked her long, straight hair behind one shoulder. "It's a lot more fun than clipping coupons."

"You know how it is," Mercy said, finally handing him that beer. "Handsome hunk, poor, bored housewives…"

"Hey!" Rosie said, smacking Mercy in the shoulder. "Take that back!"

"Yeah," Livvie said, peeling the older child off her lap so she could get up to yank a paper towel off the roller under the cabinet. "With four kids, who has time to be bored?"

"And may I remind you," Carmen said in her husky voice, adjusting the big collar on her sweater, "that some of us aren't wives at all, bored or otherwise."

Ben saw Anita and Mercy exchange a quick glance before his brother's wife carried the casserole from the room. "She okay?" Carmen said in a low voice to Mercy, who shrugged, at which point Carmen's gaze cut to Ben's.

"Hey," he said, lifting his hands. "I just got here. Don't look to me for answers. Or expect me to take sides."

"Yeah, easy for you to say," Carmen said, shoving her hair behind one ear to reveal a hula-hoop sized earring, "since you'll be outta here again in a few weeks, anyway."

And because there is a God, somebody's husband picked that moment to wander into the kitchen, said, "What the hell are you doing in here, man?" and dragged him away before he suffocated in all the girl-cooties.

But for all Ben willingly let himself be sucked into the football-and-food frenzy of Mercy's brothers-in-law, she was rarely far from his line of vision as she shepherded kids and adults through the various stages of a party only marginally less elaborate than an embassy dinner, often with some little niece or nephew hanging off her hip. She was totally in her element, with that silly little hat perched on her head, her long tiered skirt gracefully swishing around her legs as she zipped from room to room in a pair of high-heeled boots that wreaked havoc on his breathing.

He realized how easily he could pick out her laugh from the crowd.

How he kept one ear cocked for it, even in the midst of a conversation with someone else. On the other side of the house. And over the next two hours, new images accumulated in his head, as clear as any saved on a digital camera: Mercy crouched in front of a pair of toddlers, her skirt billowed around her, quietly diffusing a squabble; Mercy helping Mattie cut her birthday cake, hugging the little girl from behind as she held her tiny hand steady; Mercy rolling her eyes in ecstasy on her first bite of his mother's cheese enchiladas.

Mercy listening to Anita, head tilted, forehead creased in concentration as she held her sister's hand.

Regret pierced his otherwise mellow mood, that he'd been a fool for leaving her.

Only if he hadn't, he wouldn't be the man he was now.

And now was all that mattered. That, and the future. What he'd done, who he'd been, was irrelevant. As was whatever she'd been doing during that gap. Was her still being single a sign? Did it mean that, just maybe, there was a chance? That *he* had a chance at something he hadn't even known he'd wanted until he'd seen her locked in mortal combat with her juniper bush?

But want, he did, he realized on a rush so profound he almost shook with it.

He wanted…this, he thought as the party began to wind down. The family, the craziness, the sense of being part of something.

And most of all, he wanted Mercy.

Which was where things got hairy.

Because she'd made it pretty damn clear, hadn't she, that she wasn't looking for anything serious? Oh, sure, she'd come on to him like gangbusters that first day. But that was like…like channel-surfing and running across an old movie you'd thought was so great when you first saw it, so you watch it again just see if it's as good as you remember.

Doesn't mean you want to go out and buy a copy.

His mood suddenly souring, Ben grabbed one of the few remaining beers from the cooler in the kitchen and slipped out into Mercy's small, winter-drab backyard. Typical of the neighborhood, Mercy's patio was little more than a cement slab with a corrugated metal cover over it. But pots of assorted sizes lined the edges; Ben imagined them filled with all kinds of flowers during the summer. At least a dozen wind chimes hung from the eaves, pinging and bonging in the unseasonably warm breeze. Brew in hand, Ben leaned against one of the wrought-iron support posts, listening to a hundred finches twittering their heads off, way up in one of the tall, slender cypresses bordering the back cement wall.

He took a long swallow of his beer, only half aware of the dwindling, muffled party sounds behind him, when he heard the patio door open. The jangle of bracelets alerted him to Carmen's presence a second before he heard a gravelly, "God. Can't a girl sneak a smoke anywhere around here?"

Ben looked over, allowing a grin for Mercy's older sister. "Your secret's safe with me."

"Not that it's much of a secret," she said, lighting up and taking a deep drag, the breeze whisking away the smoke the moment it left her mouth. "But Ma getting on my case is more than I can deal with. Especially since I'd actually quit. Three years, not a single cigarette. Then the rat bastard cheats on me and drives me right back to it."

Ben weighed his words for a long moment, then said quietly, "Then he's won, hasn't he?"

Carmen's eyes cut to his before she shrugged, propping her back against another post. She lifted the cigarette to her lips again, blew out the smoke. "I would've thought you'd be long gone by now."

"Haven't figured out a way to break the gravitational pull."

"Yeah, I know how that goes." She flicked her ash into an empty plastic glass, then pinned him with her gaze. "Although in your case I'm guessing 'pull' is due primarily to my sister? And don't you dare ask 'which one?'. Speaking of not exactly a secret. Before you left, I mean."

Ben squinted out over the yard. "Ten years is a long time."

"Yeah, well, the older you get, the faster time zips by." Carmen tapped the cigarette against the edge of her glass, her earrings flashing through her waves as earnestly as all those wind chimes dangling from the overhang. "Bet you anything she remembers you taking off like it was yesterday."

He frowned. "She talked to you about it?"

"She didn't have to. Not that she moped around or took to her bed or anything. Unfortunately. The world would have been far better off if she had. Instead, we were treated to weeks of Mercedes at her crankiest. Since she couldn't get to you, she took out her extreme annoyance on all of us."

"I'm sorry."

"Heh. *You're* sorry."

"She says she got over it."

"Of course she *got over it.* You didn't break her heart, you just pissed her off. But that was then. This is now. And here's a word of warning, pal—I'm already dealing with one sister with Vargas man troubles, I sure as hell don't need another one. You mess with Mercy's head—or worse, her heart—and there will be hell to pay."

Ben did his best to control the grin trying its damnedest to hijack his mouth. As the oldest, Carmen had always been fiercely protective of her younger sisters, and both he and his brother—not to mention every other male their age in the neighborhood—had the scars to prove it. That she hadn't changed on that score was weirdly reassuring, in a God's-in-His-heaven kind of way. In this instance, unfortunately, he couldn't possibly assuage her concerns without divulging a thing or two he hadn't yet shared with Mercy.

Who, judging from her sister's out-for-blood stance on the issue, maybe wasn't quite so adamant about staying single as she let on?

Ben shifted against the post, giving the grin its head. "Carm?"

"What?"

"I hate to break this to you—but you don't scare me anymore."

"Honey," she said, stubbing out her cigarette in the bottom of the glass. "You do not want to cross a perimenopausal woman with the nasty taste of divorce still in her mouth." Her smile was clearly intended to shrivel certain parts of a man's anatomy. "Trust me, you do not know from scary. But you hurt my sister, and believe me, you will."

She stuffed the glass into a metal trash can by the back door and went back inside, as Ben considered the very real possibility that, if his plan backfired, *Mercy* wouldn't be the one who ended up getting hurt. But if he didn't put his butt on the line now, take that risk, he'd regret it for the rest of his life.

Then he pulled a plastic chair out from the wall, plunked that butt into it, and waited.

Chapter Six

"No, no, you don't have to do that," Mercy heard behind her when she went to load Juanita's empty casserole dish into the dishwasher. Everyone else, including Luis, had taken off ages ago, leaving Mercy with the uneasy feeling that Ben's mother had an ulterior motive for hanging around. "I can take it home," Juanita said. "Clean it myself."

Smiling, Mercy firmly shut the dishwasher and turned it on. "Too late. I'm only sorry there weren't any leftovers," she said as she hauled a half-full garbage bag out to the living room. "I was hoping to score lunch tomorrow. I've always been crazy about your enchiladas," she said, dumping a stack of frosting-smeared paper plates into the bag.

"And maybe that's not the only thing of mine you're crazy about?"

"Oh. Well, I sure wouldn't complain if some of your tamales found their way over here, either—"

"I'm not talking about my cooking, *querida.*"

Okay. She could play dumb, or cut to the chase. Either way, she was screwed, but playing dumb would only prolong the agony.

Another bunch of plates met their fate. "I take it you mean Ben?"

"*Si.*"

Mercy wasn't sure what she'd expected to see in Juanita's eyes when she finally looked over, but *misgiving* hadn't been in her top ten. "There's nothing going on between Ben and me. Well, except for being old friends."

Juanita gave an annoying if-that's-what-you-choose-to-believe shrug before saying, "Then I don't suppose you noticed how he couldn't tear his eyes away from you all afternoon?"

"What? Oh, um, well…no." Flushing, Mercy spun around to swipe a small herd of paper cups off the coffee table into the bag. "I've been kind of busy. And anyway, I really doubt that."

"You're calling me a liar?" Juanita said softly, the smile evident in her voice.

"No, of course not…" On a huff, Mercy plunked down on the trunk, the bag squished between her knees. "So are you trying to push us together, or warning me off? Because you can save your breath either way. You know Ben, he doesn't stay in one place long enough to gather dust. And I took myself off the market a long time ago."

Ben's mother slowly walked around the breakfast bar, laying one hand on Mercy's shoulder and looking deep in her eyes. "I have always loved you and your sisters like you were my own, you know that. And I see that look on Ben's face and part of me thinks…" Sighing, Juanita gently tugged at a wayward curl dangling by Mercy's temple. "Perhaps he *would* stay, if he had a good enough reason. Unfortunately, the other part of me worries that he's in danger of giving his heart to someone who doesn't really want it."

Mercy blanched. "Juanita! I—"

"Shush, little one, I'm only telling you how things look from where I'm standing. I only want what's right for both of you. But Ben—"

"—is your son. I get it."

After patting Mercy's shoulder, Juanita headed for the front door. "I need to get back, Luis wants to go see some new action movie." She rolled her eyes. "So would you tell Ben we won't be home until after nine?"

Mercy frowned. "What do you mean, *tell Ben*?"

One hand on Mercy's door, Juanita smiled. "What is it they say about 'right in your own backyard'…?"

The patio door ground across its track when she pushed it open. And yep, there he was, sprawled in one of her plastic lawn chairs, eyes shut, legs extended, feet crossed at the ankle.

"Dude. Didn't you get the memo that the party's over?"

Ben swung that hazy, lazy gaze to hers, one corner of his mouth slowly tilting. "Did you think I'd leave without saying goodbye?"

"You? Leave without saying goodbye? Can't imagine why I'd think that."

He grimaced. "Nothing like setting myself up," he muttered, then shifted forward, as if to rise. "I'll be on my way, then…"

"No, no, it's okay, I just—"

Some bizarre centrifugal force spun his mother's words faster and faster inside her head, splattering them against the back of her skull. Why was he here? Why *had* he been fixated on her for most of the afternoon (because, yeah, she'd noticed), especially since he'd made it more than clear that down and dirty, they were not going to get?

Half curious, half wary and frankly too tired to worry overmuch about anything, Mercy came all the way outside, collapsing into somebody's left-behind folding chair. The cold, hard top of the chair dug into her neck when she leaned back, letting her own eyes rest for a second.

"Pooped?"

"Heck, I passed 'pooped' an hour ago. And I didn't even do any of the cooking. What are you doing?" she said, her eyes popping open when she felt her foot swing up onto his knee, her boot being unzipped.

"Giving you a foot rub."

She snatched her foot back, hiked the zipper up again. "You can't do that, I've got a huge hole in my sock."

"You're wearing *socks* inside these?"

"I hadn't exactly planned on anybody seeing them."

Chuckling, he reclaimed her foot, slowly undid the zipper. Her fingers tightened around the arms of the chair. So did her nipples. Although thankfully not around the arms of the chair.

"W-why?"

"There you go again," he said, rolling off the white cotton sock before settling her foot on his lap, gently shoving the pads of his thumbs into the ball. Uh-boy. "Anybody ever tell you that you overthink things way too much?"

"Other than you?"

He smiled. "How's this feel?"

"Like it's a shame you don't want to have sex with me, 'cause what you're doing right there would be a surefire way to get lucky."

His eyes lifted to hers. His thumbs kept up their magic. And that damn crooked smile never wavered. Mercy sucked in a breath.

"You *do* want to have sex with me?"

"Oh, *wanting* to was never in doubt." He carefully lowered the first foot, lifted the other one. Stripped it bare. Ravaged it with his thumbs. Ye gods. Somehow, Mercy didn't think his mother had considered this particular possibility. Then again, maybe she had. Ugh, now she was creeping herself out—

"Whether I should was something else again."

What? Oh, right. Ben. Sex. As in, looking good. "And…now?"

Those shoulders shrugged. "Now…let's just say I'm…reconsidering things."

Okay, *very* good.

"Um, not to be pushy or anything…but you got any idea when you might reach some kind of conclusion? Because what you're doing there is kinda getting me worked up."

"You mean, this?"

"That would be it."

"And here I was so proud of myself for finally figuring out how to extend foreplay."

She swallowed as his fingers inched up to stroke the area right above her ankle. New erogenous zone, *hel*-lo.

"Okay, remember back? How getting me warmed up was never a problem?"

He stilled. Thought. Smiled. "Oh, yeah…"

"Well, I got news for ya, toots. Things haven't slowed down on that score. So unless you want me to, uh…" She shifted in the chair. Bad idea. "…scandalize the neighbors, I suggest we move this inside."

"Now?"

"Now would be good."

Her foot dropped like a stone when he stood, grabbed her hand and hauled her to her feet. And before you could say *Who's got the condom?* they were on her bed, very naked and very cozy.

Very cozy.

Oh, my, she'd forgotten how nicely he fit in there, how extraordinarily good he was at multitasking. In fact, she idly mused as they slowed down for a second to savor their reunion, her hands tightly captured in his, above her head, as he tongued and nuzzled and nipped at her jaw, her neck, her breasts, that he was the only man she'd ever done this with who could telescope the preliminaries and the main event with such panache. She couldn't help it, she'd never been one to tarry, whether the guy could keep up or not. Especially the first time.

And bless him, Ben had no trouble keeping up. In more ways than one.

Those first, delicious stirrings of warmth flared, consuming every reservation, every *This really isn't a good idea* that tried to crop up in her thoughts. She was woman, hear her roar.

Quite literally.

Oh, no, Mercy had never been one to keep things locked up inside. Especially when, with one last, amazingly wonderful thrust, Ben set off an orgasm that might have made her brain explode if she hadn't been able to release the pressure vocally.

Damn, he was good.

They were good.

And then it was over—for the moment, she had no doubt there'd be an encore or two—and he pulled her into his arms, and she thought, *This is pretty nice, actually.*

If a little weird. Because this felt very different from the last time they'd done this. More…real. Or something.

"Why?" she finally asked.

He laughed, the sound rich and warm. "You'll never learn, will you?"

That he hadn't asked for clarification was both reassuring and unsettling. She wasn't all that sure she liked the idea of a man accessing her brain that easily. Even if the guy was Ben. "So sue me," she finally said. "You must have had some reason for changing your mind."

His fingers traced lazy circles between her shoulder blades. Also apparently an erogenous zone, sheesh. "What can I tell you? Being here today put me in the mood."

"Five thousand kids and all their nosy parents turns you on?"

"Being part of something turns me on." He stopped stroking to tighten his hold, rubbing his lips over her hair. Rubbing other things over…other things. "Finally admitting I've missed all this turns me on." He paused, grinning, watching her expression as his jolly sidekick sprang to life again. God, he was such a man. "Watching you with your family turns me on."

"You are one strange dude, you know that?"

Ben chuckled. "I'm sure. Of course, if you've changed *your* mind, I'd completely understand."

"I'm here, aren't I?"

"But for how long?"

Mercy pulled back to look at Ben, her chin resting on her palm, leaving the jolly sidekick to its own devices for a moment. "It's my bed, where would I go? But let's go back for a sec to the 'being part of something' comment. Are you saying… Hell, what *are* you saying?"

He stilled, his eyes steady in hers. "That I hadn't fully realized how tired I was of being alone until I came home."

Her blood came to a complete standstill in her veins. Ohmigod—his mother hadn't been imagining things. "Ohmigod," she said. "You're ready to settle down."

One deftly executed maneuver, and she was on her back once more, pinned underneath him. He kissed one nipple, circled it with his tongue. Gently tugged it with his teeth. Blew on it for good measure. "At the very least," he said over her whimper, "I'm more ready to consider it than I ever thought I would be. What are you doing?"

"Trying to sit up," she said, wriggling out from under him to sit on the edge of the bed, her hands forked through her now-matted hair. "Oh, God, Ben…this…this isn't at all what I'd expected. I mean, really, I thought it would be fun to have sex with you again, but…"

"But what?"

She twisted around, shivering at the take-no-prisoners look in his eyes. "You know what."

"Why not?"

"Because while you were gone, doing whatever it was you were doing, I was back here making a life for myself. Becoming something, *someone,* I didn't even know existed ten years ago. If being around all these kids has got your pro-creative juices going, then maybe you need to go find some little honey who'd love nothing more than to give you a batch of baby Bens, who wants nothing more than to play the devoted wifey. Because I seriously doubt I can fill the bill on that score."

Ben sat up, skimming one warm palm down her arm, kissing her shoulder. Sending up shouts of joy from every skin cell. "But you're terrific with kids, Merce. You always have been. You adore your nieces and nephews—"

"And at this point," she said, not listening, "who knows if I could even *have* kids, what with the fertility factor taking a dive after thirty-five and all? And I can't think when you're doing that," she said, swatting his hand away from her breast.

"For heaven's sake, Merce, older women have babies all the time—"

"Yeah, except it's harder for us geriatric types to conceive a *first* baby. And here's a head's up—reproductive hoop-jumping isn't my thing."

Seemingly unfazed by her outburst, Ben moved behind her, wrapping her up in his arms and resting his chin in the crook of her neck. For a good minute or so, he simply held her until her heart stopped trying to claw its way out of her chest.

"Can I say something?" he said quietly, his breath warm against her ear. She nodded. He hugged her a little tighter. "Okay, first off, for the record? I'm not looking for a brood mare. And secondly…I hate to point this out, but for somebody so set on nothing coming of this, you sure do have an awful lot to say about things that wouldn't even be an issue."

"I'm just—"

"Covering *your* butt. I know. And in some ways, I can't blame you. But honestly, Merce, does it really make things easier, worrying about every eventuality at once, right from the get-go?"

"Yes," she mumbled, stubbornly, and he chuckled, kissing her temple. And her neck. Then her shoulder, as he palmed her breasts from behind, thumbing what had to be the most sensitive nipples in the lower forty-eight, damn them. She bit her lip but the whimper escaped anyway, betraying her, and he laughed again, slipping one hand down her belly, between her legs, two fingers sliding into the wetness that would have betrayed her, anyway.

"You want me to go?" he murmured, stroking her, and she said, "Uh, no, *going* isn't the word I had in mind," and she let him roll her back onto the bed, arching her back as he loved her with his mouth, his tongue, and then she heard the rip of foil, the snap of latex, her own unhurried sigh as he entered her again.

Filled her as only Ben could.

"Damn you," she whispered, tears gathering at the corners of her eyes, and he cradled her face in his hands, thumbing away the moisture.

"I don't know what the future will bring, Merce," he said, softly, "but for sure I'm not the least bit interested in going out and looking for some little 'honey,' as you put it." He partially withdrew (no!), then plunged (yes!), then stilled, his breathing labored served him right. "If that's all I'd wanted," he gritted out, "I could have had that a long time ago."

An odd combination of jealousy and pleasure made her skin tingle. "You were…holding out for me?"

A slightly startled look crossed his features before he grinned. "Who knew?"

He lifted her knees to sink more deeply inside her, and a shower of the most beautiful glitter burst behind her eyes, and she cried "Oh!" and he chuckled, even though she sank her fingers into his shoulders and said, "You do realize this has disaster written all over it?"

Again, he retreated, his arms braced on either side of her head, a trickle of sweat meandering through the black hair in the center of his chest. "Because it's a risk? Because it might not work out?"

"Yeah."

"Then how about we don't think about anything more than *this*," he said, pushing into her so hard, she gasped, then sighed, relishing the shiver of delight. "Think you can handle that?"

Her eyes caught his, held it fast.

"Bring it on, big boy."

"Hmm," Cass said the next morning when a brisk, bone-chilling wind blew Mercy through the front door to the shop. "You look different. New coat?"

Fighting a blush, Mercy shrugged out of her leather jacket and made her way back to the office, flinching from the heat of those big turquoise eyes squinting at her through shaggy bangs. "Nope, had it for years. Boots are, though." She lifted one foot, admiring the luscious expanse of black suede stretching out below the hem of her leather miniskirt, the pointed toe, the killer heel. Her heart pitty-patted. "Sixty percent off at Dillard's."

"Can't beat that. But that's not it…ohmigosh! You had sex!"

"Who had sex?" Dana said, popping up in the doorway. "Wow. You're actually *glowing*."

Oh, God, not before coffee. Already ruing whosever bright idea it was to open the store on Mondays, Mercy poured herself a cup from the maker behind the desk, then split her glare evenly between the two of them. "And *how* old are we, exactly? You know, I could've just had a good night's sleep. Or run for three miles this morning. Or maybe I overdid the blusher. Not that it's any of your business."

Cass grinned. "It was that hottie who was here last week, wasn't it?"

"What hottie?" Dana said, then sucked in a breath. "You did it with your *brother-in-law?*"

"Man, what is it with you two today? You don't hear me grilling you two about your sex life, do you?"

"Only because we made the preemptive strike," Cass said. Mercy stuck her tongue out at the blonde.

Standing in front of the three-quarter-length mirror next to the door, Dana pulled a comb from her purse to run it through her long hair, plucking a stray off her bright green sweater. "You may as well fess up now, sugar," she said, dimpling at Mercy in the reflection, "and save yourself a whole lot of grief."

"You're ruthless."

"We learned from the best."

They had her there. Since she might have tormented the two of them about their love lives a time or six in the past. "Fine," she said on a sharp breath. "You're right. On both counts," she added with an eye-roll at their fist bump. "Although this isn't really breaking news." At their frowns, she added, "Because Ben and I sort of had a…thing once before. Ten years ago."

"Wow," Dana breathed, her green eyes the size of kiwis. "Y'all must've had *some* catching up to do." Then she giggled. Fortunately, her cell phone rang, her sappy grin at seeing— Mercy assumed—her husband C.J.'s number on the display giving Mercy an excuse to leave the office. Unfortunately, that still left Cass.

"So. Is this serious?"

"What it was," Mercy said, straightening out a jumbled rack they'd been too tired to deal with on Saturday, "was sex."

"Yes, I got that part. And?"

She met her partner's concerned gaze. "This is the first time the man's been home in a decade, Cass. I'm not exactly seeing a future here. And I'm fine with that. Really…Dana?" she said when the redhead appeared, dragging her poncho and purse and looking slightly dazed. "What is it, sweetie?"

After a couple of blinks, Dana shook her head as if to clear it. She slipped the poncho over her head, yanked her hair out from the neckline. "D'you think you could hold the fort for a couple of hours? Something's come up, I need to meet C.J.…."

She was gone before either of them could answer her one way or the other. But if nothing else, Dana's sudden disappearance—not to mention one of the busiest mornings they'd had since Christmas—took the heat off Mercy.

Until, a little after noon, she looked up when the bell over the door jingled and there was Ben, all big and bad-looking in solid black—jeans, Henley, pea coat, cowboy boots.

The three dozen or so yellow roses, however, kinda killed the Bad Bart effect.

"Damn," Cass whispered behind her. "You must be really, *really* good."

Judging from her wide eyes, Ben guessed he'd knocked her right off those adorable pins of hers.

Point to him.

He watched her struggle to regain control of the moment—the slow, deep breath, the deliberate toss of her curls. The breath-stealing, blood-heating direct gaze. "Subtle," she said.

His eyes lowered to the flowers. "Overkill?" he asked, frowning slightly as he twisted them in his hand.

She laughed. "Just a touch. But very sweet." *Sweet?* "Here, let's get them in water. I think we've got an old vase around here somewhere...." He followed her past the sales rooms and down the hall, admiring the view. The butt, the curls, those boots...how she could be so damn cute and so damn sexy at the same time, he had no idea. It was a gift.

He leaned one forearm against the bathroom doorjamb, surveying the room as she crouched down to rummage in the storage space underneath the sink. The aqua sink. Against gold-and-green flocked wallpaper.

"Charming."

"I think the word you're looking for is *retro,*" she said, plunking a pot of some kind into the sink and filling it with water. "Kinder owners would have put it out of its misery. But it amuses us, so we left it." She carted the filled pot back out front, relieving him of the flowers to plop them into the water.

"They're really gorgeous," she said softly, fingering one blossom. "Thank you."

"Huh." Ben folded his arms. "I half expected you to give me grief. Or do that whole 'you didn't have to' crap."

"Uh, no. This is the chick who spent the first ten years of her life convinced that somewhere, a small but very wealthy principality was missing its princess." She buried her face in the blooms, then grinned up at him. "I was born to be spoiled, but apparently nobody else seemed cognizant of that fact."

"Well, then…can you get away for lunch?"

"Yes, she can," Cass called from the other end of the room.

"Not that you're eavesdropping or anything," Mercy said as her partner snaked back to the register through the circular racks.

"Are you kidding?" she said. "I'm the mother of a teenager. I have hearing like a bat. Anyway, Dana called, she'll be back in a half hour or so. And Trish only has classes this morning, so she'll be in soon, too. So go." The blonde smiled at Ben, before her gaze slid back to Mercy. "Enjoy."

Why did he get the feeling Mercy was fighting the urge to smack the woman?

"So…" Ben said once they were safely out on the sidewalk. "I take it she knows we…?"

"Trust me, it's not like I announced it or anything. We're walking?"

"It's only three blocks, it's not worth driving."

She shrugged, then said, "Do I look like I'm glowing to you?"

He reached out to capture her chin in his fingers, pretending to angle her head to get a better look. "Now that you mention it, you do, kind of."

"I rest my case."

"I made you glow?"

"Oh, for God's sake, wipe that smug look off your face. After five orgasms, I could probably guide ships into harbor."

"Yes, but who gave you those five orgasms?"

She smacked his arm, and he laughed. Then Mercy glanced up at him, skepticism oozing from every square inch of that terrific little body of hers. "So, is this, like, a date?"

"Considering the five orgasms and all, I didn't think I was exactly rushing things."

"Well, no, but…" She hiked her purse up on her shoulder as they walked. "We don't date." Her eyes angled to his. "Do we?"

"We do now."

They walked in silence for a few seconds. He could practically feel her struggle to keep her mouth shut. But this was Mercy they were talking about. And sure enough, ten seconds later, out it came.

"Okay, I can't stand it…why?"

He commandeered her hand, lifting it to his lips and kissing her knuckles. "Because it's lunchtime and I'm hungry and I don't want to eat alone. *And* the only person I wanted to eat with is you. So deal."

"And that's it?"

He chuckled. "If I say 'no,' I'm screwed. If I say 'yes,' you'll run. So since I can't win, I'm saying nothing."

"Coward."

"No, smart. I like what you're wearing, by the way."

"Yeah? You don't think it's too…"

"What?"

"I'm not sure. I mean, I've always dressed like this. But sometimes these days I look in the mirror and I think maybe I should take it down a notch."

He frowned. "Why would you do that?"

"Because maybe I'm getting a little old to pull off the Latina pop tart look?"

"So what are you saying? You're ready for orthopedic shoes and those awful print blouses like our grandmothers wore?"

"Wash your mouth out. But maybe something a bit more…subdued. Grown up."

He let go of her hand to wrap his arm around her shoulders, tugging her close. "Honey, all I see when I look at you is a sexy, beautiful woman. Not old, not young, just…you. Subdued is for everybody else. And what the hell is mature, anyway?"

She shrugged under his arm. But he could tell she was pleased. "Beats me." After a second, she said, "I color my hair, by the way. In the interest of full disclosure."

"Yeah, I know."

Her head snapped around. "What do you mean, *you know?*"

"Because…" He tugged her closer, kissed the top of her head. "I found a couple of grays."

"Ohmigod, you're kidding!" She grabbed a handful of her hair, yanking it in front of her face. "I certainly didn't notice any when I did my hair this morning!"

"They weren't on your head," he said quietly.

She squawked, turned bright red and tried to pull away. Laughing, Ben caught her and twisted her around, holding her firmly by the shoulders. "Mercy, honey…I don't give a damn what you wear. Or whether you color your hair, or use makeup or not. None of that means squat. All I know is, I like being with you. I'm *happy* when I'm with you. And that's because of who you are, not what you look like. Because you're open and honest and generous and I don't have to drive myself nuts trying to figure out what you're really saying."

Then he took advantage of her apparently thunderstrucked-ness to add, "That you happen to be one of the hottest things going is just a bonus."

She gave him one of those pitying looks women were born knowing how to do. Then her forehead knotted. "You haven't been happy in all the time you've been away?"

Damn. She was too smart for her own good. And certainly for his.

"I'm not sure *happy* is the right word," he said with a tight smile, lifting her hair away from her face. "Not unhappy, certainly. It's not like I feel I've *wasted* the last ten years of my life." He waited out the swirl of memories, good and bad, then said, "Just that it's time for a change."

Their gazes tangoed for several seconds before, without comment, she pulled away, stuffing both her hands in her own pockets as they walked. "So where are we going, anyway?"

That she hadn't bolted was a good sign. He thought. "Little Chinese joint in the next block. Not much to look at, but great food."

"Huh," she said when they reached the place, which Ben had to admit looked a little seedier than he remembered. Still, the rich aroma of fried rice and stir-fry swirled around them, seductive and tantalizing.

"I take it you're not exactly dazzled."

"It takes a lot to dazzle a princess," she said, and he thought he'd do well to remember that.

Chapter Seven

Upscale the place wasn't, the decor running mostly to gaudy posters and paper umbrellas. In one corner, a large, fake dumb cane plant indifferently shielded the listless broom, mop and vacuum cleaner behind. But Ben was right, the food *was* good. In fact, the food was fabulous. A "secret" that had gotten out, judging from the dearth of empty tables in the shoe-box-sized restaurant. The two little waitresses were about to run themselves ragged, trying to keep up.

"You," Mercy said, jabbing chopsticks in his direction, "are brilliant."

"Not really," he said, not even trying to hide his smile. "I've just gotten really good at pegging the best cheap places to eat within a half hour of setting foot in a new town."

Mercy picked up her nearly empty water glass, the ice

rattling when she drained the last few drops of water it . "A highly prized survival skill, to be sure."

"You betcha… You need water?"

"Um, yes," she said, chewing. "But they're so busy, I don't have the heart to bug them."

Ben glanced over at the water pitcher, sitting on a table by the kitchen door, then shrugged and rose, striding to the table. "Anybody else need water?" he asked, holding up the pitcher, then proceeded to top at least a dozen glasses before he finally got to Mercy and filled hers, too.

"No, no…you don't have to do that!" Half laughing, but clearly embarrassed, one of the waitresses scurried over, taking the pitcher from him and filling his glass.

"It's okay," Ben said, grinning as he sat back down. "You guys looked like you had enough to do. By the way, this is the best garlic chicken I've ever had."

She flushed, nodding and smiling, nodding and smiling. "Thank you, thank you so much. I get you more noodles, yes?" And off she went.

"That," Mercy said, "was way cool."

Ben looked over at her from underneath his thick, dark lashes, his mouth slanted. "Yeah?"

"Oh, yeah."

And this could be yours.

The ice jittered in her glass when she picked it up, downing half of it at once. How had this happened? *When* had this happened? Before, the sex had been just sex, and the friendship had been just friendship, but now…

Oh, God. This was bad. Really, really bad.

"Hey," Ben said softly from across the table. Grudgingly,

she met his gaze. "Call me crazy, but I worry when you get quiet." He made a rolling motion by his ear with his chopsticks. "You're thinking again, aren't you?"

"One of the hazards of a functioning brain," Mercy muttered, spooning the last of the lemon chicken onto her plate. She hesitated, then leaned forward. "Look, Ben, taking me to bed is one thing. But this…uh…"

"Is what people do when they want to see where things lead."

"Well…yeah."

Dark eyes flashed to hers. "Funny, I thought I'd been pretty clear about that. So if you're so dead set against this, why'd you come to lunch?"

"Because Cass made me?"

One side of his mouth kicked up. "Like anybody can *make* you do anything." When Mercy lowered her eyes to her plate, he reached across the table, snagging her wrist in his fingers. "So is the obvious terror on your face because you don't believe that I'm tired of drifting, or because I'm pushing you in directions you don't want to go?"

"I'm not terrified, Ben, I'm being practical. After being alone for so long, I *can't* see me doing the cozy family thing, frankly. Which I also made clear. But even if I did, can you blame me for being a little…skeptical? Oh, come on," she said when he dropped his chopsticks on his plate and pushed away, his jaw set. "You enlisted in the army like five seconds after you graduated. You hardly ever came home on leave. After, what? A year working with your father after your discharge, you took off again. For ten *years*. Why would I, or anybody else for that matter, believe you'd want to stick around this time?"

"And I told you," he said darkly, "it's time for a change."

"Oh, for God's sake," she said gently. "How many places have you lived in over the past decade? How many different jobs have you had? *It's time for a change* is your motto! It's more than my not believing you're ready to put down roots. I don't think you're *capable* of putting down roots. But I do think you're running from something, seeking some kind of, I don't know, sanctuary—"

The word caught in her throat. Dear God—where had that come from? But if the startled, cornered look in Ben's eyes was any indication, she'd just hit a bull's-eye she hadn't even known she was aiming for. Without warning, a host of sharp, achy feelings burst to life inside of her, prompting her to reach for his hand. But he jerked away before she could make contact.

"Ben…?"

"Are you finished?" he said. Too quietly. Too calmly.

"Oh. Uh, sure, I guess." Mercy twisted around to unhook her purse off the back of her chair, feeling unaccountably sad. And extremely confused. "I should have been back to the store twenty minutes ago, anyway."

The waitress had already left their check and fortune cookies; Ben tossed one of the cookies toward her, then stood, swiping the check off the table and striding toward the cashier. He paid, held open the door for her, insisted on seeing her back to the store, even though they walked the three blocks or so in painful silence. When they reached the shop, however, he grabbed her shoulders again and jerked her around to face him, not roughly enough to hurt or frighten her, but definitely enough to get her attention. Every muscle in his face had gone rigid, his eyes glittering like polished onyx.

"I don't know how to make you believe something you

don't want to believe. But trust me, I'd *never* expect you to change your life for me, or give up what's important to you. But dammit, Merce…"

His shoulders heaved with the force of his breath. "If *you've* changed, why can't you give me the benefit of the doubt that I've changed, too? That I want different things now? And that maybe, just maybe—" she wobbled when he gently shook her "—one of those things is the shot at a life with *you?*"

He let her go, his eyes fixed on hers for a heart-stopping moment, then strode away, a menacing slash of black in the blindingly bright midday sun.

Mercy stood, frozen, staring, her brain buzzing with static. No man had ever spoken to her like that before. Looked at her like that before. Made her so weak in the knees she didn't dare move for fear of falling flat on her can.

And if that didn't scream WATCH OUT! she didn't know what did.

Finally, she forced herself to turn around, clutching the handrail for dear life as she hauled herself up onto the store's porch, through the door to the shop, back to the office, like an extra from *Night of the Living Dead*.

She barely noticed Cass's glance in her direction as she passed, although she was dimly aware of her partner's here's-your-hat, what's-your-hurry? act with her customer immediately afterwards. Yeah, talking about this was real high on her priority list. But after all these years of working with each other, *privacy* was a pipe dream.

"I hope to God that's food poisoning making you look so wretched," Cass said when she found Mercy a few minutes later, desultorily rearranging items in the game and toy room.

"Now that you mention it, I do feel like puking. So close enough. Dana's not back yet?"

"Uh, no. She called and apologized, said she'd be in as soon as she could make it." After a moment of silence, Cass plunged her hands into the pockets of her droopy, oversize cardigan and said, "Okay, Tinkerbell, what's wrong with this one? And don't give me that 'I have no idea what you're talking about' face, you find fault with every single guy you go out with. Not that I haven't agreed with you most of the time, but still. You do have a bit of a rep for being…picky."

"Gee, thanks, *Mom*. And this has nothing to do with being picky, it's…"

"It's what?" Cass said gently when the words bottlenecked at the base of Mercy's throat.

She picked up a craft set like the one Ben had given Mattie, then sank onto a nearby ottoman, unconsciously picking at one corner of the cellophane wrapping. "The whole time I was growing up," she began, "Ben was just the obnoxious boy next door. Since he's four years younger than I am, we might as well have come from different planets. Our mothers regularly traded off, so we were always at each other's houses, but we didn't exactly hang out together. Not by choice, anyway. I mean, really, when I was a seventh grader, he was still watching Saturday morning cartoons. And by the time I was a teenager, I sure as hell wanted nothing to do with some squeaky-voiced adolescent."

She got up, replacing the craft set, then folded her arms across her middle. "Then, one day my second year of community college, I came home to find Ben in my parents' living room with Rosie and two other girls, working on some project for their English class. He was sixteen by then, nearly a foot taller than I was, and cocky as only a really, really cute sixteen-year-old boy can be, and I remember thinking *Whoa, when did that happen?* Except then he realized I was there, and… This is going to sound stupid."

"Oh, you can *not* quit now," Cass said. "Not when it's just getting good."

Mercy glowered at her, then said, "Okay. So he looked at me, right? And his whole expression changed."

"He came on to you at sixteen?"

"No!" Mercy said, giggling. "In fact, just the opposite. Somewhere along the way, he'd turned into…a real human being. *Totally* full of himself, and God knows he'd flirt with anything with breasts, but even then he positively radiated integrity." She shook her head. "And somehow after that, we each become someone the other one could talk to. About all sorts of stuff. He had girlfriends, I had boyfriends, but Ben…"

She blew out a sigh. "Ben knew me better than anybody. I don't know how it happened, it just did."

"So you were friends?"

"Like this," she said, tightly crossing her middle and index fingers. "At that point, I figured that's all we'd ever be. And that was okay. Then he went into the army, and for six years we hardly saw each other. But whenever he'd come home on leave, we'd fall right back into the same comfortable pattern. We even double-dated once, me with whoever I was going with at the time and Ben with an old high school girlfriend. That was a trip, let me tell you. And then," she said on a pushed breath, "he got out of the army, and came home 'for good'—" Mercy drew quotation marks in the air "—and suddenly…things shifted. Neither of us were kids anymore, or in a relationship, and…" She shrugged.

"It wasn't good?" Cass said softly.

"Oooh, it was a helluva lot better than *good*. What it was, was mind-blowing. But weird. Very, very weird. For both of us. But before we had a chance to figure out what to do about that, he was gone again." She looked at Cass, the ache reasserting itself like a long-healed broken bone bitching in damp weather. "No goodbye, no warning, nothing. He just left."

"And somehow, he still lives."

"Only because jailhouse orange is hideous with my skin tone."

Cass laughed, then said, "And now he's back, and let me guess—he's playing the Serious Card."

Mercy blinked. "God, you're scary. But how did you know?"

"Because I know that look *very* well. Remember?"

Blake, Cass's husband, had walked out on her and their now sixteen-year-old son when the kid had been a toddler, only to pop back into her life a dozen years later, asking for a second chance. Which, eventually, he got. Mercy sighed. "I half expected him to pull a golden retriever out of his back pocket."

"Wow," Cass said. "Forget *good*. You must be downright *phenomenal*." At Mercy's halfhearted smirk in her direction, the blonde smiled sympathetically. "Sorry. So. You don't trust him."

"It's not a matter of trust."

"Of course it is. He betrayed your friendship, Merce. In your shoes, I'd be leery, too. Hell, I *was* in your shoes. And leery doesn't even begin to describe it."

"But it's different with you and Blake. He left you because of a misunderstanding. Ben took off because he's incapable of staying in one place for more than ten minutes. That he'd come home and suddenly decide he wants the very thing that gave him hives before… It doesn't make sense. *This* doesn't make sense."

After a moment, Cass said, "So you're not falling for him."

"Of course I'm not falling for him! What do you take me for? I mean, sure, he's funny and kind and sexy as hell, but…minivans and retrievers? Get real!"

Several seconds of intense scrutiny later, Cass said, "So tell the guy to take a hike and put both of you out of your misery. I mean, if you're not falling for him, what's the big deal?"

"Besides the sex? Not a thing."

"You could get sex anywhere."

"Not this sex, I couldn't," Mercy said on a mildly despondent sigh.

"And, as an added bonus," Cass said dryly, "Ben seems like a really nice guy."

"What are you, the little devil on my shoulder? Besides, you've met him exactly twice. And what the hell happened to 'I'd be leery, too'?"

"I got over it," Cass said. "And you of all people should know the farther past thirty you get, the quicker you can size 'em up. Besides, if Ben's into you, he obviously has excellent taste."

"Yeah, for crazy people."

"Oh, please," her partner said as the bell over the door jingled, announcing a customer. "The world would be a far better place with more crazy people like you." Then she shrugged. "Well, it's up to you, baby cakes. Just remember, though, if you do decide to play along and he screws up again, Blake and C.J. would be delighted to take him out, no problem."

Mercy laughed. "Yeah, I'm sure your husbands would love to know they've been volunteered for goon duty. Thanks, honey, but that's Carmen's province."

A fact which Ben knew all too well, she thought as they both went out front to help customers. So she could add courageous to the rapidly growing list in Ben's plus column.

Too bad she couldn't add it to her own.

Because, frankly, this whole thing had her rattled out of her wits, like expecting to land in Cleveland and finding yourself in Rio. Or in this case, maybe the other way around. A fling, she could handle. In fact, she'd become the Queen of the Flingers in the past few years. In her world, men were like shoes—pick something flashy and trendy that catches your eye at the moment, wear 'em constantly until you get bored, then toss 'em in the Goodwill bag at season's end without a second's regret. Because who wants to wear the same boring old pumps year after year?

Never mind that her feet were constantly blistered from breaking in new shoes.

Thankfully, a steady stream of customers for the rest of the afternoon kept her reasonably distracted. Then Dana finally returned, with a funny look on her face that Mercy immediately surmised would be far more than a distraction.

"Dana? Sweetie—what is it?"

"Okay, y'all…" Her dimples playing a nervous game of peekaboo, the redhead shooed Cass and Mercy back toward the office. "We need to talk."

Cass and Dana exchanged glances, but it was obvious from the blonde's shrug that she had no more clue than Mercy what was going on. Since it was near closing, anyway, Cass killed the front lights, except for the display windows, then trailed Mercy back to the office. Dana was sitting at her desk, her face buried in her hands.

"Dana! Ohmigod, honey…" Cass perched on the end of an old chair, her voice choked with worry. "Is something wrong?"

"No, no…" Her laugh sounded almost frantic. "I'm sorry, guys, I didn't mean to scare you. But…Oh, God, there's no easy way to say this." She looked from one to the other, her mossy green eyes riddled with apology. "I want out."

Cass clicked in first. "Of the *business?*"

Tears pooled on the redhead's lower lids, one dribbling overboard when she nodded. "You know how C.J. and I went to an open adoption agency a couple of months ago, to get the ball rolling to give Ethan a little brother or sister? Well, we figured it would take months, probably, before we found a match." She pressed both hands to her mouth, then said, "Turns out we're going to be parents again in about three *weeks.*" She gave a wobbly smile. "To a little girl."

"Oh, my God," Mercy said softly, then both women lunged for Dana, wrapping her up in a group hug. "Ohmigod, sweetie…that's *fantastic!*"

After the hugging and squealing died down, Dana said, "I'm so excited I can hardly stand it. I mean, yeah, I know the mom might still change her mind, but we met her today—that's why I was gone so long, we took her to lunch and we all really clicked—and I don't think she will. She's a real sweetheart, but she's only sixteen, she's just not ready to be a mama yet. Anyway, we're going to have a newborn and a toddler, and as much as I love bein' here—especially with the two of you—" she got all teary again "—I've waited too long for this. I want to be home with my babies, at least for a couple of years. I could still handle the decorating service, probably, since that's only part-time, but…if y'all want to buy me out, or find another partner, I'd completely understand."

"Well, I can only speak for myself," Cass said, her gaze flicking to Mercy, then back to Dana. "But as long as you want to keep a hand in, I see no reason why you'd have to bow out completely."

"I agree," Mercy said immediately. "I'm sure we can work around this, honey." A couple of years ago, a devastated Dana had lost not only her ability to have a baby of her own, but a jerk of a fiancé who apparently only wanted a wife with a working uterus. Now she was happily married to a guy who scored off the Richter scale in the "good" department, had already been having a blast raising her cousin's little boy with his father, and soon would have the infant nature had seemed determined to steal from her. Not every woman's definition of paradise, certainly, but definitely Dana's. And Mercy was delighted for her. "This is such great news! You must be floating!"

"You have no idea," Dana said. Then she laughed. "Ohmigosh—I've got three weeks to get a nursery ready!" And with that, she bounced up out the chair and flew into the small room they'd set aside for furniture catalogs and wallpaper books.

"You think there's any point in even trying to steer her away from pink?" Cass asked Mercy.

"Not a chance in hell," she said.

Yeah, she thought as she slipped back into her jacket and gathered up her purse, nice girls not only finished first, but way, way ahead. Which is how it should be. Both her partners, in fact, had seen their lives do a serious one-eighty in the past year, a thought which produced the strangest little twinge in the center of her chest. Like mild heartburn.

But as oddly as both their happy endings had come about— Cass remarrying her ex-husband, Dana and C.J.'s shared custody of Trish's son leading to their falling in love—there'd at least been compelling reasons for them to be together to begin with. Not so with Mercy and Ben. All they had in common was sex, history and family ties. Right?

Mercy hollered her good-nights and went out to her car, thinking Cass was right. Not about playing things by ear, but about cutting this thing with Ben off at the knees.

Because, really, what was the freaking point in pursuing something that was doomed, anyway?

"We have to talk."

Amazing, how such quietly spoken words could cut right through the whine of the power saw.

Releasing the power button, Ben looked up from the two-by-four straddling a pair of sawhorses to see Mercy standing at the foot of his father's driveway. The harsh, unforgiving beam from the security light did nothing to soften that obstinate set to her mouth he remembered all too well from their childhood. While Carmen had been protective and Anita nurturing, Mercy's nickname had been *La Cabezudita,* Little Miss Stubborn, hell-bent on controlling everything—and everyone—in her path.

"What about?"

"Maybe we should go someplace where the entire neighborhood can't hear us?"

The one thing Mercy underestimated, though, was how transparent her show of toughness had always been. In fact, the more that chin jutted out and her eyes flashed, the more flustered she really was. And the protective part of him hated forcing her hand, disconcerting her like this. But Ben knew making her mad was the only way to lure her out from behind that steel wall he suspected she kept up to keep anyone from hurting her.

And God help him, Ben was not above savoring the thrill of power that came from understanding that about her. Of knowing he could allow her that little illusion of control when he was actually the one calling the shots.

Only this time, he wasn't yielding an inch.

"Whatever you've got to say, you can say right here," he said, revving the saw once more.

"Fine. Oh, for God's sake—turn that damn thing off!"

So he did. In fact, he even set it down on the metal table he'd dragged out from the garage. Then he waited, thumbs hooked in pockets. He'd gotten real good at waiting over the years.

"We can't do this," she said.

Just what he'd figured she'd say. Would have been disappointed, in fact, if they'd skipped this step. Since after all, challenges were right up his alley.

"Can't do what?"

She gestured back and forth between them. "*This*. And not because I'm scared, before you play that particular card. Because it's…pointless."

He caught her eyes in his, saw exactly what he'd hoped to see. And it wasn't at all what she probably thought was there. "Says who?"

Now her lips pressed together so tight her mouth disappeared altogether. A breeze ruffled all those curls. "Dammit, Ben," she said in something close to a snarl. "You can't bully me into a relationship!"

"Is that what I'm doing?" he said quietly.

Her chest rose once, twice, three times before she finally said, "This isn't going to work, it's over, end of story."

Then she spun around on those spiky heels of hers and started off, and he watched, giving her time to get almost all the way across the street before he called out her name. And, yep, she turned around. One day he'd have to give her a lesson in following through on her convictions, but not today. Today, it was all about following through on *his*.

"You're wrong, Merce. Because it's not over. Not by a long shot."

They stood there, staring each other down from across the street. As he imagined, he could see the steam coming out of her ears from thirty feet away. Then she spun around again and trounced into her house, because it was either that or stand out there in the middle of the street and argue with him, and he knew she wasn't about to do that.

Still, he thought on a satisfied chuckle as he picked up the saw and cut off the next marked piece for the built-in shelves in the family room his father had been promising his mother since before he'd gone into the Army, for godssake, he'd given her due notice of his intentions now, both in private and in public. In fact, he imagined her mother was probably already on the phone with her, asking her what on earth was that all about.

Not that he expected Mercy to give in without a fight. And

he would lay odds that she was chalking up whatever had gone on between them to nothing more than chemistry.

Oh, they had chemistry, all right. The kind of chemistry that blew up stuff, brought about cataclysmic changes. They always had, although he doubted even Mercy would argue that things were ten times more combustible now that everybody had a better handle on what they were doing and all. Yeah, there was a lot to be said for being with a woman who knew exactly what she wanted and wasn't afraid to ask for it.

Who wasn't shy about returning the favor, either, he thought with a very sly grin.

But if she thought this was only about sex, she was crazy. And while Mercy was definitely crazy, she wasn't *that* kind of crazy.

And if she thought Ben was going to simply give up and walk away because she was having doubts, or running scared, or whatever the hell it was she was doing, she was dead wrong about that, too. Because, yeah, he was *real* good at waiting, a thought which sent a twinge of guilt sliding through him, that he was keeping such a large part of who he'd been from the woman he now knew he wanted to spend the rest of his life with. Some folks would undoubtedly say he wasn't playing fair. And, in many ways, they'd be right.

But to tell her now would only muddy the waters. Shake her up more than she already was. When the time was right, when he felt she could deal with it without going ballistic on him, he'd tell her. Until then, this was about being patient. In fact, you might say patience was one of his strongest attributes.

What he wasn't good at, however, was failing.

Especially when it wasn't only *his* welfare at stake.

* * *

Over the incessant pounding reverberating inside the half-built walls, the deafening Mariachi music blaring from the boom box in the middle of the concrete slab, Ben had no idea his father had arrived at the job site. That is, until he felt the familiar, slightly harder than necessary slap between his shoulder blades as he hunched over the working drawings—heavily annotated with Tony's nearly illegible scrawl—spread out on a makeshift table in the middle of what would be the house's family room.

"Checking up on me?" Ben asked, straightening as he rerolled the plans.

"Your mother sent lunch," Luis said, his mustache curving into a smile as he held up a metal box and a large thermos. "But that, too." He looked around, nodding in approval. "After thirty years," he said, "I still get a kick out of seeing drawings turn into a real house. Of knowing it'll probably still be standing long after I'm dead and buried."

"I know what you mean," Ben said, earning him an understandably quizzical—and hopeful—look. But his father only set the lunchbox and thermos on the table, then walked over to inspect the framing where a pocket door would go, bracing one callused, ugly hand against a pine two-by-four.

"You used to build little houses when you were this high," his father said, holding out a hand at knee level. Then he chuckled. "I taught you how to use a saw when you were four, I thought your mother would kill me for sure."

"I remember," Ben said, smiling. "That was around the time I added a few choice words to my Spanish vocabulary, as I recall."

Now his father laughed out loud. "Your mother has a real mouth on her when she gets mad, that's for sure." He angled his head at Ben. "I'm thinking that hasn't changed, no? How you love building things?"

A truth that had occupied Ben's thought almost constantly the past few weeks, although not the way his father meant it. Yes, he loved the orderliness, the satisfaction of watching a building take shape, morph from idea to drawing to reality. Nor could he deny that the fresh, living scent of lumber, the reassuring tattoo of hammers and whines of saws, both soothed his blood and made it tingle with possibilities. But even after a couple of weeks, he'd begun to realize that the thought of doing this day-in, day-out would drive him slowly insane.

Not that he was about to admit this to his father, not when the old man was counting on him to keep his business from collapsing while Tony was indisposed. "It's been fun," he said, which got the expected grin.

Luis picked up the food again, nodding that they find someplace to eat, the workers having broken for lunch a few minutes before. Ben led his father out onto what would eventually be the house's porch, overlooking a long drive and already partially terraced front yard, half thinking how ironic it was that Luis had spent the better part of his life building houses far grander than his own modest brick-facade ranch. And that he was every bit as content—probably more so—in that unassuming little house than half the people who lived in these overblown, overdone monstrosities that had sprouted like steroidized mushrooms all over Albuquerque's far Northeast Heights in the past twenty years.

Luis handed him a sub sandwich piled with enough lunch

meat and cheese to open a deli counter, then twisted the top off the thermos of coffee. They ate in silence for a minute or so until his father finally asked, "Not that I'm pressuring you or anything…but have you given any more thought to hanging around? Because I'd like to retire one of these days. I'd hate to see everything I'd worked so hard for fall apart."

This was it, then. The chance to ease into the subject Ben hadn't been sure how to bring up before this. He took a bite of his sandwich and said, "Tony wouldn't let that happen."

"Not intentionally, no. Oh, he does his best, but…" His father blew out a breath. "Half the time I think he's only doing this because he's sucking up." Dark, penetrating eyes swerved to Ben's. "Because he thinks it's a good way to rack up points. To be the 'good son' because you left. But I don't think his heart's really in the construction business."

Ben stifled the impulse to contradict his father, at least until the old man shed more light on the subject. From everything Ben had seen since his return, his father had nothing to complain about as far as Tony's work was concerned. That he was finding fault now only confirmed Ben's original gut instinct that he hadn't been wrong in staying away. Staying out of something he hadn't understood at the time, still didn't understand now.

Something that would have to be sorted out, one way or the other, if he was to reestablish his life here. With or without Mercy.

The crew's laughter drifted over to them on the breeze. "What makes you think I'd be any better at this than Tony?" Ben asked.

His father's gaze warred with his for several seconds before he said, "Because if you did stay, if you decided to come into the business with me, I'd know it would be because you *wanted* to. Not because you felt you *had* to. It's not huge, by some standards, but it's solid. And yours for the asking."

"I hope to God you haven't said any of this to Tony."

His father shook his head. "No. But if you stayed, maybe that would give him an out. A chance to do what he really wants to do. Whatever that is."

Ben sighed, thinking what bizarre, complicated creatures humans were. He knew his father loved his brother, but he also knew full well Tony would still see Ben's coming on board— an inevitability, whether it drove him crazy or not, since what else would he do if he stayed?—as the first step to push him out. As a flare-up of the competitiveness that had always marked their relationship, despite Ben's best efforts to avoid it.

"And I think you're wrong, Pop," he said. "Tony's completely devoted to the business. And he's damn good at it. Certainly better than I would be. Hell, all I'm doing is carrying out his orders. Without him, I'd be screwed."

"Don't sell yourself short, *mijo*. Yeah, I know you've got some catching up to do, but once you did…" A smile trembled underneath Luis's moustache before he looked away, took another bite of his sub.

"Dammit, Pop," Ben said softly, rubbing the heel of one hand over his thigh. "By rights you should hate me."

"For what? Leaving?" His father shook his head. "Your mother, now *she* didn't understand, that sometimes a man has to leave home in order to find it. But I do. Hell, I did the same thing, when I was eighteen. Maybe it didn't take me as long to find my way back," he said, "but I always understood what was going on. Just as I think maybe I understand what's going on now. Why you're finally ready to sink those dusty, dry roots you've been dragging behind you all over the country. You want some of this coffee? It's still hot."

Ben took the thermos from his father, staring at it for a long moment before finally lifting it to his lips. He couldn't ever remember talking to the old man like this. But then, he hadn't exactly provided many opportunities for long conversations, had he? Even when he'd called home, he'd kept the exchanges deliberately short, sidestepping any chance of questions he didn't feel were in anybody's best interest for him to answer.

"I didn't know you'd done the wandering thing, too," he now said, handing back the thermos.

"Yeah. Five or six years. Just like you, I went where the jobs were. Of course, even then there was plenty of work right here, but the thought of spending my entire life where I was born…it gave me the willies, you know?"

Ben nodded. "Why'd you come back?"

His father bit off a chunk of his own sandwich, chewing for some time before saying, "I didn't like it much. It gets lonely, drifting like that."

Ben waited out the zing of recognition before he said, "Did you know Mama before you left?"

"No, that happened afterwards. And it wasn't like there weren't girls I could have married before I met your mother. But I didn't feel like I had anything to offer anybody, you know what I mean? Not that I did when I met your mother, either," he said with a soft chuckle, "but she wasn't taking 'no' for an answer."

He stuffed the last bite of sandwich in his mouth, then wiped his fingers on a napkin. "You know, everybody always talks about how women are so anxious to get married and have a family, that it's the men who fight it. But you know something? I think women are a lot better at being alone than men are. We need them a lot more than they need us."

Ben grinned. "I think you may be on to something there."

"It's true! And anyway, if it weren't for women, we'd probably all still be running aroun' in animal skins, clubbing things over the head for our suppers." When Ben chuckled, his father glanced over, then averted his gaze again, his hands linked between his knees as they sat on the steps.

"Family's everything. *Everything,*" he said with a vehemence that made Ben frown. "Something your brother seems to have forgotten somewhere along the way. And yes, I know all about him and Anita having problems, so you don't have to preten' you have no idea what I'm talking about." He sighed. "First rule of marriage, you learn to compromise. Otherwise known as agreeing with your wife," he said with a grin, then sobered. "Tony has no idea what a good deal he's got going there. Anita's a good woman. A good mother. So what if she works? If you ask me, sometimes I think Tony's just jealous because his wife has a job she loves, an' he doesn't."

It was all Ben could do not to slam his hand into his forehead. Had his father not heard a thing he'd said? Why did the old man have such a blind spot about this?

"Anyway," Luis said, "if Tony screws up his marriage, I will never forgive him. Maybe you could talk to him?"

Ben nearly choked. "No way. My toe still smarts from sticking it in that particular tub of scalding water. In case you missed it, Tony and I aren't exactly buddy-buddy. Not to mention the fact that I'm the last person to be advising anybody about marriage."

"It's not a buddy he needs," his father said, ignoring the marriage comment. "It's someone with the *cojones* to knock some sense into him."

"Maybe. But I'm not that person. Sorry."

"Even though Mattie and Jake are suffering?"

The one comment guaranteed to make Ben's stomach roil. Because it killed him, watching his niece and nephew unwittingly stuck in the middle of Tony and Anita's crisis. If Tony even had a clue…

Still, he shook his head. "I feel awful for the kids, I really do. But you know if I intervene it's only going to make things worse. For everybody."

Luis shrugged, then dragged a hand through his thick salt-and-pepper hair. "You never answered my question. You gonna stay or not?"

His lunch finished, Ben leaned back on his elbows, one knee bent. The noonday sun made it feel as warm as spring, the few puny clouds overhead barely breaking the expanse of clear blue sky. "Depends," he said. "Maybe."

Without looking, his father reached around and briefly squeezed Ben's knee. "You know, Anita's not the only Zamora girl I've got a soft spot for." When Ben remained silent, Luis twisted around. "Or did you think I hadn't figured that one out, either? She's why you're thinking of sticking around, yes?"

Ben sat forward again, his brows drawn. "Not much point in denying it."

"Yeah, that's what I thought. But you don't think she's been sitting in that little house of hers, never dating anybody while you've been gone, do you?"

Despite the odd, unexpected surge of jealousy, Ben laughed softly. "Hardly. Although you could spare me the details."

"Details, I don't have. But I'm not blind—or deaf, although your mother and Mercy's mother seem to think I am, considering the things they talk about when I'm aroun'—and I can see that as the years go by, she goes out less and less. All I'm saying is, maybe you've come home at the right time."

"I'm not sure she'd agree with you." When his father lifted one brow, Ben said, "She's not exactly making things easy."

"Which only makes the victory all the sweeter. Or so your mother tells me," Luis added with a grin that almost immediately softened. He looked out over the front yard. "She doesn't trust you, does she? That you'll stay?"

"That's certainly part of it. But she also keeps saying it's too late, that she's past wanting to get married, have a family."

"You believe her?"

"Some women don't, you know."

"We're not talking about some women, we're talking about Mercedes."

Ben laughed, then said, "She said I can't bully her into a relationship. And I can't. Wouldn't want to. But for damn sure I'm not going down without a fight."

"Good for you." Luis paused. "The part about her thinking she doesn't wanna get married—you're on your own with that. But the other thing, about you sticking around…"

He reached into his jacket pocket, pulling out a long envelope which he handed to Ben. "Maybe this will help convince her, no?"

Chapter Eight

Mercy felt like a mouse in its hole, knowing the cat was just outside, waiting, biding his time. Not that she was into stalking fantasies, but…

Four days had passed since she'd told Ben it was a no-go. Four days during which she'd decided it was not in her best interest to mention to anybody exactly how gratifying—not to mention stimulating—she'd found his adamant refusal of same. Four days during which his compelling voice repeatedly sauntered through her head, sending wickedly delicious chills over her skin.

Some feminista she was.

Logically, she knew she'd made the right decision. Emotionally—and heaven help her, physically—turning away from Ben was like vowing never to eat chocolate again. And by chocolate, she was talking the good stuff, not that lethicin-laden crap they sold at the checkout.

But by her reckoning, she only had to hold out for a few more weeks, since Tony would be out of his cast by mid-February and thus able to resume his full workload. Once that happened, Ben would go back to wherever he'd come from, and she could resume her normal life, and all would be well.

At least, that was the plan, she thought as she pulled forward into the pick-up lane at Mattie and Jake's school, in answer to a frantic call from Anita who'd been roped into starting the second shift when her replacement didn't show and neither grandma had been available. Since Mercy had taken the day off herself, she'd won the coin toss. Not that she minded, she thought, grinning, as her niece and nephew spotted her car and raced toward her, visions of all sorts of auntie-indulgences undoubtedly dancing in their little heads.

"Cool!" Jake announced as he clambered into the front seat, ramming home his seat belt. Even under his open jacket, Mercy could see his uniform shirt untucked from his black pants, his tie completely askew. Mattie, by contrast, still looked as though she'd just left the house. Even her hair was combed. Ah, yes, this was Mercy's niece, all right. "Where's Mom?"

"Still at work," Mercy said, her forehead crinkled as she carefully maneuvered the car out of the lot. Last thing she needed was to cream some little kid. "So you're stuck with me."

She had no idea what was going on with Anita and Tony—since Anita's surprise visit the other night, she'd been oddly quiet about the subject. Mercy glanced at the kids, but judging from their smiling faces she was guessing their world was still fairly intact. "But don't think this is all fun and games. I've been given strict orders to make sure you get your homework done. And don't tell me you don't have any," she said, cutting her eyes at Jake, who already had his mouth open. "Your mother said this teacher *always* gives you homework."

Jake clamped his lips together and slumped down in the seat, clearly annoyed at being thwarted. Then he brightened. "C'n we go to McDonald's?"

Mercy glanced over at the kid. Since a stiff wind would blow him into the next county, she decided fast-food-induced obesity probably wasn't an issue. At least not within the next three hours. Still, since she knew Anita was making a concerted effort to cut down on the junk food, she had to make it look good.

"What did they serve for lunch?"

"S'ghetti an' salad an' peaches," Little Bit piped from the back seat.

"Did you actually *eat* it?"

"Uh-huh," both kids said. And indeed, that would appear to be tomato sauce stains on Jake's shirt.

"Okay, I suppose. But don't you *dare* tell your mother."

"That's lying." Again from the back seat.

Jake swiveled around as much as his seat belt would allow. "No, s'not. It's only lying if, like, Mom asks us if we went to McDonald's and we tell her no."

"I *know* that," Mattie said with clearly exhausted patience. "But what if she does? Then what?"

Jake's eyes popped back to Mercy. "I'll handle your mother," she said, figuring she'd deal with it when she had to. And not a moment before.

Fifteen minutes, two Happy Meals, a Spicy Chicken

sandwich and three chocolate shakes later, they all tumbled into her house, their nonstop chatter instantly banishing the heavy silence that normally cloaked the space. Jake threw himself down on the sofa in front of the TV and Mattie trailed after her into the dining nook, thunking her glittery Hillary Duff backpack onto the table and wriggling out of her puffy pink coat, letting it land on the tile floor.

"Where's Homer?"

Mercy stopped sucking on her milkshake long enough to mutter, "Off on one of his jaunts. And pick up your coat, peanut. This floor isn't exactly clean." Damn cat had been gone since Monday. And it had been below freezing every night. She told herself he was fine, that he was smart enough to get out of the cold. But then, he clearly wasn't smart enough to stick around, so there you were. "So," she said, "do you have homework?"

That got an eye roll. "Aunt Mercy."

"What?"

Little hands flew up in the air. "Hello? I'm in kindergarten? We don't *do* homework."

"Boy, Catholic school's certainly different than it was in my day. *We* had homework in kindergarten."

"Yeah, well, that was then and this is now," the kid said, and Mercy gawked at her. "I got my Valentines, though," Mattie said, ratching open the zipper and digging around inside the backpack. "We could do those, if you want."

Mercy stopped short of saying "Blech." Bad enough she'd been railroaded into the whole Valentine's decorating thing at the store. If she never saw a heart-shaped anything again, it would be too soon.

"Isn't it kind of early? Valentine's is ages away yet. And why do you have them with you, anyway?"

"I know, I'm not s'posedta, but they're so pretty I didn't want to leave them at home. See?"

Ah, yes. Princess Barbie. What was up with this kid and blondes?

Mercy settled at the table with what was left of her sandwich and the shake, feeling all warm and filled up inside. Yeah, grease and chocolate'll do it every time. "Wow. What are you going to do with forty-eight cards?"

Another eye roll. "Aunt Mercy."

"What?" she said again, her mouth twitching.

"The *family?*"

"Of course. I forgot," she said, then turned away so Mattie wouldn't see her smile when the little girl shook her head at her aunt's obvious cluelessness.

"An' maybe we could put some of the extras on Annabelle," Mattie said, pointing toward the tree, standing naked and forlorn in her corner, waiting patiently for Mercy to get off her duff and put her away already.

"Sure," Mercy choked out, then yelled to Jake, "Need any help with your homework?"

"Nope, I'm good," floated back. Along with assorted TV-land voices. Mattie spread all her cards out on the table.

"Mama said Valentine's Day is for telling people you love them. Except I don't get it—what if I *don't* love them?"

"Then you just avoid the issue." When the little girl frowned at her, Mercy said, "You don't have to give a Valentine's to someone you don't like."

"That's not true. Mrs. Miller says we gotta give one to

everybody in class, so we don't hurt anybody's feelings. Even the dumb boys."

"Well, that's a little different. When you get older, it's okay to be more selective."

"What's that mean?"

"That you don't have to give Valentines to anyone you don't want to."

"No dumb boys?"

"Nope. You can scratch the dumb boys right off your list."

The child looked immensely relieved. After a few minutes of painstaking copying, complete with tongue sticking out of her mouth, Mattie said, "Should I give one to Uncle Ben?"

"Don't see why not. He's part of the family, after all."

"*And* he's not a dumb boy."

"No," Mercy said, telling herself now the grease and chocolate was making her feel all trembly inside. "He's definitely not a dumb boy." Just a dumb bunny.

Mattie frowned, pencil poised, then looked up at her with a wrinkled nose. "How do you spell it?"

"U-N-C-L-E B-E-N."

When she was done, the kid held up the envelope with a satisfied sigh, admiring her handiwork, backwards B and Es notwithstanding. Then she stuffed the card and envelope in with the others, got down off the chair and climbed into Mercy's lap, and Mercy felt the strangest *sproing* inside her chest. "How come grown-ups don't give out Valentine's cards?"

"They do. Just not to half the free world."

"Huh?"

"Never mind. Your grandma used to give me and my sisters

Valentines when we were little, just like your mama does to you. But when we got bigger, she stopped doing that."

"That sucks."

Mercy chuckled. "We survived. Now Grandma only gives a card to Grandpa. Because he's her *real* sweetie."

"Do I have a sweetie?"

"I have no idea," she said, rubbing her cheek against the little girl's soft, silky hair. "Is there a boy at school you like better than any of the others?"

Mattie seemed to ponder this for a second, then shook her head. "No. They're *all* dumb. They keep chasing me and pullin' my hair and stuff."

"Ah. That's because they like you."

"Then they should give me candy or somethin' instead of pulling my hair."

"You might have a point there."

"Aunt Mercy?" she said after a moment.

"Hmm?"

"How come you don't have kids?"

"Because I never got married, I suppose."

Mattie twisted around to look up at her. "Jake says a lady doesn't have to be married to have babies."

Thank you, Jake. "Well, that's true. But it's harder that way. To be a mommy. Besides, not every lady has kids, you know."

"You should be a mommy, though," she said, very seriously. "You're real good at taking care of Jake and me."

Mercy laughed. "Thanks for the vote of confidence. But being a good auntie doesn't necessarily mean I'd be a good mommy."

Mattie shimmied off Mercy's lap to dig around again in her backpack. "Here," she said, handing Mercy a blank card.

"What's this for?"

"It's for you to give to Uncle Ben."

Mercy froze, looking at the card as if expecting it to strike. "Why would I do that?"

"Because maybe then he'd marry you and you could have babies."

She burst out laughing, only to pull the little girl to her again when her face crumpled. "I'm sorry, sweetie, I didn't mean to laugh. But…it doesn't work that way." Although, she thought with a squirrelly sensation in her midsection, considering the way Ben had looked at her the other night, she half wondered if giving him a Princess Barbie Valentine would be enough to elicit a proposal from him. And wasn't *that* a scary thought?

"But you like him, right?"

"Well, yeah, but—"

"Aunt Livvie says you two make a cute couple. So does Aunt Rosie."

Somehow, Mercy refrained from suggesting the child tell her other aunties to mind their own damn business, just as Mattie added, "But Aunt Carmen said once a badass, always a badass, and you should stay away from him."

On a bark of laughter, Mercy said, "Um…maybe you shouldn't let your mother hear you say that word."

"'Kay." Mattie gathered up the remaining cards and headed for the living room, where she randomly stuck them amongst Annabelle's branches, then said, "C'n I go outside to play? Maybe Homer'll come back if he sees me outside."

"Sure, knock yourself out."

Because far be it from her to disillusion the child by telling her that wanderers don't come home simply because you want them to.

Ben no sooner alighted from his truck when his niece and nephew yelled out to him, standing at Mercy's chain-link fence and waving their arms, which left him no choice but to cross the street to see them.

Laughing, he hauled Mattie up into his arms from the other side of the fence, hugging her back when she threw her arms around his neck and buried her sweet-smelling little self in his neck, all the while listening to Jake's nonstop litany about everything that had gone down in his life since they'd last seen each other.

Then Mercy came out of her house to see what all the commotion was about, her smile going a little stiff when she saw him. Ben set Mattie back down in the yard and stuffed his hands in his jacket pockets, aiming to look as relaxed and cocksure as he knew how. Because to tell the truth, after his ultimatum or whatever that had been the other evening, he'd realized there was a big difference between resolve and having a clue about how to carry through on that resolve.

Until his father had handed him that envelope.

"You draw the short straw?" he asked, grinning.

"Two of them," she said, not exactly grinning back. But not exactly not grinning, either. He guessed he'd be pretty wary, too, if he were her. They hadn't spoken since the night she'd tried to break things off and he'd said *no,* so she was probably a trifle perplexed about what, exactly, their relationship was at the moment. Other than being related through their siblings' marriage, that is.

"Where's Tony?" she asked.

"With Pop, working out some kinks on that job out in Placitas. He probably won't be home for another couple of hours." He got an idea—a probably stupid one since he hadn't thought it through, but what the hell. "You guys up for going for a short ride up into the mountains?" he said to the kids, and of course they both jumped up and down like he'd offered to take them to Disneyland. "With dinner at Dion's after?" he added, which made them jump up and down even more.

"How about you?" he said to Mercy, smiling. "You look like you could use some pizza."

"Oh, I don't know…they already had Mickey D's," she said, which immediately set off a chorus of *"Pleeeease, Aunt Mercy?"* and she made the requisite feeble protesting noises because she had to at least *try* to sound adult and responsible and all. Except Ben knew from the moment he'd said *Dion's* she was a goner. She'd once said, when they'd done this dance the first time, that if she were stranded on a desert island with all the Swiss chocolate and Dion's pizza she could eat, she'd never even miss civilization. Although unless that island had a mall and cable, Ben sincerely doubted she'd last a week.

"I'll just call your dad and make sure it's okay," Ben said, pulling out his phone, which his niece and nephew took as a signal to take off for his truck, zipping around and tripping over each other like his mother's dogs.

"Look…why don't you go ahead and take the kids?" Mercy said after he'd gotten Tony, who'd sounded relieved as much as anything. "I've got, um, stuff to do here."

Ben slipped his phone back into his shirt pocket. "What kind of stuff?"

She made a lame gesture with her hand. "Just...*stuff.*"

He held her gaze in his for several seconds, considering his options. He could cajole her into going, or shame her, or even trick her, if it came down to it. Or he could cut the crap and go the direct route.

"You know I'm crazy about the kids," he said, "but it's your company I want right now. Besides, I've got something to show you."

Curiosity flared in her eyes. "What?"

Gotcha. "Guess you'll have to go with us to find out."

Several seconds passed. Then she said, "No funny stuff?"

"With the kids around?"

"Okay, fine," she said on a sigh like she was making the sacrifice of the century. "I'll go. But only because pizza's included in the deal."

Mercy told herself this was only about going for a ride with the kids, and pizza. She was thinking in terms of chicken, jalapeños, black olives. There was a lot to be said for having a cast-iron stomach. But the minute Ben pulled onto the vacant lot with the view of the mountains to the east and the entire city below to the west, she knew this was about far more than dinner.

At a little after five, the sun was just beginning to kiss the Sandias with the watermelony light that had given the mountain range its name so many years before, as the sky stretched benignly, limitlessly overhead. Although the surrounding area was littered with huge, sometimes pretentiously Southwest-style homes, this particular parcel was situated so that nobody could ever build behind it, impeding the incredible view.

"Wow," Mercy said as a chilly breeze messed with her hair. The kids had taken off, infected with the instant exuberance that comes from feeling boundary-less. "This is really something. Is it one of your father's building sites?"

"No," Ben said after a moment. "It's mine."

Her head whipped around. "You *own* this?"

"Yep. My grandfather left it to me when he died. Tony's got one, too, about a mile away. The old guy had bought them up probably forty, fifty years ago for practically nothing, then never did anything with them." His hands shoved in his pockets, he walked to the edge of the property, the wind rustling his hair, looking more relaxed than she'd seen him since he'd gotten back. As if he'd finally come to terms with whatever it was he'd needed to come to terms with. "I hadn't thought about the lot in years."

Mercy overlapped her jacket closed, hugging herself against the breeze. Against the internal trembling making her voice shake. "It must be worth a small fortune."

"So Dad tells me. Amazing what some people will pay for a bunch of lizard-infested rocks and sagebrush."

She looked away. Swallowed. "I know a great R-Realtor if you want to sell. He'd make sure you got the b-best price for it."

"You cold?" he said behind her, and she shook her head. His boots crunched the uneven ground when he came up to stand at her back, close enough for every one of her skin cells to vibrate from his proximity. "Or I could build on it."

"Oh. Well, yeah, that makes sense," she said, the trembling getting worse. "Because you could make a killing, developing the property and *then* putting it on the market…why are you laughing?"

"Because I've never known anyone who could be as deliberately obtuse as you, Mercy." Now he took her by the shoulders, turning her to face him, the heat from the gentle pressure of his fingers searing her through the jacket, the heat in his eyes searing her far more. "I think it's about time I had a home of my own. Don't you?"

Oh, God. She ached for the sincerity behind his words, the earnestness in his eyes. And had this been ten years ago, she might have been sorely tempted to take those words at face value. For a brief moment, however, she saw an earlier Ben, the one she used to be able to pour her heart out to, knowing he'd listen, and even commiserate, but never judge her. And in that flash of recognition bloomed a revelation, that her trust had never been fully reciprocated, had it?

Because when all was said and done, she honestly didn't know who this man was…because he'd never let her far enough in to find out.

What really drove you back here? she asked him with her eyes. *To me?*

And when his own eyes flickered, then shadowed, she knew she'd hit her mark. Damn.

"You haven't even been home a month, Ben," she said quietly. "It's like somebody who goes on vacation and falls in love with Tuscany or Mexico or the Outer Banks and decides on the spur of the moment to move there. No, listen to me," she said when he tried to interrupt her. "It's not that I don't believe *you* think you're really ready for this. And maybe you are, I don't know. But odds are, you're going to change your mind in six weeks, or six months, or maybe even a year, and where would that leave me? So I'd be an idiot to believe you'd had a complete change of heart—that basically you'd become someone else—in such a short time."

There, she thought. *There's your opening. Go for it.*

Instead he said, "So this has nothing to do with whether you want to get married or not, does it?"

Well, one of them should be honest, Mercy thought even as annoyance shot through her. Never mind that she'd nearly bought into it herself. She pulled out of his grasp, walking away, the wind whistling mournfully in her ears. "Not really, no."

"You never used to be so cynical," he said softly from a few feet away. But she knew he wouldn't argue with her. That he wouldn't dare.

"Not cynical. Realistic. One of the hazards of growing up. It's getting cold," she said, turning toward the children. Away from Ben. "Maybe we should go get that pizza, huh?"

An hour later, after Ben took the kids back to their house, Mercy let herself into hers. This time, the cus-tomary, and usually welcome, silence seemed to heckle her. Her already unsettled mood darkening by the second, she draped her jacket over the back of one of the bar stools, then unlocked and shoved open the patio door, calling Homer, just in case. But no tank-sized kitty barreled across the yard, roared past her into the kitchen, begged for food and attention.

Disappointment settled over her like a fog.

Well, get over it, sister, she thought as she rammed the door closed again and relocked it, then yanked the drapes over the cold glass. Homer was just like that. Always had been, always would be. Why get her panties in a twist about it now? After all, it wasn't as if he was the greatest conversationalist in the world, anyway.

She grabbed the remote off the coffee table and jabbed the On button, surfing through fifty channels in less than thirty seconds, only to realize the boxed voices were making her grind her teeth more than the quiet. Except the minute she turned off the TV, all the thoughts she'd refused to entertain for the past hour crowded into her head like crazed shoppers into stores the day after Thanksgiving.

Strangling a pillow to her stomach, Mercy wondered— and not for the first time in her life—if something was seriously wrong with her. Because what woman in her right mind would keep pushing away this superb specimen of masculinity as hard as she was? So she'd gotten used to being single. So she even liked it. Where was it written that she couldn't get used to being *un*single? After all, she'd been all for it at one point in her life. So why not now?

Then she remembered that shuttered look in his eyes and had her answer.

On a groan, she keeled over onto her side, still hugging the pillow, only to jump when her land line rang. She was up and off the sofa in a flash, pouncing on the poor hapless instrument faster than Homer on a lizard. Didn't even bother to check the caller ID first.

"Hey, there," Dana said, sounding nearly as desperate as Mercy. "You busy? 'Cause for the life of me I cannot decide between a carousel or fairies theme for this nursery, and C.J. is no help whatsoever."

Hmm. She loved Dana and all, but… "I don't blame him. Those are your only two choices?"

She heard a frustrated breath on the other end of the line. "Better than some cartoon character that'll be out of style before the baby's first birthday."

Marginally. "Then again," Mercy said, "you *could* ditch the whole 'theme' idea altogether. Just paint the room pink and be done with it."

"How'd you know I was goin' with pink? Never mind— d'you think you could come over? I'm about at my wits' end."

"I'll be there in fifteen minutes," Mercy said, hoping that, if nothing else, the effort of keeping a straight face whilst considering the relative merits of fairies over horses in drag would keep her from thinking about other things.

Like the six-foot-tall hunk of temptation across the street who had taken the concept of "bad for you" to a whole nother level.

Chapter Nine

C.J. Turner, Dana's hubba-hubba hubby, opened their massive, carved front door when Mercy rang the bell. On his face, a killer smile. In his arms, a sleepy, pajama'd toddler, clinging to his side like a blue-eyed, towheaded koala bear.

"Cavalry's here," she said, stepping inside the marble-floored vestibule.

"Thank God. Two more minutes," he said, his bourbony Southern accent swirling around her as she came in, "And I'd've lost it for sure."

"I heard that!" came from down the hall a second before Dana appeared, her round figure sausaged in skintight jeans and a low-cut apple green sweater that made her mossy eyes sparkle like gemstones underneath her bangs. Long auburn tendrils snaked around her pale neck and collarbone, escapees from what was left of the topknot listing off-center at the top of her head. "Although it's true," she said, cupping Ethan's head. "Five minutes was all it took to do up this guy's room. Why this one's bein' such a bear, I do not know."

Mercy grinned as she unwound her scarf, dumping both it and her purse on a small wrought-iron table by the front door. "Of course you do. Males could care less about their surroundings. Girls, however…" She laughed. "You're probably afraid she's going to wake up one morning and wonder what on earth you were thinking."

"Yeah, that'd be it," Dana said, and burst into tears, clearly overwhelmed with happiness.

"Ohmigosh…sweetie!" Mercy put her arms around her friend, blinking pretty rapidly herself.

"She's been doing this a lot," C.J. said with that half sympathetic, half panicked edge to his voice common to men in the presence of a weeping woman. Except then Mercy glanced up and saw that C.J.'s deep blue eyes seemed brighter than normal, too.

Brother. At this rate she'd be lucky to get out of here alive.

"I'm okay, really," Dana said, swiping at her eyes and giving an embarrassed giggle. "It's just all happenin' so fast, I've hardly had a moment to catch my breath!"

C.J. leaned over to give his soggy wife a quick kiss, then disappeared with Ethan, leaving Mercy and Dana to trot off the mile or so to the other side of the house, where C.J.'s old office was being converted into a very frilly, girly nursery. Heaven help them all if the kid turned out to be a tomboy.

"So where are these wallpaper swatches?" Mercy said.

Still sniffling, Dana dragged over two sample books the size of the Ten Commandments plaques, plopping them open on the floor at their feet. Yep, fairies and carousel horses, all right.

"Of course, if I go with the fairies," she said, producing a catalog out of nowhere and flipping to a dog-eared page, "I could do this with her bed later on."

Mercy blinked at the picture of some gauzy, flower-littered, tentlike thing floating evilly over a twin bed. "You're not serious."

Dana bit her lip. "A bit much?"

"Uh, yeah. But you know," she added gently when Dana's forehead puckered, "maybe you should wait and ask your daughter if she'd like it. Because I'm not the one sleeping in here, she is… Honey? What is it now?"

Two more tears tracked down the redhead's cheeks. "That's the first time anybody's said 'daughter.' I just wasn't expectin' it, is all."

Mercy tamped down a sigh, then pointed. "Fairies."

"You're sure?"

Heh. "Absolutely."

Like the sun coming out from behind a cloud, a huge grin burst across Dana's face. "That's what I thought, too! In fact, I've already talked to a faux painter about havin' a big old white castle painted on that wall!"

Just shoot her now. But, you know, the only thing that mattered was that her friend was happy. And yeah, that the kid shared her tastes or Dana and C.J. would be footing wonker therapy bills down the road, but hey—not her problem.

"So. Is that it?" Mercy asked.

"Actually…" Dana threaded an arm through hers and led her back out into the hall. "No."

"Tell me you're planning the kid's first birthday and I'm outta here."

Dana laughed, then shook her head. "No, I'm savin' that for next week. Actually…I didn't really need your help pickin' out the nursery wallpaper. But Cass and I are worried about you and—"

Mercy dug her boots into the stone floor. "You got me here under false pretenses? I will so get you for this."

"Oh, come on," Dana said, tugging Mercy toward the kitchen, a granite-and-cherrywood masterpiece straight out of a decorating magazine. "My mother brought pineapple-upside-down cake, you have to help me eat it."

"And plying me with baked goods doesn't change anything," she said, hauling herself up onto a bar stool in front of a kitchen island the size of Maui. "You and Cass can stop worrying. I'm fine."

"Yeah. Like I was 'fine' before C.J. and I finally stopped runnin' from each other. Like Cass was 'fine' when Blake waltzed back into her life after all that time, suddenly lookin' to get back together." She cut them both huge pieces of cake, dumped forks on the plates and slid one across to Dana. "Trust me, sugar. We know the look."

"And what 'look' might that be?"

"The 'what the hell do I do now?' look."

Mercy rammed a forkful of blissfully moist, sweet cake into her mouth. Dana's mother could be hell-on-wheels, but *day*-um, the woman could cook. She chewed, swallowed, took another bite, then finally said, "Actually, I took Cass's advice and broke it off. She didn't tell you?"

Dana looked at her from underneath her lashes. "Why do you think we're worried? So? What happened?"

Mercy sighed. And forked in more cake. Dana held up one finger—the universal signal for *Hold on a sec, I don't want to miss anything*—and poured them both glasses of skim milk. "Go on, I'm listening," she said.

"Ben didn't seem real interested in taking 'no' for an answer. And then," Mercy said, chewing, "he takes me up into the mountains to show me this piece of land he's apparently had since birth or something, tells me he's going to build on it." She waved her fork. "As, you know, proof that he's not going anywhere."

"And?"

Edging closer to despondent by the second, Mercy shrugged one shoulder. This time, Dana sighed.

"And I can tell from that hangdog look on your face that all that hooey you gave Cass about you not being the domestic type is just that. Hooey."

"Actually, I—"

"Well, let me tell you something, missy. You're just sayin' that because it's the only way you can figure out how to save your skinny little butt. And anyway, there's all kinds of 'domestic.' Making a home for somebody doesn't mean havin' to stand behind the stove all day or make sure people could eat off your kitchen floor. Obviously, Ben looks at you, just the way you are, and sees exactly what he needs. And wants. And there's a lot to be said for that, you know."

A point that was hard to argue against, considering everything Dana had gone through before she'd met C.J. Still, Mercy wagged her head. "Yeah. *Now.*"

Dana frowned. "So maybe the timing wasn't right before.

And if y'all had tried to make it work back then, before he'd gotten whatever this was out of his system, you probably *would* have had a holy mess on your hands."

Mercy stabbed at the last piece of cake on her plate, trying to keep her breathing even. She knew Dana meant well, but *damn,* the woman was getting on her last nerve. "You really don't know anything about this, Dane. Anything about us."

"I know this sad-sack routine isn't like you. At all. And it's only gotten worse since you supposedly 'broke up' with the guy."

She couldn't argue with that, either. With a groan, Mercy propped her head in her hands, her fingers tangled in her hair. "You're right, this isn't like me." She peered up at her friend through her eyelashes. "I've never been this ambivalent about a man in my life. I don't get it—why can't I just make a decision about Ben and stick with it? Why do I keep feeling, no matter which path I take, I'm making a huge mistake?"

On the other side of the island, Dana set down her own fork to lean both hands against the granite's smooth edge. "If this were ten years ago," she said softly, "would you be this cautious?"

"Moot point. He left, remember?"

"And it hurt more than you wanted to admit."

Her mouth twisted, Mercy picked up the fork again, pulverizing the remaining crumbs on her plate. Then, finally, she nodded.

"So what this really boils down to," Dana said, "is that you're afraid to risk it again. Because this time, there's more on the line than there was before. And don't tell me I'm talkin' outta my bee-hind, because I wouldn't believe you. Any more than I believe this story you keep feedin' everybody about how you don't want a family of your own anymore, that you're perfectly happy living by yourself."

Dana sliced off another sliver of cake, plopped it onto Mercy's plate, then did the same for herself. "Trust me, I know all too well how easy it is to convince yourself of something you think's never going to happen. So what are you gonna do, Merce? Take a chance on getting what you've always wanted, or take the easy way out now and maybe regret it for the rest of your life?"

"I hate you," she muttered around a mouthful of cake, and Dana grinned.

"Long as you make me godmother to your first baby," she said, "I'll forgive you. Except..." She leaned back, her eyes narrowed. "How come you *didn't* tell me I was talkin' outta my butt? Don't tell me you'd already figured this out, all by yourself?"

Mercy snorted. "It does happen, you know. And anyway, you didn't exactly give me a chance, did you?"

"Oh. I guess not, huh?"

They ate in silence for a minute or two while Mercy contemplated how much her world seemed to be tumbling upside down all around her, with Dana's leaving the business and whatever was going on with her sister and Tony and now this thing with Ben. Ben, who was the last person on earth she'd ever expect to be promising stability. Permanence. Solidity. The very things she'd never thought mattered to her, the very things she now realized she couldn't live without.

There was irony for you.

"It's funny," she said, "how everybody's always thought of me as the free spirit of the family. The one who wasn't afraid to put myself out there, who did everything the hard way." Frowning, she looked up at Dana. "When did I become such a stick-in-the-mud?"

"Oh, honey, it happens to the best of us," her friend said, smiling, then collected both their plates, carrying them to the state-of-the-art dishwasher on the other side of the kitchen. "So you just have to ask yourself, would you be more unhappy with Ben, or without him? Once you figure that out, the rest is—" she grinned "—a piece of cake."

Mercy groaned. Then frowned. "The thing is…I can't help feeling there's something he's not telling me. Something that has to do with his time away. Something that's at least partly responsible for why he wants to stay."

"So ask him. If he's so hot to work this out with you, he'll tell you."

"And if he isn't?"

"Then at least it will make your decision easier."

"Thank you for being no help whatsoever."

"Anytime. Although…" The redhead swallowed the last bit of milk in her glass, then said, "If he is keeping something from you, maybe there's a good reason. Men aren't real good at coming right out and saying what's on their minds, in case you haven't noticed. Sometimes you just gotta be patient. Trust you'll find out whatever you need to know, when you need to know it."

And on that comforting note, Mercy drove home again, where, as it happened, Ben was sitting on the tiny slab of concrete that passed for her porch, his long legs stretched out in front of him. Long legs that Homer hurdled gracefully in his zeal to reach her, meowing nonstop as he told her all about his latest escapades.

Ben got to his feet. "He was meowing at your door so loudly I decided to come over here to keep him company until you got back."

Mercy slammed shut her car door. "Really?"

"Okay, I'd already decided to wait until you came back and the minute I sat down, Homer showed up."

Hands in his pockets, Ben stayed right where he was. Waiting for her to make the next move. Still, he couldn't have known what she'd been thinking, all the way back from Dana's, that she'd already figured out what she needed to do. Sort of. Mostly. She swallowed.

"It's cold out here," she said, rubbing her arms. "How long have you been waiting?"

"Ten minutes." His smile was gentle. Wistful. "Ten years."

Her eyes stung. "You're like a pesky fly, aren't you?"

Ben glanced down at the ground, shaking his head, then back at her, his expression downright rueful. "I keep thinking, stay out of the woman's way. Give her whatever space she needs. And then I think…how else can I prove that I *want to be with you?*"

Mercy hugged her jacket closed a little more tightly as Homer writhed around her ankles, complaining. "The first time somebody broke my heart," she said, "I thought I'd die—"

"Ricky Gonzalez," Ben said, startling her. "I remember. You were sixteen. When you hadn't shown your face in almost a week," he said at her stymied expression, "I asked Rosie if you were sick."

"And she told you about Ricky?" Mercy squeaked. "I'll kill her."

That got another chuckle. "Rosie and I were both twelve,

your boy troubles were all the excitement we could dredge up that summer. She thought you were being a drama queen."

Mercy rolled her eyes, then shook her head. "Anyway. My point is, after that, I thought it would get easier. Why I thought that, I don't know, but I did. I was wrong." She took a step closer, her heartbeat thundering in her ears. "I'm not as tough as I look, Ben."

"Neither am I," he said softly. "Honey, I would never, ever knowingly hurt you. Especially not now. All I'm asking for is a chance."

She could barely swallow past the knot in her throat. "It's just that, after all these years..." She shook her head. "It all seems to be happening so fast."

"Call it making up for lost time."

So confront him already, rang in her head. *Right here. Right now.* Only she opened her mouth and the words refused to budge. Because maybe he needed her to trust him. To be patient with him. Because maybe he thought she was the only person who could really do that, which was pretty amazing, when you thought about it.

Then again, maybe she should shove him out of the way, run inside and lock the door.

Only then she'd be by herself on the other side, wouldn't she?

"Oh, what the hell," she said, moving into his arms.

Sometime around midnight, the grating crash of a closing minivan door jarred Mercy awake, propelling her instantly from the bed.

"What is it?" Ben rumbled behind her, yawning, as she wrestled her robe out from the underneath the cat, stumbling the short distance between bed and window as she clumsily put it on, yanking the tie closed. A quick twist of her mini-blinds revealed Anita's sandy-beige Voyager in her mother's driveway, her sister marching Jake up to her mother's front door with a sacked-out Mattie slumped against her chest.

"Crap," Mercy muttered, leaving the blinds open to ransack the chair by the closet for the jeans and sweater she'd been wearing, sparing a brief glance for Ben propped up on one elbow in the bed. "Anita's brought the kids to Mom's."

"You're kidding?"

"Nope." Mercy grabbed clean underwear out of her dresser drawer and rushed into her bathroom. "That can't be good," she called out through the open door, only to jerk slightly when she turned to find Ben in the doorway, already dressed, clearly furious.

She knew what he was thinking, that everyone had hoped the relative quiet from that front had meant Anita and Tony had somehow patched things up. Wishful thinking, obviously. For her sister to disrupt the kids' sleep on a school night meant something was seriously wrong.

"I assume you're going over there?"

"What do you think?" she said, wincing as she rammed a brush through her guess-what-I've-been-doing? hair. "In fact, wanna bet my phone rings before I finish up in here?"

Right on cue, her land line rang. Ben snatched the portable out of its charger by the bed and tossed it to her, then wrapped his arms around her waist from behind as she answered. Just to hold her, absorbing her trembling. She glanced up at their reflection in the mirror, at his strong, serious eyes looking back at her, and relaxed. A little.

"Anita's over here with the kids!" her mother's agitated voice came through the line. "She says she's left Tony!"

"Yeah, Ma, I know. About her being over there, I mean. I heard the van."

"You don't sound surprised."

Uh, boy. "Actually, 'Nita and Tony have been having problems for a while. And before you jump down my throat, I didn't say anything because 'Nita asked me not to. She didn't want to worry you and Papi."

Her mother muttered something in Spanish, then said, "He's not..." She lowered her voice to a whisper. "He's not hurting her, is he?"

"No! God! At least, I don't think so, she never said anything. I just think he...doesn't get who she is," she added over her mother's whoosh of relief. "He never really has. Are the kids okay?"

"Mattie's still half asleep, 'Nita's putting her down in your old room. But Jake...Jake's a mess. He's in the family room, he won't talk to anybody. Poor little thing...so much to put on those small shoulders." Then she heard a tiny intake of air as her mother started to cry, as if this was somehow her fault.

"Oh, God, Ma...hang on, I'll be there in a minute."

Ben took the phone from her, putting it back while Mercy sat on the edge of the rumpled bed to stuff her bare feet into a pair of shearling boots she'd grabbed from the floor of her closet.

"This is what you do, isn't it?"

At the wonder in his voice, Mercy looked up, shoving her hair behind her shoulders. "What do you mean?"

"Give the parties, watch the kids, keep everyone from losing it in a crisis."

Breathing a little harder than she'd like, Mercy sat upright, her hands curled around the edge of the mattress. "Is that a criticism?"

"Hardly. I just think it's ironic that you can't watch the news because it depresses you so much, yet you're the one everybody else relies on."

She stood, shoving her arms into a down vest. "Maybe because my family's across the street, not halfway around the world. So I feel like I can actually be of some use, you know?"

In the half light, she saw Ben's mouth curve into a smile. Then he peered out the window, slipping his corduroy shirt back on. "Huh. My mother's on her way to your folks' house." His eyes touched hers. "You really ready for this?"

"No. But I suppose it was bound to come to a head sooner or later. You going to stay here?"

He stared out the window another few seconds, apparently considering his options, before turning away to pocket his cell phone and wallet. "Tempting as that is," he said with a half smile, "I've dodged my family responsibilities long enough. Maybe I can talk to Jake while you help the women sort things out. Then we'll see. If my mother's at your house, odds are my father will head to Tony's. An impartial third party might come in handy."

Suddenly Mercy remembered, or at least half remembered, Anita's comment about Ben and his father—something about Luis favoring Ben? Tony's feeling left out? In all the backings-and-forthings of the past little while, she'd forgotten. Now, seeing the pained look on Ben's face, she wondered if there was more to her sister's words than she'd realized.

"Impartial?" she said.

"Compared with my father? Or Tony? Yes. Not that I have any idea what I'm supposed to do, but…" He shoved his hand through his hair, and Mercy thought, *Yeah, definitely something going on there.* She doubted, however, if this was the time to get into it. "Sometimes," he said, "I guess all you can do is play it by ear. Whoa," he said when she threaded her arms around his waist and nestled up against him. "What's this for?"

"You're really not the same Ben as before, are you?"

"Finally," he said, dropping a kiss in her hair. "The light dawns."

Seconds later, they stepped outside, the brisk, clean high-desert air banishing the last vestiges of sleep. The door clicked closed behind her, but before she could head down the walk, Ben grabbed her, turning her around to kiss her quickly, softly, his lips warm, solid, reassuring. "Just remember, this has nothing to do with us," he said, and she nodded.

Then he took her by the hand and they crossed the street, and she had to admit there was something to be said for not going into battle all by her lonesome.

Chapter Ten

By the time Ben reached his brother's house a half hour later, he was loaded for bear.

Not that he'd let on before this how angry he was, although he guessed from Mercy's solicitous frown that she pretty much figured his blood was boiling. Two people taking their frustrations out on each other was one thing. But to put their children in the middle of it…

Idiots, he thought as his truck door thundered shut, setting off a chorus of dogs. Over their crazed barking, his footsteps ricocheted into the night as he trudged past his father's SUV. The raised voices inside came to an abrupt halt when he rang the bell; his father opened the door, eliciting a bitter "What the hell are *you* doing here?" from Tony on the other side of the living room.

"Seeing if I can knock some sense into that thick head of yours, that's what," Ben said, sidling past Luis and jabbing one hand toward the east. "I've just spent nearly a half hour trying to calm down your son, who has no idea what the hell is going on, or why his parents can't see past their differences long enough to see how much their fighting is upsetting their kids!"

Tony recoiled like he'd been sucker-punched, only to immediately lurch in Ben's direction on his crutches. "This is none of your business! And don't you worry about me taking care of my own kids! I managed just fine without your help up until now, I sure as hell don't need it now!"

"Well, you sure as hell need *somebody's* help!" Ben yelled, half tempted to grab one of his brother's crutches and smack him upside the head with it. "You and Anita, both! Because she's not exactly on my list right now, either, dragging the kids out into the middle of the night!" He muttered a choice swear word, then leveled his gaze at his brother again. "You're supposed to be the older brother, dammit! So maybe it would be nice if you acted like it, you know?"

"Benicio, please…" Luis had slumped down onto the edge of Tony's sofa, his stubby-fingered hands limp on his knees. "Everybody's on edge, maybe this isn't the best way to go about fixing things—"

"You want me to stick around, to be part of the family again?" Ben said, reeling on his father. "Then you can't dictate how that plays out. And you," he said, turning again on his brother, "have no idea how good you have it! When you asked me what I had to show for my life, did it occur to you to take five seconds to appreciate your *own?* That you found a woman who put up with you for all these years, and who would continue to put up with you if you'd get your head out of your butt long enough to figure out that her wanting her own life isn't some kind of threat to *you*. And your kids," he said, his throat clogging on the word. "God, Tony—is this what you want for them? To put them in the middle, to make *them* suffer for their parents' hardheadedness?"

His words echoed in the resulting silence. Until Tony, his face purpled with rage, stamped one crutch ineffectually into the carpeted floor…and lit into their father.

"Dammit to hell, Pop—Ben's home for, what, five minutes? And you *ask* him to stick his nose in my business?"

As angry as Ben still was with his brother and sister-in-law, the chronic pain in Tony's voice tore him up inside. The pain that had made him less than enthusiastic about getting in the middle to begin with…the pain that had been a large part of his leaving all those years ago.

"*Why,* Pop?" Tony said, the word wrung from his throat. "Why was Ben always the good one, even though I was the one who stayed, worked my butt off for you? *With* you? Why was he *always* the better son?"

His expression ravaged, Luis pushed himself to his feet and reached out to Tony, who rebuffed him. "I never thought Ben was better than you, Tony—"

"No, only that he would have done a better job than me," Tony hurled at the old man.

"Which was wrong," Ben said, purposely drawing fire. "Why *did* you always seem to favor me?" he asked his father. "Especially when it was completely unwarranted."

"I told you," his father said, "I wasn't put out with you for leaving—"

"I'm not talking about that. Tony's got five times more on the ball about the construction business than I ever did. Or ever would have. And maybe if you'd start appreciating *him* more, he'd stop taking out his frustrations on his wife." He shifted his gaze to Tony, who stood there openmouthed. "Part of the reason I left was because of you. Not the only reason, God knows. But getting out of the way so maybe you and Pop could work things out between you definitely had a lot to do with it."

Somewhat recovered, Tony smirked. "Nice try, little brother. The fact was, you couldn't wait to get out, to leave the family. There was nothing for you here, and you know it."

A tight smile pulled at Ben's mouth. "You have no idea how much there was here for me. What I gave up in some obviously misguided attempt to save this family, even if I didn't fully understand it at the time. What I gave up for *you,* Tony." His gaze veered back to Luis. "Because as long as I stuck around, you refused to see Tony for who he was. And I hated it, Pop. *Hated* it."

He spun around and headed toward the door, tossing a glance in his brother's direction. "So you'll have to forgive me if I seem a little put out that you seem determined to destroy the very thing I sacrificed for you. Now if you'll excuse me, I've got a life to get back."

Before Ben had stormed off into the night, presumably to knock some sense into his brother, Mercy had slipped him the spare key to her house from the hook by her mother's back door. She hadn't even thought about it, it simply seemed like the logical thing to do. Even though she'd neither hoped nor expected him to return. She'd just thought he should have the option, that was all.

And giving him a key avoided all that messy having-to-wait-up business.

Not that she wasn't awake when he let himself in, sometime around two. Or if she hadn't been, she would have awakened anyway, when he undressed again and slipped into her bed to spoon up against her. When his arm snaked around her waist, she automatically skootched into his warmth. This wasn't about sex, however, but about something far more precious and real and heart-stopping. What they'd had so long ago, multiplied by a hundred. A thousand.

Or could be, if he'd ever let that little—maybe not so little?—piece of him he was holding back out to play.

"So?" she murmured, and he nuzzled her hair. "Is everyone still alive?"

He chuckled tiredly, tightened his hold. "Barely."

A moment passed. "You okay?" she whispered.

"I'm fine," he said after a beat. "Go back to sleep."

As if. Mercy skimmed her fingers up and down his arm. "What is up with you and your brother, anyway?" When he didn't respond, she said, "Anita seems to think your father always pitted the two of you against each other. That he favored you, at Tony's expense."

Ben went very still. "It would seem that way."

"Why would he do that?"

"No idea. Can we go to sleep now?"

Resisting the temptation to pluck out one of his arm hairs, she said, "You do realize that everyone now knows we're sleeping together?"

"Mm-hmm," he said, his breathing slowing. "They can deal. They're grown-ups, we're grown-ups…" She felt him shrug. "No more lies, babe," he mumbled. "No more secrets…"

Oh?

A nanosecond later, he was sound asleep, while Mercy lay there, eyes wide open, thinking, *Be careful what you wish for…*

Except two days later, she still had no clue what Ben had been talking about. And whenever she brought up the subject, he frowned, like he had no idea what *she* was talking about. Which, come to think of it, sounded pretty much like every married couple she knew, so maybe they were on the right track with this relationship thing, after all.

Anyway. So here it was, Morning *Numero Dos* since she and Ben had officially Become a Couple, and there her sister was, in bright pink scrubs and her down jacket, standing at the counter and looking about as forlorn as a girl could, pouring herself a cup of the lovely, strong coffee Ben had put on when he'd gotten up a half hour before. On the other side of the breakfast bar, Mercy sat alternately guzzling said coffee and yawning, listening to the shower running from down the hall and wishing there was some way to politely tell her sister the sounding board wasn't on duty for at least another hour. Or two.

"What I don't get," Mercy said after another yawn, "is why you just don't call Tony already, if you're so bummed."

"Can't do that." The coffee sloshed over the edge of the blurred carafe when Anita shakily set it back on the warming plate. "He's the one who has to come to his senses," she said over the sizzling.

"But the kids—"

"The kids are fine. Really. Ma and Papi are overcompensating like mad, and Tony talks to them twice a day. And they went over there last night for a little while…" Her voice trailed off, then she pulled her shoulders back, shoving her hair behind one ear. Oh, hell, her bottom lip was trembling. "So…" She sucked in a steadying breath. "How are things going between you and Ben?"

And a deaf person could have heard the "I hope to hell you know what you're doing" in her sister's voice. Not that Mercy needed the warning. Or the meddling, well-meaning though it might have been.

"Not bad, actually. Although maybe you shouldn't be here when he gets out of the shower."

"He's still pissed with me?"

"He's pissed with everybody. Why do you think he's been staying over here? He and his father aren't even talking."

Anita gave her a hard look. "Like I'm gonna believe Ben's staying with you has anything to do with his father."

Mercy sighed. "You know, if you'd asked me six weeks ago how I would have felt about sharing my house and my bed and my life with another human being—especially this particular human being—I would have broken out in hives."

"And now?" When Mercy only shrugged, her sister leaned across the breakfast bar, laying a hand on her wrist. "*Chica,* take it from someone who knows…do not get yourself into anything you're not one hundred percent sure about. When I think back about how young I was when I got married…" Her hair grazed her shoulders when she shook her head. "Love really is blind, you know?"

"Yes, I do. I also know there's no such thing as one hundred percent. Or are you saying I don't get to take the same chances the rest of you did?"

Anita's mouth fell open, but at the sound of the shower being turned off she hurriedly finished her coffee, then grabbed her purse off the counter. "Just be careful," she said, then hustled around the bar, through the living room and out the front door.

A minute or so later, Ben had replaced her sister in the kitchen, all damp-haired and yummy-smelling in a corduroy shirt and jeans, chatting away to the cat while leaning against the counter waiting for his toast to pop up. Like he belonged there or something.

Unbelievable.

"I take it Anita was here?"

"How'd you know?"

He held up her empty mug.

"She misses your brother," Mercy said, holding out her own mug for Ben to refill while he had the coffeepot in his hand. "I told her you're staying over here because of all the stuff between you and your dad."

A smile played around his mouth. "What other reason would there be?"

She threw her spoon at him, which, laughing, he dodged only to laugh harder at Homer's double axle when it clattered to the floor. "Anyway," she said as he bent over to pick up the spoon, "I get the feeling she thinks we're being a trifle impetuous."

His gaze never leaving her face, Ben took a long sip of his coffee, then set his mug on the counter. "Do *you?*"

Aside from than the occasional spurt of anxiety about whatever it was he wasn't telling her?

"No," she said, deciding not to let on that, actually, his being around felt a lot like, after years without a sofa, she'd been sure the room would feel cramped once she finally decided to live like a grown-up and get one. And yet, amazingly, the minute the delivery guys set it down it was as if it had always been there.

Except having Ben around was much nicer, since sofas don't ask how your day was or make coffee in the mornings or listen to you bitch or give you orgasms.

Of course, they also stay where you put them, which was a big point in their favor.

His toast shot out of the toaster; he caught it midair and plunked it onto a plate. "So did you tell her to mind her own business?" he asked while he buttered it, giving her one of those skin-prickling, tummy-fluttering looks that immediately brought on the Naughty Thoughts. Even at this hellacious hour.

"She's probably a little vulnerable right now for the direct approach. But yes, basically."

Ben set a piece of harmless, glistening toast on a plate in front of her; this early, it might as well have been something from Fear Factor. Still, to show she appreciated the thought, she picked it up and nibbled on one corner. Carrying his own toast into the living room, Ben reached over to reinsert one of Mattie's Valentines that had fallen out of Annabelle's branches.

"Are we sending our parents to early graves?" he asked.

"Hey. If they've survived everything the seven of us have put them through thus far, they'll live through this, too." She lowered the toast to the plate, flicking crumbs from her fingers. "Why? Have yours said something to you?"

Ben walked back into the kitchen, shoving the rest of his toast into his mouth. "They're a little preoccupied with the Tony-and-Anita Show at the moment, so no," he said, chewing. "Yours?"

"Oh, we had an agreement," she said lightly, waving one hand. "If they wanted me to live across the street, they had to stay out of my private life."

Ben's eyes crinkled at the corners. "Yeah, I can see your mother agreeing to that."

She blinked at him, then slapped one hand on her cheek in mock astonishment. "Ohmigod—you don't think Anita was a *spy,* do you?"

Chuckling, he checked his watch, then grabbed his jacket off the back of the chair, leaning across the bar to give her a soft, lingering see-you-later kiss as he slipped it on, and she sat there for twenty minutes after he'd gone feeling as dreamy and mush-brained as a fourteen-year-old with her first crush.

And almost as willing to believe in happily-ever-afters.

Go figure.

If it hadn't been for Mercy, Ben thought as he shuffled through a stack of invoices in his father's office, he'd've lost it by now for sure. Nearly a week after Tony and Anita's split, Tony and Ben and Luis only spoke with each other about business, and then as briefly as possible. Even so, the hurt in his father's eyes, and the confusion in Tony's, nearly took him under. But what else could he do? At least he'd dragged the problem out into the open, half-decayed though it may have been after having been buried for so long. Getting past the layers of grime and identifying it, however…that was up to them. Especially his father.

So Mercy had been his bulwark through the whole ordeal. Except, despite her repeated assurances that she was fine with the way things were going between them, Ben could practically smell her lingering insecurities. Willing to give this a shot though she might be, only a fool would believe she completely trusted him. And he could hardly blame her, could he? Especially since—

His cell rang, derailing his thoughts. Ben glanced at the display, frowning when he saw Tony's number.

"You about to knock off?" his brother said.

"Soon. Why?"

"It's okay," Tony said on what sounded like a defeated sigh. "I'm not gonna bite your head off or anything. It's just that it's taken me this long for a lot of what you said to sink in. An' now I'm thinking maybe it's time you and I talk. Finally. So you wanna pick me up when you get off, we could go to Applebee's or something? I'd say here but there's nothing in the house except cereal and yogurt, and I can't face another pizza."

Deciding he didn't detect murderous undertones in his brother's voice, Ben agreed to pick Tony up shortly, then called Mercy to tell her his plans.

"O…kay…" she said. "And you're telling me this why?"

"In case you were counting on me being there for dinner, why else?"

"Actually, Rosie strong-armed me into helping her with a Pampered Chef party tonight, which I'd totally forgotten about until she called me a little bit ago. So I wasn't going to be home, anyway."

"A Pampered what?"

"Never mind. Girl thing. So…does this mean we're officially living together now, or what?"

The cell reception wasn't the best down in the Valley, but even so, Ben couldn't tell if Mercy was surprised, annoyed or strangely pleased. Nor was he about to jump in with an answer guaranteed to elicit the wrong result.

"Call it anything you like. I was only giving you a heads-up. In case you were expecting me."

"I wasn't *expecting* anything," she said, a little shortly, he thought. "It's a lot safer that way."

"In other words, you still don't think you can count on me."

"How about I'm good with taking this day by day."

"Then how about I make it clear, so there's no misunderstanding," he said, leaning heavily on the desk, the phone tightly gripped in his hand. "We're *together,* Mercy. Which by my definition means we share our meals and we share a bed, unless something comes up on either end, in which case we let the other one know what's going on. You got a problem with that?"

Finally, he heard her chuckle. "And if I did?"

"Then tell me to back off, and I'm gone."

"Yeah. Like that worked so well before."

"Only because I didn't think you really meant it."

"God, you are such a man."

"You complaining?" he said, leaning back in his chair, a grin sliding across his face. "In fact, being as I'm the guy and all, guess what I'm thinking about right now…?"

"And maybe you should hold that thought, since I'm here at the store and all?"

His smile broadened. "Thought I was gonna talk dirty, didn't you?"

"You weren't?" she said, sounding slightly disappointed.

"Guess you'll never know," he said, disconnecting the call.

"I take it that was Ben?" Cass said, wrapping up a vintage christening gown in tissue paper while the customer—a pint-size, white-haired thing who had to be in her seventies, her blue eyes positively radiant over the birth of her first granddaughter—floated amongst the racks, seeing what else she could add to her already prodigious stack of goodies for her seven grand*sons.*

Mercy rolled her eyes. There'd been little point in pretending to her partners that she and Ben weren't back together. Although she could have done without the smug expressions on both their faces when she'd fessed up. "Get this—he called to tell me he wouldn't be available for dinner. Because he didn't want me to feel, I don't know, stood up or something."

The tissue paper stopped rustling. Mercy glanced over to see Cass frowning at her. "I don't suppose I have to tell you how much a considerate man goes for on the open market these days?" At Mercy's weak laugh, Cass tilted her head. "So…is this a good thing or no?"

"I'm not sure," Mercy said on a sigh. "Although he did indicate if I felt crowded, he'd back off."

Cass resumed her rustling. "Not that I was listening or anything, but I don't recall hearing anything that sounded like telling him to go jump in a lake."

Mercy thought about that for the next few minutes, while the grandmother toted more stuff up to the counter and finally pulled out her credit card, which Mercy swiped for her. Once the woman, gleefully laden down with a half-dozen multicolored Great Expectations shopping bags—and a bilious pink heart-shaped balloon for good measure—bounced off, Mercy looked at her partner and said, "Actually, what I feel is…hold on to your hat—happy."

"It's okay, you'll get used to it," Cass said.

Yeah. That's what worried her.

For the past thirty minutes, Ben and Tony had been sitting at the Applebee's bar, watching some college hoops game on the closest TV and nursing a pair of beers. Since his brother had initiated the contact, Ben was more than willing to let him initiate the conversation as well. Although at the rate they were going, they'd be into a new administration before that ever happened.

They'd been close when they'd been kids, Ben supposed, being only two years apart. But by the time Tony started middle school, they had little to do with each other, a gap that only widened after they moved into separate bedrooms when Ben turned nine or ten.

Now, though, despite the awkwardness of the moment, Ben felt as though the impenetrable wall of animosity that had been wedged between them for as long as he could remember had finally begun to dissolve. A little, anyway. Especially, when—at long last—his brother slid a glance in his direction and said, "I called 'Nita this morning. Said if she wanted to go to counseling or something, that would be okay with me."

"Miss her, do you?"

"Worse than *ESPN* that time I forgot to pay the cable bill."

Ben smiled. "You can't back out this time, you know."

"I won't. I *swear*," Tony repeated at Ben's skeptical expression. "I love that woman, Ben. Yeah, we make each other crazy, but the thought of life without her…" He shook his head. "I would die, man. Just curl up in a ball and freakin' *die*. I guess it took her actually walking out for me to realize that maybe I've been a little…stubborn. That maybe I could be a little more, you know, supportive. Show her how much I appreciate her."

Ben hid his smile behind his glass as he swallowed his beer, then said, "You do know, don't you, if you so much as think of backsliding—"

"Not gonna happen. I know people think I'm dumb as a rock, but I'm not *that* dumb."

Ben clunked down his glass. "You're not dumb, Tony. Shortsighted, yes—a quality you share with me, for what that's worth—but not dumb."

"Thanks," Tony said, and Ben nodded, then Tony said, "I think maybe I owe you an apology, too."

"What for?"

"For blaming the wrong person all these years. For not realizing it wasn't you who was the problem, it was Pop."

Ben stared blankly at the TV screen, fingering the condensation dripping down the side of the glass. "I don't think it's that simple."

"Like I don't know that? But at least now I've got some idea what I'm really dealing with. After you left the other night, I came right out an' asked Pop why he never thought I was good enough, and he looked like I'd slapped him in the face. Of course, he was already shaken up pretty good, after what you'd said, but…" Tony wagged his head back and forth. "It was like he'd suddenly woken up or something. And he apologized."

"Did it sound sincere?"

Tony seemed to mull that over for a moment, then shrugged. "I think he's really sorry for everything that's happened. Whether or not he would've, or could've, changed the way he felt, I don't know. But when you stood up for me like that…" His dark gaze swung to Ben's. "That meant a lot. Especially since I didn't get the feeling you were just blowing smoke up my ass."

Ben smiled. "No. I wasn't." He released a breath. "I have no idea why Pop's always thought I'd be better at running the business than you. From everything I've seen since I've been home, there's absolutely no reason for him to think that. Although…" He pushed the beer away, leaning back to cross his arms over his chest. "*Are* you happy? Working for Pop, I mean?"

One side of Tony's mouth quirked up. "I'd be a lot happier if he'd get off my case an' trust me every once in a while, you know? I mean, sure, I screwed up a couple of times when I started out. But that was years ago. An' even then, it wasn't anything serious. Just stupid stuff." Again, Tony's eyes cut to Ben's. "You really left because of me?"

"In a roundabout way, at least. Because Pop was driving me nuts, too, putting me up on some damn pedestal that I didn't deserve. And for sure didn't want. I despised what he was doing to you, but I couldn't figure out any other way to solve the problem except by removing myself from the picture."

Tony got very quiet. "All that you were saying, about me having no idea what you'd had here…you were talking about Mercy, huh?"

After a moment, Ben nodded. "Yeah."

"And you really gave her up because of me?"

"That's how it played out."

"And people think *I'm* stupid." When Ben started to protest, Tony raised a hand. "Okay, fine, I'm not stupid. But, damn— what were you thinking?"

"It's okay, it wasn't that serious between us, anyway."

That got a narrow-eyed look. "On your part? Or hers?"

Smiling, Ben shook his head. No, if it was one thing Tony wasn't, it was dumb. "Far as Mercy was concerned, it was just a passing thing. If not an outright mistake. I don't think it ever even occurred to her to associate the word *permanent* with what we were doing." He twisted his glass of beer around by its base. "And I figured I might as well make my move before it did."

"Man," Tony said on a rush of air. "I mean, I hear what you're saying, but it's not registering. That you'd do something like that. For me." He took a long swallow of his beer. "It didn't work, you know."

"Yeah. I can see that. I'm really sorry."

"Me, too," Tony said on a short laugh, then added, "But it's not your fault. Apparently, it never was."

"I've never been in any kind of competition with you, Tony. I swear."

"I know. At least, I know *now.*" His brother lifted his beer to his lips, taking several swallows before saying, "So. You hoping to start over or win her back or what?"

"That's the plan, yep."

"Is it working?"

"I'll let you know."

Tony chuckled, then said, more seriously than Ben could ever remember hearing him before, "For sure, you are definitely not the same person you were when you left."

"Is that good or bad?"

After a noncommittal shrug, his brother said, "I'll say one thing, though—I think maybe I could learn to like the dude sitting beside me right now." He hesitated. "If you'd be interested, I mean."

"I'll take it under advisement," Ben said, and they both smiled.

Only then Tony came up with, "Does that mean you might consider telling me what you really been doing all this time you've been away?"

Startled, Ben frowned in his direction. Tony misunderstood and immediately started backpedaling. "Not that it's any of my business, so if you don't want to tell me, that's cool—"

"No, it's not that, it's…" Ben shook his head. "I just don't—"

"—get how I figure that? For one thing, for somebody's who's supposedly been working in construction all along, you're practically clueless about the newest materials and techniques. For another, I've run into too many guys over the years with stuff in their backgrounds they don't want me to know about not to recognize the signs." When Ben looked away, Tony said, "So am I right?"

"Yeah," Ben said on a sigh. "You're right." Their waiter brought their steaks; Ben picked up the salt shaker, staring at the sizzling meat for several seconds before looking over to run smack into a combination of curiosity and expectancy in his brother's eyes.

And he realized it was time to come clean.

So, as they ate, Ben filled Tony in on what had really kept him away from home for so long, and Tony's eyes got wider and wider until eventually he said, very quietly, "Wow." Then, in a rare demonstration of understanding, he said, "I can sure see why you kept this to yourself," only to then add, with a fork jab for emphasis, "but if you don't tell Mercy, like, yesterday, you can kiss any chance you have of winning her back *adios*. 'Cause keeping something like this from her…" Tony shook his head.

"I know, I'm working up to it," Ben said, grabbing the dessert menu, reasonably sure his stomach's churning had nothing to do with his dinner. He'd left that life behind, of his own accord; there was no reason, none, for the sudden surge of ambivalence his conversation with his brother had provoked. He'd stuck it out longer than most, for God's sake. Didn't he deserve a life of his own now? "Although you do realize if you breathe a word of this to anybody—"

Tony's laugh cut him off. "Are you kidding? An' spoil the joy of for once being the only one in the family that knows something the others don't? Not on your life," he said, turning the small laminated menu over. "I can't decide between the apple pie and this brownie thing, whaddya think?"

Ben smiled halfheartedly, wishing with all his heart for just *some* of his decisions to be that uncomplicated.

Chapter Eleven

When Mercy returned from the Pampered Chef party, Ben was sprawled on the sofa watching TV, hands behind his head, his crossed, socked feet propped on her coffee table. He'd turned Annabelle's color wheel on, the goof. And speaking of goofs, Homer was stretched out on the sofa beside Ben, flat on his back, looking positively filleted. Mercy shook her head.

"How was your thing?"

"It wasn't *my* thing," she said with a yawn, sinking into the cushions beside him, melting into his side when he put his arm around her and drew her close. "And please, shoot me if I ever even suggest doing a home party. But it was fine. I bought one of those pizza stone dealies for the oven."

"Does that mean homemade pizza in our near future?"

"Probably not. But Rosie kept giving me the evil eye so I

caved." She laid a hand on his stomach, toying with a shirt button. "How was dinner with your brother?"

"Okay," he said, and she thought, Sheesh, men, only then he said, "More than okay. We talked, really talked, more than we ever have before." He gave her a little squeeze. "Speaking of caving…he's going nuts without your sister."

"Yeah?"

"Oh, yeah. I think we can all strike that particular crisis off our list. Until the next time, at least."

The furnace kicked on with a whoosh, then a rumble; seconds later, heat murmured through the vent. Outside, some old truck rattled by. She could hear a dog barking on the next street over. All sounds Mercy normally wouldn't have even noticed, if it hadn't been for the profound silence that had suddenly taken her living room hostage. Anxiety sparked inside her; before it had time to flare, she twisted around to find Ben staring blankly at nothing, his forehead bunched.

"Hey," she whispered, dragging a knuckle down his rough cheek. "What's going on in there?"

He sucked in a quick, sharp breath, as if to clear his head, then took her hand in his, stroking his thumb over one fingernail. "I haven't exactly been honest with you," he said quietly. "About the time we've been apart."

Finally, Mercy thought, even as she wondered why, instead of feeling relieved, she felt like a character in a Japanese horror movie, waiting for the oogly-woogly to git 'er.

She pushed herself up. Looked him straight in the eye. "Tell me you have a wife and four kids in Boise and you are so dead."

"No," he said on a dry chuckle. "No wife. No kids. Never been to Boise."

"Then what?"

Ben lowered his feet to the floor, leaned forward. "For the past eight years, I've been working with this P.I. based in Dallas, helping to rescue lost and abducted kids."

For who-knows-how-long, she just sat there, staring at his profile, his words clanging in her head. Then she shifted to sit on the trunk so she could face him. So he'd have to face her. "You're telling me you haven't been drifting from place to place all this time, working construction?"

"Not after the first couple of years, no."

After that, she only heard bits and snatches of his explanation, about how he'd gotten to talking to this P.I. who'd specialized in rescuing kids when they'd both ended up in the E.R. one afternoon, the "click" when he realized that maybe this was something that would give him a sense of purpose.

"I was a real mess at that point, Merce," he said. "I had no idea what I was supposed to be doing, I was getting real tired of the freelance construction routine, and I couldn't come home. Not then, at any rate. Roy took me under his wing, showed me the ropes, helped me to get my own license a few years ago." He shrugged, then pushed out another breath. "And that's it. The truth."

"So all this time…you've been a private investigator? And nobody knew?"

"No."

Her eyes burned. "You bring babies back to their parents?"

"That's pretty much the job description, yeah."

Mercy released a huge breath of her own. Well, that explained a whole lot, didn't it? Why he'd been so concerned about the little boy at the store, why he'd questioned her about

Mattie's friendliness with strangers…just his connection with kids in general. Then, even as the first stirrings of anger began to bubble inside her, she said, *"Why?* Why on earth did you keep it a secret?"

"Think about it, honey—can you imagine my mother's reaction if she'd known what I'd really been up to? Yeah, for the most part it's a lot of Internet searching and talking to the authorities and sitting on your butt behind the wheel, watching and waiting for hours on end. But sometimes…" He scrubbed a hand down his face. "Let's just say things can get kind of hairy."

The inside of her head felt like a presidential news conference with a hundred questions being shouted at once. Only in her case, it was which one to ask first, not answer, that had her stymied. "But…isn't that what the police and the FBI are for?"

"You'd think," Ben said with a tired, tight smile. "But there are far more cases than the authorities can handle. And frankly, in many jurisdictions, if it's a parent who's taken the kid, they still don't treat it as a kidnapping. The parents left behind…they're desperate. Beyond desperate."

Just the thought sent a wave of nausea through her. "So, what? You did the commando thing and went in and rescued the kids?"

"Not unless we absolutely have to," he said. "It's dangerous, borderline illegal and a Rambo number can definitely traumatize the kids more than they already are. If we're lucky, the abducting parent gives up without a struggle, once they're discovered."

"And if you're not?"

His eyes searched hers for a long moment. "The kid's welfare is always, always the first priority. But the longer a child's kept in essentially a hostage situation, hiding out, not allowed contact with his or her other parent or friends or family, the harder it is on them."

"In other words, you did what you had to do."

When he looked away, the muscle in his jaw working overtime, she felt like a kid playing that searching game where somebody tells you if you're getting warmer or colder, the closer or farther you get to whatever it is you're looking for. Even if you don't know what that is. And right now, she guessed she was pretty damn warm.

"Sometimes, yes," he said, and she thought, *Warmer...*

"And...?" she prodded.

Several beats passed before he met her gaze again, the haunted look she'd seen that first day back in spades. "Last fall I had a very close call—no, the kid's fine," he said at her swift intake of breath. "Back home with his mother in Oklahoma. It was my partner. Who's fine, too. Now." When he paused, she realized he had no intention of elaborating, at least not then. "But it shook me. Not because I might have gotten hurt, but..." He swiped a hand over his mouth. "I've never lost a kid, Merce. But what happened, it really drove home..." She saw his throat work. "For the first time, I found myself wondering how long my lucky streak could hold out."

Almost soundlessly, his fear crept out of the shadows to stand before her, awaiting her judgment. Mercy reached out to wrap her hand around his as snapshots flashed in her mind's eye, of an obnoxious ten-year-old, reduced to helpless laughter over farting noises; a charming teenager, too full of himself for his own good; the easygoing young man who'd somehow become her friend, sitting across from her at her mother's kitchen table the night before he left for boot camp, his eyes brimming with a cocktail of excitement, anticipation and sheer terror.

The passionate young lover she'd catch watching her as though he couldn't believe his good fortune.

All gone now, leaving in their place a man of conviction, compassion and quiet courage. A man who she realized she loved so much it hurt. The last man she'd have never thought would meet all her requirements for a perfect mate.

Except for one, she thought as the anger she'd been holding back erupted to the surface, propelling her off the trunk and into the middle of the room.

Ben knew the instant realization hit. Now all he could do was batten down the hatches and weather the storm.

Her arms tightly crossed over her ribs, Mercy paced the small patch of empty carpet in front of the TV, her curls bobbing nonstop as she shook her head. "I knew something was up," she muttered. "I *knew* it." She stopped long enough to shoot daggers in his direction. "But did it occur to you to *tell* me what was going on in your head? What you'd been doing all this time? To tell me the *real* reason you'd come home? Dammit, Ben—you *lied* to me!"

He shot to his feet. "I didn't lie to you! I would *never* lie to you!"

"Well, you sure as hell sucked me into this relationship under false pretenses, didn't you? My God, Ben, how could you keep something that important from me? How can I possibly think about a future with you if I don't even know who the hell you *are?*"

"Because I'm *telling* you who I am, Merce," Ben said quietly, standing his ground. "Who I *was*."

"So glad you finally got around to it."

"I never intended on keeping it a secret forever."

"Then why keep it a secret at all?"

"Because I didn't dare tell anybody with the way things were between my father and me!"

Her brows crashed together. "What does your father have to do with it?"

"How about everything? He's always had this crazy idea that I'm supposed to take over the business. Not Tony, me. He's always…favored me—and I know how that sounds, but I don't know how else to say it. God knows, I've never done or said anything to encourage him, especially when I could see how much it hurt Tony. I mean, yeah, if I have to go into the business with them, that's one thing. But taking it away from my brother was never part of my game plan."

Her arms still crossed, Mercy stood absolutely still, apparently trying to absorb what he'd said. Then something shifted in her face. "Ohmigod. That's why you left, isn't it? To save your brother's butt?"

The cat hopped off the sofa to rub up against Ben's calf, doing his little broken meow thing. "Mainly, yeah."

Finally, though, she shook her head, hurt and distrust littering her eyes. "And what does that have to do with me? With us? Okay, keeping this from your father—maybe I can understand that. To a point. But not from me. Oh, wait a minute…this is some macho don't-worry-the-lady's-pretty-little-head-about-it thing, isn't it?"

"No! Okay, maybe a little," he said, when she blew a disbelieving breath through her nose. "Hey, you're the woman who still can't watch the news because it upsets her too much! So yeah, every time I thought about telling you, you'd say or do something and I'd think…not yet. But it wasn't just that. It's…"

One hand hooked on his waist, he began some pacing of his own. "The people I help, they act like…like I'm this big hero or something. But I'm not, I'm just a guy doing what needs to be done, and it makes me real uncomfortable when people make more out of it than it is. Maybe this only makes sense to me, I don't know. But the last thing I want to do is come across like some fatheaded jerk who thinks he's hot stuff."

"So you decided it was better not to say anything at all?"

He stopped. "Basically," he said on a rush of air.

She glared at him for another several seconds, then stomped into the kitchen and yanked open the fridge door, pulling out a bottle of fruit juice.

"Well, *that* was stupid," she said, wrenching off the top.

"I'm sorry, Merce," he said softly. "And you're right, it was stupid, not telling you. But since that part of my life is over, I honestly didn't think it mattered."

"You were wrong," she said. "And anyway, what, if I may ask, is so terrible about being a hero?"

"Because it's not me. I don't know, maybe Pop wouldn't've blown things out of proportion, but I wasn't about to take that chance. To give him anything he could use as another wedge between Tony and me. And yes," he said to her eye roll, "I know, I know—that has nothing to do with us. Bad call, okay?"

"*Really* bad call." Mercy tilted the bottle to her lips, then lowered it, saying, "And I think you've gotta accept the fact that to those parents, to the kids, you're definitely Super Ben.

Yeah, yeah, yeah," she said, cutting off his protest. "Just a guy doing his job, I got it." Another sip. Another dead-aim look in the eyes. "But it's over? You're really giving it up?"

"Yes," he said, shoving aside the niggling doubt that had been plaguing him more and more over the past few weeks. He cocked his head. "This mean you're not mad at me anymore?"

"Don't kid yourself. I'd smack you silly if I didn't have to get up on something to reach that big fat head you're so worried about. But I don't understand." Her gaze was steady. And far too discerning, like it had always been. "Why would you give it up? I mean, yeah, I can understand having to take a break, I can't imagine how rough it could be to keep putting yourself on the line like that. But to just…walk away and not look back?" Her brow creased, she shook her head.

Ben sighed. "Because working with all those families drove home what was really important. The more parents I reunited with their kids, the more I realized what I'd really given up. What I really wanted. And being ready to go wherever, whenever, not to mention the constant stress—that's hell on a family. I can do one or the other, but not both. And I've made my choice."

He watched her chest rise and fall, rise and fall, underneath her soft sweater. "So Tony's broken leg had nothing to do with it?"

Ben smiled slightly. "I wouldn't say that. It provided the kick in the butt I needed to get back here and fix some stuff that sorely needed fixing. To see if…"

"What?"

"To see if my memory had been playing tricks on me all these years."

"And?"

"It hadn't."

Mercy set down the juice bottle, then propped her elbows on the breakfast bar, sinking her face into her hands. When she looked up, hope peered cautiously from her eyes. "Honest to God, you're here to stay?"

Even though Ben could hardly blame her for asking him virtually the same question three times in as many minutes, her obvious skepticism and uncertainty cut him to the quick. Helluva lot to fix, here.

Helluva bridge to burn behind him. But for crying out loud—he'd devoted a good chunk of his life to taking care of other people. Was it so wrong to want to grab a little happiness for himself?

Even if that meant, once again, giving up one thing for another, Ben thought as he looked deep into the eyes of the woman he hadn't fully realized how much he needed until he'd thought he'd lost her.

No. The woman he hadn't realized how much he'd needed until the promise of actually *having* her shimmered like El Dorado in front of him.

The cat scooted out of his way as he crossed to the breakfast bar in three strides, leaning across it to thread his fingers through Mercy's thick, lush hair. He pressed his lips to her forehead, then eased back, taking her hands in both of his, kissing her fingers. "You're as much a part of me as my own heart, Mercy," he said, banishing those niggling doubts to a galaxy far, far away. "I *love* you, you crazy woman. So I swear, as long as you want me in your life, I'm not going anywhere."

In the space of a second, a hundred emotions played over

her features. Then she pulled away to put the half-drunk juice
back in the fridge. Well aware that she hadn't returned his dec-
laration—and trying his best to be a man about it—Ben
straightened, wondering what was coming next.

She suddenly whirled around, her eyes huge.

"You almost died," she said.

"What? No, I didn't, it was my partner—"

"No, not then. When you were a baby. Maybe around two,
because I think I was in first grade. You got really, really sick,
spent something like a month in the hospital. I remember
Tony was at our house a lot because your parents were with
you. Your mother…ohmigod."

She pressed a hand to her mouth; he could practically see
the memory shuddering into focus. "Carmen and I had come
home from school, we'd walked, nobody knew we were there,
and our mothers were together in the kitchen. Yours was
crying. Sobbing, actually, so hard I could hardly understand
her. But I got the gist of it. And I…I ran into the kitchen,
yelling, 'The baby can't die! Babies don't die, only old people
die!' I can still see the horrified look on my mother's face. I
thought she was going to knock me clear into the next week."

Ben frowned. "You're sure of this?"

"Yes."

He blew out a breath, shaking his head. "But I didn't die."

"No," Mercy said, smiling weakly. "You didn't. In fact, I
think they brought you home a few days later. But I was only
a little kid, I'm probably not the most reliable source." She
tilted her head. "They never told you?"

"No. Oh, when I went into the army, there was some stuff
in my files about having had a bad case of the flu when I was

two, but I certainly never knew it was that serious." He felt his forehead cramp.

"Not that I'm any expert," Mercy said, "but if your father thought he'd nearly lost you…"

"That might have accounted for the preferential treatment."

"It's a thought," she said, lapsing into silence, during which Ben felt far more anxious than he ever had during any of his operations. All he wanted was to wrap her up in his arms and promise her the moon. But one did not promise Mercy the moon. One either delivered it, or shut the hell up.

Finally, she said, "Okay, this isn't about you leaving to save your brother's butt, or any of the other stuff you've been doing while you were away, because I don't want you to think I'm all blinded—" she waggled her hands by her shoulders "—by the glory or anything stupid like that. And it's going to take me a while to get over being ticked with you for not telling me the truth sooner than you did. That was so wrong, buddy, and if you *ever* do anything like that again, I swear I'll sic Carmen on you without a moment's hesitation. But…"

She propped her hands on her butt. Stuck out her chin. Looked him right in the eye. "But in the interest of full disclosure, I guess I should tell you this is it for me, too." When he frowned at her, she rolled her eyes. "I'm in love with you, too, you big turkey."

His ears heard her words, but his brain had clearly stepped out for a moment. Then it hit. Hard enough to knock the breath out of him. Finally he got back his breath and said, "Then what the *hell* are you doing over there?" and next thing he knew, *whoomph!* She'd launched herself at him like a linebacker, and they fell onto her sofa, laughing, the stupid cat

frantically meowing at them from the trunk as Ben kissed
Mercy over, and over, and over, determined to banish the lingering doubt lurking at the edges of her words.

However, it wasn't until a long time later, after they'd
made love until neither of them could move and she was
tucked safely, securely against his chest, that he remembered
that thing about promising her the moon, and he smiled.

One moon, he thought, *coming right up.*

Her hand tucked underneath her pillow, Mercy lay in bed,
staring blankly at the digital readout inches from her nose,
waiting for seven-thirty, only dimly remembering Ben's
goodbye kiss before he'd left a half hour before. Sunlight
bled through the blinds; with her orange walls, it was like
waking up inside a fat, juicy orange. Through the closed
window, she could hear a lone, overachieving dove hoo-
hooing its head off outside.

He loves me.

She stretched and rolled over, not even trying to resist the
pubescent impulse to gather Ben's pillow to her, inhale his
scent. Anything to jumpstart the contentment that by rights she
should be freaking *drowning* in by now.

But no.

Because even two days later, it still hadn't fully registered.
That he loved her and she loved him and that they'd both
actually said the words, so that must make it real.

On a groan, she tossed the pillow aside and sat up, vaguely
aware that no pushy orange cat was bugging her to feed him.
Ben must have done the honors, let him outside.

Ben. Ben, Ben, Ben, Ben, *Ben.*

Grimacing, Mercy shook her head.

Had she been too rash, admitting how far gone she was? Except the look on his face afterwards…well. Some things a girl just can't dismiss out of hand. Especially when those things had been *so* long in coming. And anyway, it wasn't as if he'd asked her to marry him or anything. Gosh, it might be months…years before the subject even came up. If ever.

*In…out…*she breathed, her heart rate slowing. *In…out…*

There. Much better.

Stealing a glance at the clock—two minutes to go—she wrapped her arms around her knees. Life was never perfect, God knew. But Anita and Tony seemed to be on the mend ("Ay, you should have seen his face, Mercy," Anita had said, laughing. "I've never seen a man so scared!") And Danas and C.J.'s new little girl had arrived yesterday, two weeks earlier than expected, and they were both disgustingly happy, if poleaxed. Ben and his father were still on the outs, but Rome wasn't built in a day, either—

"*Dios!*" Mercy yelped when the alarm finally blatted. She slammed it off, then dragged herself out of bed. Yawning and exaggeratedly hoisting her eyelids open as she tugged her robe tie closed, she shuffled down the hall toward the aroma of coffee, thinking that Ben's having repeatedly witnessed her in all her first-thing-in-the-morning glory—and not bolting—spoke volumes about his character. In fact, when she'd gotten up the other morning and cried out in alarm at her reflection, he'd only shrugged and said, "So?"

So, indeed, she thought, yawning again…

Then she blinked.

What the…?

Stumbling closer to the breakfast bar, Mercy rubbed her eyes and looked again, in case it had been a mirage the first time. It hadn't.

"Holy…" she murmured, picking up the tiny velvet box with trembling hands. Popped it open. Then, on a whimper, she sagged against the countertop, her free hand pressed to her mouth.

The emerald-cut stone, and its companion baguettes on either side, winked up at her. The ring wasn't huge, but then, neither was her hand. It was, however, perfect and exquisite and perfectly exquisite and exquisitely perfect and…

She clamped shut the box and grabbed her phone. Ben answered on the first ring.

"Made it out to the kitchen, did you?" he said, sounding both so tickled and so nervous, her outrage shrugged and left the building.

"You're asking me to *marry you?*" she squeaked. Or, more accurately, croaked.

"Just letting you know where I stand. I'm not expecting an answer."

This was far too much for the caffeine-deprived to process.

"You're insane," she said.

"True. Anyway, I was going to wait until Valentine's Day, but it seemed so…"

"Tacky? Clichéd?"

"Far away."

Mercy realized she was sniffling. But really, she'd've been happy with a box of Godiva and a card. She'd've been *thrilled* with a box of Godiva and a card. She grabbed a napkin and swiped at her nose. "It's in less than two weeks."

"Like I said."

She crumpled up the napkin, tucking it against her ribs when she crossed her arm over her waist. "Um, you do realize that most guys do this in person?"

"I know," he said, so gently her insides hurt. "But I didn't want to put you on the spot."

"Huh?"

He laughed softly. "I know you're probably not ready for this. And that's okay, that's fine. I just wanted you to know, to *really* know, that I am. But I thought if I sprang this on you—"

"Which you just did."

"—in person, you might…well, I didn't want you to feel pressured to, I don't know, put on a show or something."

She opened the box again. Again, the diamonds winked at her. The box sounded like a firecracker when she snapped it shut. "Since when have you ever known me to BS you—or anybody else—about anything?"

"True. Okay," he said on a sigh, "so I was afraid you'd say no. Or, worse, hate the ring."

"Uh, no. The ring…" She blinked. "The ring is gorgeous."

"Really?"

"Really. And if you had help picking it out, I don't want to know."

Another laugh—but no volunteering of information, she couldn't help but notice—before he said, "I'm serious, Merce."

"Yeah, I got that—"

"No, I mean about not pressuring you. I know what I want, but I don't know what you want. If and when you're ready, you put the ring on. But if you don't, I'll completely understand. I swear."

Then he said he had to run, and he loved her, and after he hung up Mercy stared at the little blue box for a long, long time, as though it was going to explode in her face or something. Finally, however—because she was female and breathing—she opened it. Pulled the ring out of its cozy little nest. Wriggled it a bit, just to see how the light played over all the darling little facets in the stones.

Slipped it on.

And let out a long, trembly breath.

It couldn't have been a more perfect fit.

Chapter Twelve

"Okay," Mercy's mother said, handing her a stack of the "good" dishes to put back up on the top shelf of the freshly-scrubbed and repapered kitchen cupboard, "you going to tell me what's going on with you and Ben or do I have to beat it out of you?"

From her precarious perch atop the step stool, Mercy now remembered why the prospect of helping her mother with her annual scourge-and-purge of the kitchen hadn't exactly filled her with gleeful anticipation. But everybody else was busy either minding babies or having babies or mending their marriages or fixing their lives or—in her father's case—out playing golf, so that left her. As it always did. Normally she didn't mind—the job went much more quickly with two people, she usually got a good lunch out of the deal, and when you're one of five it never hurt to suck up a little—but she'd known this conversation was coming.

Funny thing, though, how the older you get, the more you realize you don't have all the answers. Which meant that, instead of her standard knee-jerk "Stay out of my life, Ma!" response, all she said now was, "As if you don't know."

"I'm not talking about sex," Mary Zamora huffed, signaling for Mercy to return to terra firma. In more ways than one, most likely. Hmm…had her mother's honey-colored hair always been nearly the same color as the cabinets? "I know how things work these days. Okay, how they've always worked, for some people. But this is *Ben*," she said, worry crowding her eyes. "Doesn't that make things more…complicated?"

Braced though she may have been for the conversation, actually knowing what to say was something else entirely. Trying to order her thoughts, Mercy poured herself a cup of coffee from the never-empty pot on the counter. "You don't know from complicated," she muttered into her cup.

Taking the carafe out of Mercy's hands and filling her own cup, her mother barked out a laugh. "With you five? Believe me, I'm no stranger to 'complicated.'" She glanced over. "So…it's not only about sex?"

"Geez, Ma, would you quit saying that?"

"Hey. I didn't find you five in the cabbage patch, you know."

The oversize castered kitchen chair wobbled when Mercy pulled it away from the table, sank into the vinyl-covered cushion. A second later, her mother joined her, waiting. Mercy took two, then three swallows of coffee before she grabbed her purse off the table, searching through the depths until her fingers closed around the little velvet box. After a week, her heart still bumped whenever she touched it or saw it or thought about it.

She opened the box, set it on the table between them. Her mother let out a little "Oh…" Then a more forceful, more understanding, "Ohhhh…" Her eyes lifted to Mercy's. "You're not wearing it."

"Boy, nothin' gets past you, does it?"

"Don't be a smarty-pants." Then her mother's expression softened. "You don't like it?"

A half laugh climbed out of her throat. "Liking the ring—" which glittered at her when she scooped the box back up "—isn't the issue. Liking *Ben* isn't the issue. But that's the thing—half of me wants to jump up and down like a sixteen-year-old who got asked to the prom by the cutest guy in school. But the other half… Oh, Ma," she said on a long breath. "I feel like somebody's split my brain in two. I'd honestly thought I'd be single for the rest of my life. And frankly, when I looked at my future, I liked what I saw—complete autonomy, being able to make my own decisions, the whole nine yards. So what happens? Here comes Ben, offering me something I'd pretty much thought I'd never have, and…"

"It scares you?" her mother said gently.

"You have no idea. Except then I look at Dana and Cass…and I envy them," she said, literally jumping at her own words. "I want what they have." Her mouth stretched tight. "Sometimes so badly I think I can't stand it."

Her mother chuckled. "Wondered how long it would take."

"But is that really *me* talking, or am I just feeling…left behind? Just because Cass and Dana got their happy-ever-afters, so, what? It's my turn now?"

"And what's wrong with that?"

"Because I'm not a lemming?"

Smiling, her mother rested her chin in her palm. "Do you really love Ben?"

Tears pricking at her eyes, Mercy nodded. "Yeah. Go figure."

"So screw all the other stuff," her mother said, and Dana choked on her coffee. "I'm serious. So maybe it is your turn now."

"But with *Ben?*"

"Why not? That spacey kid he used to be doesn't exist anymore," she said, and Mercy thought, *And you don't know the half of it.* "*Querida,* this is a good man. Grab him before he changes his mind. Because I don't care what you say, the face I see before me is not the face of a woman who really wants to spend the rest of her life alone." Her mother leaned forward to cup Mercy's cheek in her warm hand. "Just scared to death of having her heart broken."

Mercy pulled away, shaking her head. "That's crazy. At my age—"

"—it's harder to take a chance."

"That's not what I was going to say."

"I know it wasn't. But it's true. You're afraid he'll leave again, aren't you?"

"He swears he won't."

"But you don't entirely believe him." When Mercy shook her head, Mary said, "Why? Has he done or said anything to make you doubt him?"

Mercy got up to refill her coffee cup, trying desperately to pinpoint the source of the anxiety that only seemed to increase with every promise Ben made. Considering everything she now knew, how could she even think of questioning the man's integrity?

Because, she realized, it was that very integrity that kept keeping her from taking him completely at his word.

She turned, holding her coffee close. "Okay, this is going to sound completely out of left field, but bear with me. When we were kids, did you ever notice Ben's father playing favorites with him?"

Her mother smirked. "Baby doll, when you were kids, I had my hands full keeping you and your four sisters alive. I can't say I was all that aware of what was going on between Ben and his father. Why do you ask?"

"Because Ben told me the real reason he took off, especially the second time, was because his father was making him crazy, always building him up and making a fuss over him. And unfortunately Tony got the short end of that stick."

"That's crazy, Luis would never have done that—"

"Yeah, he did. I didn't remember it, either, until Ben brought it up and then a whole lot of pieces I hadn't even thought about until then started to fall into place. Anyway, Ben finally decided things were never going to get better as long as he stuck around. That if he left, maybe his father would finally start appreciating Tony."

"And it took him nearly ten years to realize what a dumb idea that was? Especially considering he'd already been in the army, for heaven's sake."

Mercy smiled. "This is the male brain we're talking about. But that was only why he *left*. There was another reason that kept Ben from coming home," she said, then filled her mother in on Ben's activities in the intervening years. The more she talked, the larger her mother's eyes got behind her glasses until Mercy thought they'd pop out of her head altogether.

"*Madre de Dios,*" her mother breathed when Mercy was done. "I knew he'd changed, but…my goodness. And Juanita and Luis don't know?"

"No. And don't you *dare* tell them. That's up to Ben, when he's ready."

Her mother's mouth tightened. "Not to worry. Since that whole mess with Tony and Anita, we're barely speaking."

Mercy frowned. "Even though 'Nita and Tony are back together?"

Her mother's round, capable shoulders shrugged. "I may have said some things to Juanita…about Tony…" Contriteness pinched her mother's features. "I was angry and hurt for Anita's sake, I wasn't thinking. I apologized, but…"

"Ma. You guys have been friends for a million years." The old dishwasher's door whined when Mercy opened it. "She'll get over it."

"You're probably right, it's just…all these changes…"

"Yeah," Mercy said, staring out the kitchen window with her arms crossed. The middle of February and her mother's Japanese cherry was already budded out, honestly. "I know." Then she turned, sinking into her mother's embrace. "I hate this feeling," she mumbled into her mother's shoulder. "Like I'm seeing spooks in every shadow. And it's not that I don't believe Ben, when he says he's missed family, that he wants one of his own. With me." She lifted her head, seeking—and knowing she wouldn't find—answers in her mother's eyes. "But I still can't shake the feeling that it's too soon for him to really know what he wants. To be sure."

"Which is why you won't wear the ring."

"Right."

"But you haven't given it back, either."

When Mercy only shrugged, her mother laughed softly, then said, "Ever since you were a little girl, you've always worried yourself half to death about what *might* happen. Maybe it's time you stopped doing that?"

Heh. Easy for her to say.

Now this was the way to spend Valentine's, Ben thought as he lay on his side in Mercy's bed, his head propped in his hand. Streaming through the partially open miniblinds, the Sunday afternoon sunshine lapped at Mercy's golden skin as she crossed to the closet to get a robe, something weightless and red and shimmery. The same color as her toenails, as it happened.

"No," he said as she started to slip it on. "Wait."

The robe dangling from one hand, she cocked her head, then shifted, uninhibited, to let the pulsating light, like a hundred white-gold butterflies, dance over her breasts, her dimpled hips, tease the shadowed thatch between her legs. In this, she withheld nothing from him. Ever.

He signaled with his other hand for her to turn around.

"Is this about to get kinky?" she asked.

"With any luck," he said.

Mercy replied, "In your dreams," only to yelp when he sprang out of the bed and started to chase her around the room, eventually catching her and tossing her back onto the bed, both of them laughing and breathless. Now pinned underneath him, her smile flickered when he swept her insane hair away from her face, and he ached with loving her so much.

And with the constant knowledge that, after nearly two weeks, she still hadn't worn the ring. A one-and-a-half carat symbol of her chronic ambivalence.

"What?" she whispered, touching his face, and he smiled.

"Just reminding myself how lucky I am."

"Damn straight," she said, laughter reigniting in her eyes, and he claimed her mouth in a kiss that was tender and hot and sweet and crazy all at the same time, prodding Ben to remind himself that he was a patient man, an understanding man. The kind of man who could tell a woman he was crazy about her, give her a ring to show her how crazy he was about her, and then get out of her way while she made up her mind what she was going to do about that.

Well. Maybe not that out of her way, he thought as she slid her calf along his, tempting. Inviting.

They had all the time in the world, he thought as he came up for air, looked deep into her eyes. "And to think, I don't even need Internet access."

She tried to slug him but he pinned her hands up by her head and kissed her until her indignation melted and his cell rang again.

"Go ahead, answer it." She wriggled out from underneath him, snatching her robe up off the end of the bed. "I need food, anyway. Want some popcorn?" she said as she stood, tugging the end of the belt out of his hand so she could tie it.

"Sounds great," he said, watching her pad away with no little regret.

Not nearly as much regret, however, as he felt when he noticed Roy's cell number on the display. As promised, Roy had left him alone, given *Ben* the space to make up *his* mind.

That it hadn't worked, at least not as well as Ben had hoped, wasn't Roy's fault. Or Ben's. Or anybody's.

Oh, yeah. He understood all about ambivalence. Just as he understood exactly what answering this call would likely mean.

He flipped open the phone. "Yeah?"

After a long moment, Roy said, "I'm gonna take the fact that you answered as a positive sign."

"Don't be so sure of yourself."

"Hell, Ben, I'm not sure of anything, you know that." He hesitated. "Except that, after all these years, I think I know you pretty well."

"I told you, Roy—"

"The father's got the kid right there in Albuquerque. Mother's a Mexican national, doesn't speak much English. We need to move fast."

Ben's chest tightened. Through the open door, he heard Mercy singing along with some pop star over the rapid-gunfire sounds of exploding popcorn in the microwave. He imagined her bopping along in time to the music in her bare feet, that flimsy little robe gliding over her body. How warm and soft and willing she'd be when she came back to bed.

Grinding his palm into his forehead, Ben forced in a deep breath. Then another. "You got a positive ID…?"

He was already dressed when she returned, sitting on her chair and tugging on one of his boots.

Her stomach plummeted like a 747 hitting an air pocket. The popcorn bowl rattled against the dresser when she set it down; sucking in a steadying breath, she met one very troubled gaze.

"That was Roy," he said.

"Oh?"

He stood, shoving his hands in his pockets. "It's a one-off, Merce. The last time. Roy only called me because the case is right here." His jaw worked. "The kid's four. Holed up with his dad in some motel over on Central." A pause. "All you have to do is say 'no,' Merce, and I'll call him back right now, tell him—"

"No," she said, cutting him off. "I mean, no, don't call him back."

"You're sure?"

Despite feeling like the mother of all exposed nerves, she nodded. "I'm sure," she said, clenching her fist behind her back when a combination of relief and eagerness flooded Ben's face.

"Since the boy's mom's Mexican," he said, visibly pulsating as he moved around the room, collecting his watch, his keys, shoving his phone into his pocket, "the police aren't all that motivated to help her. Dad didn't return the little boy after his weekend visit, three weeks ago. According to the day clerk at the front desk, he's already been there for a week. But God knows how long he'll stay—"

She touched his arm; he jerked to a stop, frowning into her eyes. "How can I help?" she asked.

"Merce…"

"Later," was all she said, even though she would've had to be dead not to not feel the cataclysmic shift in the status quo during the last fifteen minutes. But right now, all that mattered was a little boy who'd been taken from his mother.

Searching her eyes, Ben lifted one hand, stroking her hair

away from her temple. "I can't go in to get the boy myself," he said. "Or it's kidnapping. If his mother gets him, it's not. But it probably wouldn't hurt to have another woman along, to support her. Help keep her centered."

"I'm in," Mercy said, and Ben smiled.

"Get dressed. And then listen very carefully to everything I say...."

"What if tonight is the night he does not go out?" Flora Rivas, the little boy's mother, asked in Spanish from the middle seat of Mercy's parents' SUV.

For the past hour Ben, Mercy and Flora had been waiting in the parking lot of the Buena Vista motel, one of the many, mangy, fifties hangers-on sharing this stretch of the old Route 66 with the seedy bars and the mobile home sales lots. The young woman was barely in her twenties and scared out of her wits, her dark eyes huge with worry in Ben's rearview mirror. Mercy, her expression calmer than Ben would have expected, sat beside her, tightly holding the girl's trembling hand in hers. Flora had begged a family friend to drive her to Albuquerque from El Paso, but the friend couldn't hang around. How she and her son were going to get back, she had no idea.

Ben twisted around to give her as encouraging a smile as he dared. This was one courageous young woman, one who'd found the *cojones* to leave an abusive husband, despite her family's berating her for having a serious screw loose. After all, what woman in her right mind would walk away from a man living legally in the States, someone who'd been regularly sending money to her impoverished family back in some flyspeck of a town in Mexico? That he'd been also regularly beating the tar out of her was beside the point.

"The desk clerk said he's brought the boy for her to watch every night for the past week," Ben said in Spanish. "Chances are he will tonight, as well." Because clearly, they weren't dealing with the sharpest knife in the drawer. Yes, the jerk had taken his kid, but staying in one spot made him a pathetically easy target. "And even if he doesn't," Ben said, "we will simply return tomorrow, yes?"

A smile flickered across the young mother's mouth, followed by a little nod…and then a frown. "But what if he decides to leave?"

A very valid worry. Although not one Ben was going to entertain tonight.

"The clerk told me your former husband said he'd found work, so he probably isn't going anywhere too soon."

Flora shook her head. "He thinks I am not smart enough, or do not have the courage, to try to find my baby. That I would just let him take Rico from me without a fight. *Atrasado.*"

A dimwit, indeed, Ben thought as Mercy choked back a laugh, prompting the young woman to say in broken English, "You are very *considerada,* to let me stay with you."

"*De nada—*"

"*Dios mio!*" Flora said on a gasp, grabbing Mercy's arm and practically lunging through the car's window. "*Ay, Rico…nino…*" Her voice lowered to a growl. "*Que pasa to your hair?*"

Ben felt the familiar thrum of adrenaline as they watched a short, wiry young man in baggy jeans and a tatty leather jacket close the door to one of the upstairs units, then lead a practically bald little boy by the hand slowly down the stairs…across the lot…into the office. Through the large, bare window, they could see the man talking with the clerk, laughing, looking down at the child.

Ben held his breath. *C'mon, dirtwad, just leave the kid and go….*

The door to the office opened. Both man and boy emerged.

"No," Flora whimpered, rocking back and forth. "Noooo…"

Then she bolted from the SUV.

Spitting out an obscenity and tersely ordering Mercy to stay put, Ben scrambled out from behind the wheel, as Flora's shrieked *"Rico!"* knifed through his skull. Both man and boy wheeled at Flora's cry, the man bellowing *"Cabrona!"* as he clumsily grabbed the child, tried to stuff him into a beat-up sedan.

"No! *No!*"

Flora flew toward them, still screaming her son's name, when suddenly her ex let out a scream of his own, clutching one hand with the other as Rico, his tiny legs a blur, sped across the parking lot and launched himself into his mother's arms.

"In the car, Flora!" Ben yelled in Spanish, hustling the pair toward the SUV. *"Get him in the car!"*

"Ben!" Mercy cried as she hauled Rico into her arms. "Watch *out!*"

Unfortunately, she was a split second too late.

Chapter Thirteen

"Hey," Mercy said softly, one hand on the dividing curtain in the E.R. exam room. Fear melted into relief when Ben looked over and smiled. "You're sitting up. Good sign."

Smirking despite the fierce pain barely dulled by the meds they'd given him, Ben made a half-assed attempt at buttoning up his shirt over the bandage cushioning his ribs.

With a gentle "Here, let me," Mercy stepped closer to do the job for him, even though her hands were shaking. One long red nail was gone, a victim of the scuffle at the end. Ben stroked the naked finger, smiling.

"I dunno…dyed hair, fake nails. And to think the whole reason I fell for you was because of your honesty."

She made a tiny choking sound. Ben slipped one hand underneath her hair to grip her neck and pull her closer, shutting his eyes as he inhaled the scent of her shampoo. "It's okay, babe," he whispered. "Rico's fine, I'm fine…all's well that ends well, right?"

"Heh," she said.

"So I suppose you want to kill me, too," he said, nuzzling all that soft, silky craziness.

"Too?" she said, focusing on a particularly stubborn button.

"First words out of my mother's mouth."

Her task accomplished, she patted his chest, then lifted her eyes. "I can't believe you still hadn't told them. They're out in the waiting room, by the way. Basket cases, the pair of them."

"Yeah," Ben said on a released breath. "I know. Not exactly how I'd envisioned their finding out about my 'secret' life. For a moment, I really did think my mother was gonna kill me."

"And your dad?"

"I think he understood. Why I had to keep this to myself. Didn't make him any less pissed, though."

"I don't imagine so."

"How are Flora and Rico?"

"Fine, considering." Mercy stepped back, her arms crossed, looking extremely grateful to have something else to talk about besides the obvious. "They're with my folks. Immensely grateful and obscenely guilt-ridden. Well, Flora's guilt-ridden. Rico's just happy to be back with his mom." She paused. "He said his father told him his mother was dead."

"Sick SOB."

"To put it mildly. But if it's any consolation, the sick SOB's a guest tonight in one of APD's four-star facilities, thanks to the desk clerk's calling 911 as soon as she saw Flora jump out of the car. You talked to the police, I take it?"

"Yeah. A little while ago."

Mercy was quiet for a moment, then slipped her hand into his. "The clerk said the sleazebag had settled his bill. He was leaving, Ben," she said quietly. "If Flora hadn't gone for it, she might not have her son tonight."

"None of which changes what happened," he said, watching her face.

Frowning, she gently touched the bandage through his shirt. "Are you in a lot of pain?"

"At the moment? Not too much. The minute the happy pills wear off, though, I'm not making any promises."

"But the doctor said it's not serious?"

"Only because I moved when I did. The bullet sideswiped a rib and kept on going. An inch or two further over, though…"

Mercy's troubled eyes met his the same moment a round, cheerful lady in scrubs swished through the curtain, handing him his chart. "You're good to go, Mr. Vargas. There're instructions here on how to care for the wound, but feel free to give us a call if there's any problem. The P.A. wants to see you next week, you can make an appointment at the desk."

After the nurse left, Mercy moved to help him off the exam table. Ben tried to laugh. "Forget it. You weigh like ten pounds."

Hands lifted, she stood back, only to shake her head and mutter something about *stubborn man* as he wobbled for a second on his feet. She moved closer again; he decided maybe bracing his hand on her shoulder, at least, wasn't such a bad idea, after all.

"Man," he said as they started out of the room. "This is good stuff. I can't even feel the floor."

Chuckling, she slipped one arm around his waist to guide

him down the hall and back to the waiting room. His parents stood at his entrance, leftover panic etched into their faces.

"You're coming back to our house so I can look after you," his mother said, flashing Mercy a look that was equal parts defiance and plea.

To his surprise, though, Mercy said, "That's a good idea, actually. Since now that Dana's new baby's here, I can't really be away from work too much."

"I'm not in traction, for God's sake," Ben growled. "I think I can take care of myself—"

"Benicio." His father laid a hand on his arm. "This has nothing to do with being able to take care of yourself." Ben caught the look in his mother's eyes, and he understood.

The look in Mercy's eyes, however, would have freaked him out if the pain meds hadn't dulled the freak-out center in his brain. Still, he insisted on riding with her, instead of his parents, because the longer one waited to exercise damage control, the less effective it was.

After they'd been driving for a minute or two, he said, "Don't think I'm not well aware that somebody else might have gotten hurt. Flora, Rico…" He swallowed. "You."

"Well, we weren't. So let's move on, shall we?"

"Still, it wasn't exactly one of my finer moments—"

"Ben? Shut up."

His brows crunched together. "Okay. Out with it."

Her hands gripped the steering wheel more tightly. "God, this sucks," she whispered. "This totally, completely sucks."

"That I got hurt?"

"That, too. I mean, yeah, that scared the crud out of me. But that's not what…" They slowed for a stop light. Shaking her head, she stared straight ahead at the traffic streaming across the intersection.

"Did you realize, that night you finally came clean about what you'd been doing, that you never once talked about it past tense? You might have thought you'd put it all behind you, when actually you'd lugged the whole shebang right back to Albuquerque." She paused, then said quietly, "Rescuing Rico *wasn't* a one-off, was it?" When he didn't answer, she looked at him again, long enough for the driver behind them to beep his horn when the light changed. Mercy pulled ahead, muttering, "Yeah. That's what I thought."

"If I say it was," Ben said at last, "will you stop looking like your dog just died?"

"Yeah, lying to me will make me feel a whole lot better. No, hear me out. I'd frankly given up on falling in love, did you know that? On ever finding someone to really love *me*. Nobody, ever, has even come close to making me feel the way you do. But at this point in my life, I'm not naive enough to believe that people can be happy together by pretending. By burying who they really are in the name of *the relationship*. And from the moment I saw your game face after you got that phone call…"

She checked her side mirror, pulled into the next lane. "You didn't put off telling me because of your father, or me, or anybody else. You put it off because you weren't sure what you really wanted to do." A glance, then, "I think it's safe to say your down time is over."

Ben would have slumped down in his seat if his wound would have let him. As it was, though, her words—and the pain behind them—roared through him like floodwaters after a summer storm, washing away every objection in their path.

"Do you think I was..." He fought for the right words. "Using you, *us,* to avoid dealing with what had happened?"

"Intentionally? No. Not sure what difference that makes, though."

"Baby," he said over the knot in his throat, "everything, *everything,* I've said or done over the past six weeks, I meant. You've got to believe that. I did come back for you, Merce. Whether you'd have me, I had no idea. But when I walked away ten years ago, I was already falling for you. Harder than I had any idea how to handle."

Silence stretched between them for several seconds before she said, "Then what was all that about your brother?"

"Having more than one account to settle doesn't in any way lessen the one I had to settle with you. The difference was, if my *brother* and I had stayed on the outs, it wouldn't have killed me."

"I see."

"I seriously doubt that," he said bitterly, "since I sure as hell didn't. Still don't, not entirely. So let me just take a stab at explaining, and hopefully when I'm done it'll all make at least enough sense that you don't take out a contract on my life, okay?"

When her only reply was a grunt, Ben shifted, trying in vain to find a more comfortable position before continuing. "No matter how you slice it, the timing was all wrong back then. For me, at least. Not only were there all those issues with my family, but it's true, I *was* restless."

"Aha," she said, and he glared at her.

"I never denied it. I did feel like I'd suffocate, if I stuck around. I watched my brother and your sisters settle into their lives, and it gave me the willies. Definitely not for me. Then you and I got involved, and I freaked, because I felt like I was getting sucked into something I wasn't ready for. Because I would have only ended up feeling trapped. And then we would have both been miserable."

"Yeah," she said. "I knew that. That's why…"

"Why you didn't let on how you really felt, either?"

He could see her mouth pull to one side. "Okay, so maybe you're not the only person in this car who sidesteps the truth now and then. Not that I took to my bed or anything," she quickly added, and Ben smiled in spite of the heaviness in his chest.

"So I heard," he said, and a frown shot in his direction. "Carmen. Those exact words, in fact." She snorted. "So I'm glad, because even then, I never wanted to hurt you. In any case, when I took off, I really was as aimless as everybody thought. My only goal at that point was to get away from here."

"And from me?"

"Especially from you. From everything I thought you represented, anyway. I just couldn't see myself settling into family life when my own seemed to be such a mess. Only the ironic thing was that the longer I stayed away, the more I began to see what family really meant. Especially when something threatens to tear it apart. And somewhere along the line, standing on the outside looking in wasn't cutting it anymore."

Ignoring the pain, he reached over to trace her jaw with his knuckle. "I guess I finally got it through my thick head that I'm nothing on my own. And that I'm never going to feel complete without something to *call* my own. I also honestly believed that chapter of my life was closed. I wasn't lying to you."

"Even if you were lying to yourself."

They'd pulled up in front of his parents' house. Mercy left the engine running, a clear signal that she wasn't coming inside with him. Ben held out his hand. She glanced over, then let go of the steering wheel to link their fingers. "I don't want to lose you, Merce," he whispered. "Not a second time. Not after I've finally found the one thing that finally plugs me up inside. So I'm telling you again—just say the word and the subject's closed forever."

Her eyes shot to his, twin creases between her brows. "You don't honestly think I'd actually ask you to quit, do you?"

"And you don't honestly think I'd put you through that kind of hell?" He lifted her hand to his lips, snagging her tortured gaze in his. "The way you take everything so hard? And how much I'd have to be away? What kind of relationship would that be?"

"I don't want to lose you either, Ben," Mercy said, a tear trickling down her cheek. "But I was right all along, wasn't I? That staying here, doing the 'burbs thing…it's not you. Not the whole you, at least. In which case I'd lose you anyway. And besides…" She smiled sadly. "How could you possibly turn your back on the children? Not to mention all those desperate parents?"

He'd rather get shot a hundred times than feel his gut being torn out like this. "So you're saying it's not going to work?"

After a long moment, she shook her head. "I don't see how. Do you?"

Ben kept her gaze in his for another second or two, then got out of the car, slamming the door shut behind him.

* * *

She had to say, she held it together pretty damn well, all through returning her father's truck and checking up on Flora and Rico, who—thanks to her parents' generosity—were flying home to El Paso later that evening. But the minute Mercy literally stumbled into her house, she doubled over, gripping her stomach as though a huge, nasty vacuum cleaner had sucked out her insides.

To come *that* close...

Her gaze landed on Annabelle. Poor hapless Annabelle, still bedecked with Mattie's little Barbie Valentines. And underneath, a two-pound box of Godiva and the biggest, tackiest, gaudiest, mushiest Valentine's card ever created. Mercy stormed over to the tree and plucked it clean in five seconds flat, grabbed the candy and card and carted the whole stinkin' lot to the kitchen. She hesitated, then, with a cry bordering on anguished, she shoved the candy into the trash. The cards, however, she dumped into the sink and turned on the water, ramming the bleeding, pulpy remains down the garbage disposal with the back end of a wooden spoon, a multilingual array of swear words blending with the demonized grinding.

Panting, Mercy leaned against the sink, until the pounding in her head stopped long enough for her to think she heard Homer, scratching to be let in.

She whirled around to the patio door, slid it open, the sharp wind instantly freezing the tear tracks she hadn't even known were there.

No cat.

"Homer!" she yelled into the wind, holding her stinging hair off her face with one hand. "Ho-*mer!* Where the hell *are* you?"

Her eyes burning, Mercy stomped out onto the patio to kick the metal food dish she left out whenever he disappeared, sending week-old kitty kibble flying all over creation. *This time,* the wind seemed to whine, *he's not coming back.*

Mercy sank to her knees on the cold, hard cement and cried herself sick.

Chapter Fourteen

"Hey," Luis said softly from the doorway to Ben's old bedroom, where he stood in front of his unmade bed, stuffing the last of his clothes into a duffel bag that had long since seen better days. "You leaving already?"

"Tony's out of his cast," Ben said, zipping the bag, "so my work here is done. Besides, I've got a meeting with Roy back in Dallas."

"But your injury—"

"It's been a week, they said it's healing up fine. As long as I don't strain it," he said, hefting the bag to the floor. His father's mouth tightened, but he only shook his head.

"You'll be back?"

"Yeah, I've got unfinished business here to take care of."

"So you talked to that Realtor?"

"C.J.? I did. We went up to the property yesterday, in fact. He figures he can move it for me pretty quickly." And Ben had literally dropped his jaw at what C.J. said he could probably get for the land, even undeveloped.

His father came into the room, sat on the edge of the bed. "I know I should've talked things out with you before this. About what you said that night. When Anita left Tony. But I couldn't ever figure out how to go about it. I'm not real good with words." A brief smile pulled at his mouth. "In either language. But you were right, about how I treated you. And Tony. I mean, I didn't really understand that's what I was doing, but that's no excuse. It was wrong, and I'm sorry."

Ben's gaze drifted to his father, the constant tightness in his chest easing a little at the obvious contrition in his father's eyes. "Why didn't you or Mama ever tell me about how sick I'd been as a baby?"

Tears brightened his father's eyes. "Some things hurt too much to remember, *mijo*. Let alone to talk about."

It would have to do, Ben supposed. Only then his father added, "Speaking of keeping secrets…your mother and I, we were mad as hell at first that you hadn't told us what you were doing. But we're proud of you. The path you've chosen…that's not something just anybody would do, you know."

Ben felt blood rush to his cheeks. "It's no big deal, Pop. Please don't make more of this than it is."

"*Que chinga,* it *is* a big deal! Anyone who's nearly lost a child…" The older man's eyes got all shiny; uncomfortable with the rare display of emotion, Ben looked away. "Well," his father finally said, "You're a godsend to a lot of people,

Benicio. And there's nothing you can say to diminish that. But I've gotta say…you make one helluva lousy contractor."

It took a second. Then Ben's eyes snapped back to his father's, creased in amusement. "What?"

"You heard me. It's a damn good thing Tony was still doing the paperwork, otherwise we'd've been screwed to the wall. *Dios mio,* you suck at this."

Ben stared at his father for several seconds, then let out a loud laugh. "I think those are the sweetest words I've ever heard come out of your mouth," he said, grinning. "I just hope to hell you let Tony in on your little revelation."

"You bet I did." Luis rubbed his mouth, looking sheepish. "I've got some major making up to do where your brother's concerned. I don't know where my head's been all these years, but it's way past time I let Tony know how much…I love him, too. And it wasn't like I didn't, you know, it's just…"

"Don't tell me, Pop," Ben said, swinging his duffle up onto his shoulder. "Tell Tony."

His father nodded, then stood, his fingers jammed in his pockets. "Well. I guess…"

With one arm, Ben pulled the old man into a hug. "Tell Mattie and Jake I'll see 'em soon," he said, then walked away before he could change his mind.

About anything.

With an annoyingly anxious glance at Mercy, Anita set out the Chinese food and bottle of wine on Mercy's table.

"If you ask me one more time if I'm okay," Mercy said, already seated, "I swear to God I'll impale you on this chopstick."

"Sorry. It's just—"

Scooping fried rice onto her plate, Mercy glared at her sister, then said, "So Tony's really taking care of the kids tonight?"

"Not only is he taking care of them, it was his idea." Anita shoveled garlic shrimp onto a mound of steaming white rice, leaning forward with her eyes closed to inhale the fragrant aroma. Peeking out from her Grand Canyon-esque cleavage, the diamond pendant Tony had given her for Valentine's Day sparkled like it was lit from inside. As did Anita.

"He's really trying, Merce," she said, sitting up straight again and digging in. "Even if half the time he looks like he's having one of those dreams where you're back in math class, having no idea what's going on."

Mercy smiled, grateful that the sensation of having gone through a car wash—without the car—had begun to subside enough to at least be happy for other people.

"Of course," Anita continued, "I don't suppose it hurt that I cut back to three days a week at the hospital. Which I'm now wondering why I didn't do years ago. I take that back, I do know why." She twisted lo mein noodles onto her chopsticks, poking the slippery mass into her mouth before saying, "Because the worse things got at home, the less I wanted to be there."

"So you didn't need the money?"

"Not *that* much. Or the 'fulfillment.' Oh, I definitely like working, but once the kids came along?" She shook her head. "I've been exhausted for the past ten years, Merce. Only I was too damn stubborn, or proud, or whatever to admit it." Frowning, she twisted up more lo mein. "Talk about cutting off my nose to spite my face. Stupid."

Her words made Mercy's shrimp boogie in her stomach. More and more over the past two weeks she'd begun to wonder if that's what she was doing—refusing to see past the obvious, digging in her heels because she'd made up her mind that her way was the only way things could work.

"Anyway, it also doesn't hurt that Luis is finally acknowledging all the good work Tony's done over the years. Definitely a huge stress reliever right there."

"So everyone's happy at your house?"

Anita grinned. "Getting there, getting there. And since I've got some time to myself, I've even started an exercise program. I've lost four pounds!"

"Well, here's to you," Mercy said, lifting her wineglass toward her sister.

"Yeah, it's all about compromise, you know?" Anita said on a sigh. "Figuring out how to make all the pieces fit so that nobody feels neglected or put-upon or whatever. Because when you come right down to it, no relationship is perfect, right?" Mercy glanced up to find her gaze caught in her sister's. "So if you love somebody, you *make* it work."

From the greasy bag between them on the table, Mercy fished out an egg roll, tore it in half. "And your point is?"

"You know damn well what my point is, *chica*."

"It's over, 'Nita," Mercy said, dunking the egg roll in a puddle of soy sauce on her plate. "He sold the property and everything. That *hombre* is *gone*."

"Shows how much you know."

Mercy's eyes shot to her sister's. "What are you talking about?"

"Ben got back last night. He's camped out in our family room." She grabbed the fried rice box and shoveled more onto her plate. "I'm not supposed to tell you."

"Then why did you?"

A smile twitching around her mouth, her sister met her gaze. "Because he said you never gave him back the ring."

Mercy squirmed in her chair. "He didn't exactly give me a chance, did he?"

"Bull. He was here for a good week before he left, you could have given it back to him anytime."

"Still. I'm not wearing it, am I?"

"Only because it would be tacky to keep wearing it once you'd broken up. And if it's one thing you're not, it's tacky. An idiot, maybe, but not tacky."

"Hey!"

Anita lifted her wine glass, giving Mercy the evil eye over it. "He's back, honey. And believe me, there's only one reason for that." She tilted the nearly empty glass in Mercy's direction. "*You.*"

Feeling as though she had a hornet's nest in her stomach, Mercy got up from the table and returned to her kitchen, although she had no idea what she was supposed to be doing once she got there. Her arms spread, she gripped the edge of the sink, staring out into the half darkness in her backyard, as hope and fear and rampant confusion made mincemeat of what was left of her wits. A second later, she felt her sister's arm wrap around her shoulders, the gentle pressure of her hug.

"I only told you because I didn't want you to be blind-sided," Anita said quietly. "And because I was afraid you'd blow it. If you didn't have a chance to pull yourself together beforehand."

"Thanks. I think."

"*De nada.* Honey, nothing's ideal. And I have no idea what

he's thinking, really. But he's clearly miserable without you. And you're clearly miserable without him."

Mercy's face screwed up. "It's that obvious, huh?"

Anita let out a sharp laugh. "Let's see…you've been dating since you were, what, fifteen? So that's nearly a quarter century I've been witnessing your breakups—"

"And thank you *so* much for pointing that out."

"—and every time, you bounced back like Silly Putty. Except twice. And Ben was the culprit both times."

"And if you'd seen Flora's face, after she was reunited with Rico…" Mercy shook her head. "It's no good, 'Nita. There's no way I could have asked him to give that up. I wouldn't be able to live with myself. I mean, if I ever had kids, I'd sure want to know there was someone like Ben, willing to go the extra mile if God forbid something like that happened to me."

"And next time," Anita said softly, "maybe it would be more than a cracked rib. Right?" When Mercy didn't— couldn't—say anything, her sister said, "So are you going to worry any less if you never see the man again?"

"You didn't have to point that out, either," Mercy muttered.

Just then Anita jumped and said, "Good grief—what on earth is that awful noise?"

"*Homer!*" Mercy cried, rushing to the patio door, fumbling with the lock in her haste to get it open. Filthy, matted and several pounds thinner, the cat rushed inside before the door was even completely open, writhing around Mercy's shins and cussing her up one side and down the other. Mercy dropped onto her butt on the kitchen floor, hugging the rotten thing, soaking up his purr. "You came back, you big dope! You came back!"

"And apparently not alone," Anita said, bemused.

"What?" Homer still on her lap, Mercy looked over to see a very pretty white kitty with gingery splotches, sitting primly just inside the door.

Mercy looked at Homer. "You brought home a friend?"

"A girlfriend, from the looks of things. Hate to tell you this," Anita said, squatting by the visitor, who was arching up to bump her sister's outstretched hand, "but I think you need a new vet."

Now Mercy looked at the other kitty. "*You're pregnant?*"

She blinked her big blue eyes and gave an apologetic mew.

Eventually, Anita headed home and Mercy put away the leftover Chinese food, fed the cats (*Cats*. She still couldn't believe it. And yes, Marge—what else?—was indeed very pregnant. Oh, joy.) and finally got around to mulling over this new turn of events. Ben's return and all. And what that meant to her life.

If anything.

Because, yeah, so he was back. But his being "back" didn't necessarily mean he was back for *her,* no matter what Anita said. Heck, her sister had just patched up her marriage, she and Tony were probably having the best sex of their lives. At this point, Anita's brain was so hormone-drenched she'd probably try to fix up the Pope. So how would it look if Mercy marched herself over there and offered herself up and a reconciliation hadn't been part of Ben's plan at all?

And yet…if—*if*—there was a chance he really wasn't ready to give up…

Then again, what if he was hoping *she'd* make the first move so he wouldn't look like a loser? And when, *when,* did the freaking statute of limitations run out on this high school does-he-or-doesn't-he crap?

Bookended on her sofa between two loudly purring cats, Mercy laid her head back and groaned. *Could* she compromise? Could she live with Ben's being away, being in danger?

No, the real question was…could she live without him *at all?*

On a little cry, she shimmied out from between the cats (much to their annoyance) and tromped back to her bedroom to look for the hottest, highest-heeled pair of boots she owned.

If she was going down, at least she'd look good.

Don't think about it, just do it, Ben told himself as he got into his truck, he'd be screwed. Not that he hadn't done exactly that for the past week. In fact, he'd mulled over every possibility, every contingency, every objection she might come up with (and boy, there were plenty of those) until his head hurt. Nothing left now but to throw himself on Mercy's mercy and hope for the best.

At this point, he had nothing to lose. Except, maybe, his sanity. But that was already shredded past recognition, so what the hell, right?

He backed out of his brother's driveway, telling himself this wasn't his last shot, that if she couldn't see her way clear to go along with his plan there were still other options.

Like hurtling himself off Sandia Peak.

Stop that, a voice—the same voice that had talked him through all the phone calls and the discussions and the planning over the past seven days—yelled in his ear. She still had the ring. And Anita swore she'd softened her up, that she—Mercy, not Anita—was ripe for him to make his move.

Ben sucked in a sharp breath, his hands tensing on the steering wheel as some dumb cluck turned onto the street ahead of him, blinding him with his brights—

Huh?

The Firebird streaked past him. Screeched to a stop the same time he did. And then Mercy was out of her car, running—if you could call it that, in those ridiculous high heels—toward him, waving her arms and yelling, "Wait! Wait!"

Ben angled the truck into the curb, setting off a security light worthy of Leavenworth. He'd barely gotten out of the truck before Mercy threw herself into his arms.

Okay, this was looking good.

"Mercy, I—"

"It doesn't matter," she said into his chest, clinging to him like a limpet. "I don't care how much you have to be away, a part-time *you* is worth a hundred times more than a hundred percent of all the other men I've ever known, all put together." Still clinging, she lifted her eyes to his, sparkling in the glare of that damn security bulb. "Because who says we have to have a typical marriage, or that I need a husband who's underfoot all the time? It's not as if I don't have my own life or anything. And so, yeah, I'd probably worry, but I'm gonna do that, anyway, so we might as well be together, right? And by supporting *your* work, I'd actually feel like I was contributing something to the solution, for once, instead of doing the ostrich thing and not thinking about it at all."

People were beginning to come out of their houses, but apparently she didn't notice. And God knew Ben couldn't have cared less. Smiling so wide his face hurt, he bracketed her face in his hands. Her wild hair tickled his fingers, tickled his soul, making him want to laugh.

"You really think we could make this work?" he said, and she rested her forehead against his chest.

"It sure as heck beats the alternative," she said, still clinging. "If you have to stay based in Texas, then I'll just suck it up, I suppose."

Ben tucked his fingers underneath her chin, lifting her face to lap up the love in her eyes. "And I told you, I'm home for good."

She frowned. "And I told *you,* I don't want you to give up your work."

"I'm not. But Roy and I agreed it was time I struck out on my own. Right here in Albuquerque. I'd still be part of the same network, but I'd be based here. And hopefully, if I get enough funding, I can bring other people on board so I could stick around more. That's why I sold the property. Because I need the funds to start up my own operation."

Her gaze danced in his for several seconds before, finally, a soft "Oh" fell from her lips, followed by a sharp intake of breath…and a smile five times brighter than the stupid security lamp. Except then she let go to rummage in her jacket pocket, at last extricating the ring box. A frown bit into Ben's forehead—was his mind playing tricks on him? Hadn't she just said—

"Do it right, this time," she said, tossing her hair over her shoulder. "I haven't waited this long to get some half-assed proposal. Not having the *cojones* to give it to me in person…" She shook her head. "Lame."

"And my proposing to you in the middle of the street isn't?"

"With all these witnesses?" she said. So she had noticed.

"Oh, for God's sake, Ben…we've never done anything the 'normal' way. And I doubt we ever will. Why should this be any different?"

"Does that mean I don't have to get down on one knee?"

"It does not."

He sighed. "Can we at least go over onto the sidewalk?"

"Fine," she said on a pushed breath, leading him by the hand up onto the curb, where, in front of somebody's stinky juniper bush, Ben lowered himself to one knee, took Mercy's hand in his and kissed her knuckles. Then he looked up at her—at the woman who'd make his life a living hell, but in the best possible way—and said, "Marry me, Mercy," and she said, in a choked voice, "Okay," and then a whole bunch of people they didn't even know cheered and applauded, and then she shrieked when Ben yanked her down onto the sidewalk with him. Laughing, she threw her arms around his neck.

"I love you, Mr. Macho," she whispered, and he kissed her, and kissed her, and kissed her some more, feeling whole for the first time in his life.

Epilogue

Mercy sat cross-legged on her bedroom floor, her lap full of three-week-old kittens—one calico, one black-and-white and one gray tabby. No gingers. Mercy was guessing that Miss Marge had gotten around some before Homer'd come along and made her an honest woman. Especially since the vet confirmed that, yes, old Homer was shooting blanks.

Ben, however, was not, she mused as she nearly trampled the little furballs in her haste to get to the bathroom. You'd think, what with all the hoo-hah about fertility rates rapidly declining the closer a woman got to forty, it would have taken longer than five minutes without birth control for her to get pregnant. But no.

One day, she would find this amusing.

Mercy emerged to find her husband-to-be waiting for her on the edge of their bed, his face a study in cocky solicitousness, an expression only Ben could pull off and live to tell the tale.

"You okay?"

She had the feeling she was going to hear that a lot over the next eight months. A thought that, inexplicably—now that the woozies had passed—produced a sparkly, giddy feeling inside her, like champagne drunk too fast. She slid onto Ben's lap, sighing as his arms wrapped around her.

"You have no idea how okay I am. Even if I still can't believe this little monkey is on his or her way already."

"What can I tell you? When you're good, you're good."

"And you are so gonna get it. You sure we should wait to tell our parents until the wedding?"

"I think they can hang on for another month," Ben said, kissing her temple.

"Yeah, but can I? And anyway, the minute one of my sisters or either of our mothers figures it out—which, knowing them, is gonna take, like, a second—it's all over. Ma's already giving me funny looks."

His chuckle rumbled through her, as the unbridled joy and love in his eyes nearly brought tears to hers. "Never mind that it was your idea to wait until you were through the first three months." When she made a face, he laughed again and said, "Okay. We'll tell 'em tonight." His grin widened. "I'll bring earplugs."

Mercy lightly smacked his shoulder, then reached down

to scoop up the little black-and-white kitty, who was attacking her shoe.

"That's Mattie's, right?"

"Yep. Did I tell you I named him Bart?"

Ben groaned, then said, "You're nuts, you know that?"

"Too late to back out now, you knocked me up...what are you doing?"

"What do you think?" Ben said, nibbling her neck. And unbuttoning her shirt.

"Not in front of the babies, for goodness sake!"

"We're up here on the bed," he said, gently putting Bart back on the carpet, then deftly lifting her off his lap and onto the mattress, nuzzling her magically-growing breasts over the edge of her push-up bra. "They're down there. Besides..." He unhooked the waistband of her jeans. "They're cats, they're born knowing how this stuff works—"

His cell rang. Ben ignored it. Mercy braced her hands on his shoulders, pushed him back. Their gazes tangled for a second or two, until, on a sigh, he levered himself up and off, grabbing the phone from the nightstand.

Mercy sat up, listening. And watching, as compassion and resolve supplanted the tenderness and desire of moments before.

He clapped shut the phone; she laid a hand on his arm.

"It's okay, Ben. Go."

"But we were going to tell our parents—"

"They'll be here when you get back." She smiled. "So will we."

And two days later, when Mercy welcomed Ben's tired,

disheveled, exhilarated, wonderful self back home, it wasn't with relief, but the profound gratitude of an equally exhilarated woman who had only this to say to all those people who'd given her grief for being picky: *Thppppt.*

* * * * *

Happily ever after is just the beginning...

Turn the page for a sneak preview of
    A HEARTBEAT AWAY
        by
    Eleanor Jones

Harlequin Everlasting—Every great love has a story to tell. ™
A brand-new series from Harlequin Books

Special? A prickle ran down my neck and my heart started to beat in my ears. Was today really special?

"Tuck in," he ordered.

I turned my attention to the feast that he had spread out on the ground. Thick, home-cooked-ham sandwiches, sausage rolls fresh from the oven and a huge variety of mouthwatering scones and pastries. Hunger pangs took over, and I closed my eyes and bit into soft homemade bread.

When we were finally finished, I lay back against the bluebells with a groan, clutching my stomach.

Daniel laughed. "Your eyes are bigger than your stomach," he told me.

I leaned across to deliver a punch to his arm, but he rolled away, and when my fist met fresh air I collapsed in a fit of giggles before relaxing on my back and staring up into the flawless blue sky. We lay like that for quite a while, Daniel and I, side by side in companionable silence, until he stretched out his hand in an arc that encompassed the whole area.

"Don't you think that this is the most beautiful place in the entire world?"

His voice held a passion that echoed my own feelings, and I rose onto my elbow and picked a buttercup to hide the emotion that clogged my throat.

"Roll over onto your back," I urged, prodding him with my forefinger. He obliged with a broad grin, and I reached across to place the yellow flower beneath his chin.

"Now, let us see if you like butter."

When a yellow light shone on the tanned skin below his jaw, I laughed.

"There…you do."

For an instant our eyes met, and I had the strangest sense that I was drowning in those honey-brown depths. The scent of bluebells engulfed me. A roaring filled my ears, and then, unexpectedly, in one smooth movement Daniel rolled me onto my back and plucked a buttercup of his own.

"And do *you* like butter, Lucy McTavish?" he asked. When he placed the flower against my skin, time stood still.

His long lean body was suspended over mine, pinning me against the grass. Daniel…dear, comfortable, familiar Daniel was suddenly bringing out in me the strangest sensations.

"Do you, Lucy McTavish?" he asked again, his voice low and vibrant.

My eyes flickered toward his, the whisper of a sigh escaped my lips and although a strange lethargy had crept into my limbs, I somehow felt as if all my nerve endings were on fire. He felt it, too—I could see it in his warm brown eyes. And when he lowered his face to mine, it seemed to me the most natural thing in the world.

None of the kisses I had ever experienced could have even begun to prepare me for the feel of Daniel's lips on mine. My entire body floated on a tide of ecstasy that shut out everything but his soft, warm mouth, and I knew that this was what I had been waiting for the whole of my life.

"Oh, Lucy." He pulled away to look into my eyes. "Why haven't we done this before?"

Holding his gaze, I gently touched his cheek, then I curled my fingers through the short thick hair at the base of his skull, overwhelmed by the longing to drown again in the sensations that flooded our bodies. And when his long tanned fingers crept across my tingling skin, I knew I could deny him nothing.

* * * * *

Be sure to look for
A HEARTBEAT AWAY,
available February 27, 2007.

And look, too, for
THE DEPTH OF LOVE
by Margot Early,
the story of a couple who must learn
that love comes in many guises—and in the end
it's the only thing that counts.

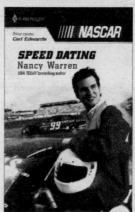

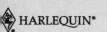

HARLEQUIN®

EVERLASTING LOVE™

Every great love has a story to tell™

Save $1.⁰⁰ off

**the purchase of
any Harlequin
Everlasting Love novel**

Coupon valid from January 1, 2007
until April 30, 2007.

Valid at retail outlets in the U.S. only.
Limit one coupon per customer.

5 65373 00076 2   (8100) 0 11302

HEUSCPN0407

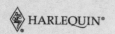

HARLEQUIN®

EVERLASTING LOVE™

Every great love has a story to tell ™

Fall from Grace

Kristi Gold

Save $1.⁰⁰ off

the purchase of
any Harlequin
Everlasting Love novel

Coupon valid from January 1, 2007
until April 30, 2007.

Valid at retail outlets in Canada only.
Limit one coupon per customer.

RETAILER: Harlequin Enterprises Limited will pay the face value of this coupon plus
10.25¢ if submitted by the customer for this product only. Any other use constitutes
fraud. Coupon is nonassignable. Void if taxed, prohibited or restricted by law.
Consumer must pay any government taxes. Void if copied. Nielsen Clearing House
customers submit coupons and proof of sales to: Harlequin Enterprises Ltd. P.O.
Box 3000, Saint John, N.B. E2L 4L3. Non–NCH retailer—for reimbursement submit
coupons and proof of sales directly to: Harlequin Enterprises Ltd., Retail Marketing
Department, 225 Duncan Mill Rd., Don Mills, Ontario M3B 3K9, Canada. Valid in
Canada only. ® is a trademark of Harlequin Enterprises Ltd. Trademarks marked with
® are registered in the United States and/or other countries.

52607370

HECDNCPN0407

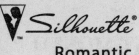

Romantic
SUSPENSE

Excitement, danger and passion guaranteed!

Same great authors and riveting editorial
you've come to know and love
from Silhouette Intimate Moments.

New York Times
bestselling author
Beverly Barton
is back with the
latest installment
in her popular
miniseries,
The Protectors.
HIS ONLY
OBSESSION
is available
next month from
Silhouette®
Romantic Suspense

Look for it wherever you buy books!

COMING NEXT MONTH

#1813 MR. HALL TAKES A BRIDE—Marie Ferrarella
Logan's Legacy Revisited
Hotshot corporate attorney Jordan Hall had never worried about how
the other half lived, until his sister asked him to sub for her at her
legal aid clinic. He was touched by his new clients' plight—and by
the clinic's steely supercompetent secretary Sarajane Gerrity. Would
the charming playboy file a motion to stay…in Sarajane's heart?

#1814 THE BEST CATCH IN TEXAS—Stella Bagwell
Men of the West
Divorced physician's assistant Nicolette Saddler wasn't buying the
office buzz about the new doctor from Houston. Then she caught
her first glimpse of Dr. Ridge Garroway—good thing he was a
cardiologist, because the younger man set her pulse racing! Alas,
Ridge suffered the same condition when Nicolette was around.
Now to find a cure…

#1815 MEDICINE MAN—Cheryl Reavis
For unhappy divorcée Arley Meehan, the healing began when
she met captivating Navajo paratrooper Will Baron at her sister's
wedding reception. But would their meddling families keep the
couple from commitment?

#1816 FALLING FOR THE HEIRESS—Christine Flynn
The Kendricks of Camelot
Assigned to protect Tess Kendrick and her son, bodyguard
Jeff Parker had no sympathy for the spoiled scion of American
political royalty who'd ended her marriage on a whim. But when
Jeff learned of her true sacrifice to save the family name from her
blackmailing ex, he quickly became knight in shining armor to the
heiress from Camelot, Virginia.

#1817 ONCE MORE, AT MIDNIGHT—Wendy Warren
Years ago, Lilah Owens had left for L.A. to find fame and fortune
after her bad-boy boyfriend Gus Hoffman was busted. Back in town,
broke and with a daughter in tow, Lilah was in for a surprise—Gus
had gone from ex-con to *engaged* success story. That is, until old
passions were reignited—and Gus learned that Lilah's daughter was
his.…

#1818 ROMANCING THE NANNY—Cindy Kirk
Widower Dan Major was Amy Logan's dream man. But falling for
the boss was a no-no for the nanny, since Dan's systematic seduction
seemed to be motivated by one thing only—his desire to have a
loving stepmother for his daughter. His careful, by-the-book plan
wasn't a substitute for true love, and Amy was holding out for exactly
that.…

SSECNM0207